Gospel Voi

A collection of short stories set ⌐⌐⌐⌐⌐⌐⌐⌐⌐ ⌐
teaching of Jesus

Caroline Greville

Faithbuilders™

Gospel Voices: *A collection of short stories set around the life and teaching of Jesus* by Caroline Greville © Copyright Caroline Greville 2020.

FAITHBUILDERS
Bethany, 7 Park View,
Freeholdland Road,
Pontnewynydd, Pontypool NP4 8LP
www.faithbuilders.org.uk

British Library Cataloguing-in-Publication Data. A catalogue record for this book is available from the British Library

ISBN: 9781913181215

Cover Design by Alexi Francis alexifrancis.co.uk © 2020

Contents

For Jesus, as knowable now as you were then.
May you be encountered in these pages.

Acknowledgements

My grateful thanks first of all to Mathew Bartlett and Laura Maisey of Faithbuilders. I have valued your commitment to this project, talking me on so readily, and your enthusiasm and dedication throughout. This book is far better for your input.

To my husband Rupert, who's been reading these stories from their early formation – thank you! I've loved sharing my ideas with you. To my children, Annie, Maddy, Eliott and Jemima, for your great encouragement. I must thank a wonderful group from church who told me to run with this idea, especially (but not exclusively) Beth Boxall, Colin and Olive Pavey, Jess Ryn and Lynn Harris. Beth Boxall – you asked us to pray in church one day for a greater love of God's word – this is the product of that day. Writing *Gospel Voices* has drawn me so much closer to God, I cannot tell you. It's an experience I wouldn't be without.

Heartfelt thanks also to colleagues and students at Christ Church University, Canterbury. Carolyn Oulton, thank you for reading and endorsing my book so quickly. I was delighted by your comments. And Bryony Williamson, your encouragement in the Moore corridor came at just the right time – I'll explain one day!

To Grace Turner, your endorsement means the world to me – huge thanks for your support of this book. And thank you to all who've listened to stories and snippets, namely my Kent Adult Education groups and the Living Well (now One Church) coffee morning.

You have all contributed to this in your own way and made me very happy!

And not forgetting Alexi Francis – your cover is wonderful. Thank you for bringing my idea to life.

Most importantly of all, thank you to the One who has inspired and blessed me beyond measure. I'm so grateful for the vision and sense of purpose you've given me, using my own voice to make you better known.

Note to reader

Gospel Voices is a between-the-lines look at accounts from all four gospels. It begins with a scene in heaven, in which the angels try to grasp the idea of Jesus coming to earth in human form, and ends with their anticipation of his return. I follow a chronological path and pick up stories that intrigue me. The book has grown out of time spent with God, praying for wisdom and insight as I have studied the Bible, asking for understanding of how the characters felt and what motivated them. Each story can be taken in isolation, but when read as a whole an appreciation of certain characters will grow.

None of the stories are imagined from Jesus's perspective and, while my inspiration comes from Scripture, I am keen for you to remember these stories are speculative. It is my hope they will trigger personal research and cause you to formulate your own ideas on what these characters may have been like as real people. I think we all identify with one or two of them. Please read with a Bible close at hand – I want this book to take you deeper into God's Word, suggest new possibilities, and enrich your understanding of him.

Bible quotes throughout the narratives are from the New Living Translation, unless otherwise stated.

Salvation song

A hush fell over the heavens now – the most profound of all pauses – But why would he? And how? Had they understood correctly? It was so like him, it *was* logical. This lavish kindness, it caught in their throats and left them searching for words that simply wouldn't come. It was deep and silent worship, for they could not articulate his goodness, his reckless, wild love that was unstoppable and defined devotion. It was as if collectively they held their breath in wonder. Throughout the entire kingdom they fell to their knees, covering their faces with wings and hands. Then, one by one, they got to their feet as if in a daze. Slowly the news began to sink in, and out in the corridor, before the throne room, discussions started in whispered and astonished words.

'He's doing what?' said the boldest angel of the throng, and the other angels stood closed-mouthed and listened, many of them still struggling to grasp this most profound of all gestures themselves. They could always rely on him to say what they were thinking.

'Going down to join them, as a baby,' replied the archangel.

'Why? I mean, why would you?' said the first angel who had spoken.

'It does sound a bit risky,' said another who was taller and more bony than the rest. 'Kind of drastic.'

'Well, I think we'll be on a few more missions with the good Lord down there,' said the most senior angel again. 'But risky it won't be,' and he lifted his sword and drew his thumb so very lightly down its silver, white-hot blade. 'I have protected those he's given to my charge before. I'll allow nothing to touch him without the Father's say-so.'

The group were silent again and he must have felt their awe at that moment, standing as he did two-foot taller and with his cold warrior-gaze. It seemed to them he was always on the alert and never even blinked; he was truer than his blade and missed nothing. 'It's in God's strength we go,' he reminded them. '*He* equips us for combat. God's very presence is alongside us.'

'Yes, we'll be straight onto any difficulties,' joined his second-in-command. 'You must all remember our Daniel's trials? I was sent by the Lord himself the very moment the faithful old fellow began his prayer.'

'He didn't see you straight away – what took you so long?' asked the forthright angel again.

'It was that accursed Prince of Persia holding him up, but I supported him,' said the archangel. 'Team effort. You were there in God's timing lad, don't feel you let him down in any way. Sometimes the Lord allows the odd obstacle; it's not a problem, you know. The humans are given time to grow, while we get to use our weapons, and keep our combat skills sharp. Yes, he might need us down there, but we'll be ready.'

'Heaven won't be the same without him,' came a quiet voice from the back of the crowd. This angel was feeling particularly morose and had seated himself on the golden floor, his wings hanging limply behind him, the privilege of wearing them all forgotten. 'I wonder if this place will still shine, or if much of the brightness will leave with him. I don't care for beautiful golden streets if he's not walking along them. And who needs jewel-encrusted walls, anyway? He brings the beauty here, the meaning.'

'Then let him take that glory somewhere else. They need him more than we do,' said the second-in-command. 'God the Father still remains here, we'll always have him, and his wonderful love is equal to the Son's.'

'I just hope they appreciate him,' said a devoted angel who had always preferred worship to her appointments with humans, though her face shone whenever she heard them understand something more about him.

'Oh, they won't,' came a voice. It belonged to an angel who'd had more than his share of disappointments. 'Do you think he knows what he's doing?'

'He knows exactly what he's doing,' explained the most senior angel again. 'You must have seen his tears, watched him pace the corridors, plead with his Father to do something, for this one and that. The discussions they've had over the most vile of sinners, the terms of endearment he uses for them. I don't quite know what he sees in many of them myself. I mean, I know he made them but they're an ungrateful lot, with one or two exceptions of course.'

'They are outrageous,' he replied. 'The bad outweigh the good by far. That donkey was more receptive to God than his prophet. Many an evil man producing equally evil offspring. Brother killing brother, first Cain and then Abimelech obliterating all his. Jezebel killing prophets, babies... Horrendous people with barely a worthy soul among them.'

'The Lord dealt with them,' said the archangel, apparently exasperated at this continued argument against God's good intentions. 'Those who do follow are all the more remarkable in the light of the darkness that's flooded the place. You need a touch more of his mercy.'

'And think of the salvation,' joined a wise and considered angel who always thought before she spoke. She closed her eyes to concentrate, raising a hand in worship as the extent of God's mercy touched her deep in her being. 'If he loves them all so much then who are we to argue? He's crazy about them, even the most hateful, despicable ones. He says they can change, throws good opportunities in their paths on a daily basis. He sees something valuable in each of them – he doesn't want to let a single one of them go. Their rejection of him pains him beyond belief. It's like there's a sadness in him at times that even the purest, deepest worship cannot shake. All these empty rooms here,' she continued, waving her raised hand over her shoulder now and causing a feather to fly, 'What's the point of them if he can't fill them? They go on for miles in every direction, while his designs for expansion never stop. His new agenda explains it all, though perhaps it's not a new vision. Perhaps he's had it all along.' The angel paused for a moment to reflect. 'And the way our Lord spoke of this plan; his words made it more like a love song than a speech.'

'Can we even begin to understand it,' said another. 'The deep love of the Lord, will it stop at anything?'

'He's going to show them his love once and for all,' she replied. 'They cannot fail to grasp it this time, and then things will be different.'

A collective cry of worship burst forth from the group, and each began to speak and sing in their own angelic tongue. The sounds and phrases merged to make a new song that was more beautiful than every individual expression. They sang his declaration of love for mankind and shivered. Wings unfurled and angels soared into the air, some turning somersaults and diving, others simply hovering with arms outstretched and meditating on God's goodness. Shouts of 'hallelujah' rebounded down the length of the corridor, bringing a coherence to their utterances of praise. It was a salvation song, soon to be sung over the fields and rooftops of Bethlehem, the heartfelt adoration of those who understood, and a proclamation of his love.

One by one they landed with balletic ease, broad smiles on their faces as they rejoiced in this new demonstration of his mercy, about to be witnessed on the earth. They rested and considered the Lord again, and an angel with a heart for the studious spoke out what had been troubling him. 'So, at what point does his consciousness leave here and take up residence in the baby? In the womb or when he's born? And will he be limited in what he knows and what he can do?'

'I can't answer that,' said the archangel, 'but I do know he's weighed this up properly, and when he wants to do something, there's no stopping him. It's what makes him so worthy of all our worship, of everything: that love of his always prevails. It's unmatched, it's extravagant and it's so pure it burns. It's why he wants to do this so much – so fires will start in the hearts of men, and heaven will be full of those he made for relationship with himself. His plans never fail. Have any of you *ever* heard of him abandon a plan as too difficult, have you *ever* known him get it wrong, in all of history?'

One by one they shook their heads. 'He is able, God be praised.' 'Who can understand the thoughts of the Lord.' 'He reigns, our sovereign Lord reigns.'

'He has my loyal following.'

'And mine.'

'Me, too.'

'I want to be there right from the start.'

'That's wonderful all of you,' said the archangel, 'but you must go where he directs you. There's a plan in place for each of you, and no one's going to miss out. Wherever he sends you, proclaim the truth of his love over them. These are indeed exciting times.'

See Luke's Gospel, chapter 2 verses 13–14.

'Suddenly, the angel was joined by a vast host of others – the armies of heaven – praising God and saying, "Glory to God in highest heaven, and peace on earth to those with whom God is pleased."'

Two sisters home alone

'Greetings,' you call in a joyful voice that we're not quite ready for. 'Anyone home?' You push the door very lightly, I can hear your hand sweep over it, and the gentle clearing of your throat. We take a little longer to respond than we know is polite, and Mary is still going on as I head for the door, 'Oh, do you really think I've lost him?'

I don't like being left at home by my parents. They say she is an adult now and can look after me. I'm not so sure – *I'm* the one having to look after her today, and she's got herself into some *serious* trouble.

You are just walking away when I reach the door and I feel shamed by my laxness. 'Hello, Uncle?' I call after you. As you turn I see a face that's tired from a day in the sun, legs ready to collapse from a day on the road. You look more ancient than ever – you're covered with dust, which isn't helping. I wonder though what you must think of me. I hope you think I'm looking very grown-up, though, like I'm running the house. I brush the chaff from my apron as I've been grinding grain between the stones to make more bread. As Mary says, we really are behind.

'You're very welcome,' I say, 'of course you are. Please just don't ask too many questions. You see, my sister's had a bit of a shock.'

We go inside together, and Mary is pretty embarrassing. She's sitting over in the corner with her knees hugged in tightly to her chest and she's rocking slightly.

'Look, I can see it's a bad time,' you say. 'I'll call again when your parents are back, or perhaps stay somewhere else.'

'Don't be daft,' I tell you. 'Come in, you're family and we *were* expecting you. It's just that we're a bit flustered right now. Let me get you a drink,' I say, 'you've had a long journey. I should wash your feet first like Imma[1] would, if you'll just –'

'No, I'm alright,' you say, and you place your basket against the wall. 'Can I just wash and have somewhere to lie down?'

---

[1] Abba and Imma (father and mother) are names of Aramaic origin and still used today. Some argue that Av and Em are the titles from the Biblical Hebrew. However, it is thought Avi (my father) described the relationship and was not used within families.

At this my older sister gets to her feet and comes over to greet you. 'You must forgive me,' she says, straightening her tunic so that it falls to the floor. She's all demure and responsible again. Abba always uses those words for her. Not for much longer. 'We must look unhospitable,' she tells you, in a rebuke to herself and me, and she pours water in a bowl that she places in front of you. I take down a goblet with two hands and fill it from the pitcher before making a space for you to sit down, removing Imma's embroidery and placing it in the hammock for now. You're still looking awkward, so I pat the low stool next to me and give you my biggest gappy smile. 'Come and join me,' I say, and you do.

Mary seems to have turned a corner and takes over now. 'I do trust you,' she says, 'and to be honest, I really need an adult to talk to, and one whose faith I respect.'

Well that's charming, I think I'm pretty wise, as little sisters go, and I'll stand by her through worse than this. I have to say, her troubles have made life pretty exciting. She has your full attention, with those beautiful large dark eyes of hers; I've always thought they should belong to a Persian deer, not a *sister*.

'I'm worried that Joseph's left me,' she says.

You raise an eyebrow. 'Surely not,' you say, 'not good old dependable Joe.'

I know what you mean. I love Joe so very much and I hope I get to marry someone like him one day. He's tall and heavy set, built for big tasks my father says, and for endurance prayer, says my mother. I've caught him praying before and he literally sweats, but then he has a great big beaming smile on his face when he's finished, like he does when he's whittled something out of wood and he hands it to me. He's usually so patient – there's always a pause before he speaks, but I think that's because he's kind. I've never known him to be hasty about anything. Sometimes I have to fill in his long pauses, it takes him so long to get his words out. Now he's gone off for a very long pause as he thinks about what my sister has told him.

'What seems to be the problem?' you say. 'That is, if you want to tell me, of course.'

'I'm pregnant,' Mary says and I hear you catch your breath, then try to look unshockable just a little too late. 'Not by him,' she says, and now you stand up, as if to leave.

'Oh, you don't understand,' she says. 'Not by any *man*. It's the Messiah. I had an angel visit me and tell me that I'm going to be carrying God's child, and that it won't be down to any man. He has it all worked out, you know. Only Joseph doesn't seem to believe me.'

'I'm not surprised,' you say.

'I knew we shouldn't have told you,' I blurt out.

I dare to look at Mary – she has started to cry again. 'If you won't believe me, who will?'

'It is possible,' you say. Then you start quoting Scripture and I don't understand. I want to interrupt but I want you to think me grown up. Your memory is good for someone old. 'Out of the stump of David's family will grow a shoot,' you say, 'yes, a new Branch bearing fruit from the old root.'[2] You lick your finger and start to draw a tree on the clay floor, the stool wobbling as you lean forward. Joseph needs to fix that dodgy leg if he's coming back. 'Branch,' you say, thinking aloud, 'the town of the branch, yes, netzer,[3] Nazareth.'

Mary is looking at you for reassurance but you seem to be off in your own little world. 'I do trust you, Mary,' you say at last. 'Now tell me about this angel. What exactly did he tell you?' and she describes that night when, unfortunately, the rest of us were all fast asleep. It's just not fair. I would *so* love to see an angel.

'I wasn't frightened for long,' Mary tells you. 'Not when he started talking about Jesus – that's the baby's name that God's already chosen. I wonder if it's happened in me by now. The angel said the Holy Spirit would 'come upon' me, and I suspect it's taken place when I've been asleep, because I haven't noticed anything strange going on just yet. I'm wondering if my stomach has started to swell,' and she smooths her tunic with her hand and holds it there.

You are starting to look like you really believe her now. You are absorbed as if listening to the best storyteller ever to visit Nazareth, but it's only Mary telling her version of things. And she's never been one for making things up. She'd always rather get into trouble than lie to Imma and Abba, but I can't even

---

[2] Isaiah 1:1.

[3] The name Nazareth is thought to derive from the Hebrew 'netzer', meaning 'branch' or 'shoot'. The significance of this would have occurred to many of Jesus's family members, friends and followers.

remember the last time that happened. It's very hard to live up to her standards.

'The angel did say that our cousin Elizabeth is expecting too. She's so very old! I have to go and visit her. If I find it is as the angel has said, then all this *has* to be true. I mean, I really know it is, of course it is. But sometimes it feels so far-fetched, like something a *child* would make up,' she says, looking at me and giving me a gentle nudge in the ribs. That didn't last long – now she's looking glum again and she's staring at the tree you've drawn. It's fading to nothing as it dries out in the heat.

'Joseph will come right,' you say. 'He just needs time. I expect by this time tomorrow he'll be back, and with a plan all worked out. You really don't have to worry. God has this sorted; you can be sure of that.' Mary's face is brightening slightly as she allows her mind to believe it. She really loves Joseph, but I think she loves God even more. 'What he calls you to, he'll give you the strength to see through. And who ever heard of his plans failing? He wants Joseph in on this, and a very good choice he was, too.'

I think you're right, and I can see Mary does, as she's smiling properly again. I mean she looks really happy and that smile just won't go away. I'm going to miss her when she's gone. Still, Joseph's house isn't far from here. Perhaps they'll let me stay with them, and then there'll be the baby I can help with. I can't wait. Not just any baby but *God's* baby. I wonder if he will cry? Will he throw his food on the floor when he gets bigger, and smear it in his hair? Will he have toddler strops? I don't think so. And I don't think he'll argue with me. He'll hold my hand, sit on my lap, listen to all my stories and will never get bored of me. Immanuel, God with us. But especially God with *us*. I'm looking forward to explaining all this to my friends, but for now, I've been told not to. Mary says they won't understand, and even if they do, their parents won't. She's dreading everyone knowing, but I'm not. I'm going to be Jesus's aunty and I'll have so much to teach him. I wonder what he'll teach me?

See Luke's Gospel, chapter 1, verses 26 – 38 for the angel's visit to Mary.

In John 19:25 we read that Mary had a sister. My story is built on this idea; while the details are purely speculation, it is certain Mary's pregnancy would have caused a stir at home.

Joseph's dilemma

At last I'm alone and no one can interrupt me. At last. I duck my head under a contorted branch that I used to swing from as a child. It was a struggle to reach then, even with a leg up from a friend, but now I have to stoop to walk beneath it. It's as good a place as any to pause, and I sit with my back against its wide trunk, my hands unable to settle on its twisted roots that are more jumbled together than my thoughts. I've sat in this olive grove more times than I can count and usually it calms me – that earthy scent, and just the sense that so many of these trees have been here hundreds of years, and will remain so. I remember sending a ball through these gnarled, arched roots when I was small, rolling it out the other side to a friend. One tree had such deep, exposed roots that we'd shelter inside them. That tree is long gone, and so is that life...long gone. No one else seems to come up here now at the end of the day, but that suits me fine.

So much has changed since last Thursday and I know I should get back to Mary soon, but I just don't know what to do. Oh, I just don't know. I surprise myself with a low groan that comes from deep within – it sends a sparrow that had started to pick through twigs near my feet flying for cover. Aww, I just don't want to let her go; that was never the plan. But what she's told me – I mean, it's so outlandish and she's made me look a fool.... I should be addressing these thoughts to you Father and asking for your help – forgive me. So dear Lord, I'm completely lost with this situation. I thought I knew her, could trust her. She had been constant these past five months and I couldn't wait for her to be fully mine. I'm a pretty tolerant fellow and I know we have base instincts – there's some rough talk amongst the builders that I can never block out completely – but Mary, really no. I had never expected this; it wasn't something I feared, for her character always seemed admirable. Always so pure. But Lord, she drew me aside, beckoned me round the back of the house, and whispered to me her terrible news: that she is pregnant. Pregnant! She stole a look at me as she said it, to gauge my reaction, and I saw no shame in her eyes. There was a degree of modesty there, yes, but she wasn't apologizing. She played with my fingers as she always did but I pulled my hand away. She blamed it on you, yes, you. I know you heard it, but the thing is, I'm still in shock.

I'm glad no one is watching me here, for the tears are coming again... Ho, Mary, can I trust you? Has something affected your mind? Do you not want to marry me? Are you making this up? Who else could there be in your life? Why did you have to go and ruin everything?

I'm up on my feet and pulling up a thorny, withered tree, roots and all. It scatters soil as it bursts from the earth, it scratches my skin, even causes a gash on my wrist, but I don't care.

Lord, what do we do? What do *I* do? Are you even there? Forgive me, I know you are but you've ripped out my very soul and set it adrift. Perhaps I thought too much of her, allowed her to take the place that should be yours in my heart... I'm sorry Lord. Please show me what to do. I have put off seeing her for too many days but I don't really want to part from her. Not from the girl I once knew, anyway... I should see her tomorrow, Lord. Yes, tomorrow. Would you show me what to do by then?

I think I'll take a stem from that young olive tree beside me, place it in a cup of water in the house to remind myself of this decision, to mark it. I will have an answer for her by tomorrow. If I follow the rules I know I should divorce her quietly, but my heart is telling me not to. What is it you're saying, Lord? What will your answer be? Help me not to miss it Lord, guide my thoughts, my steps, so that I truly know your will. Amen.

The gash on my wrist shows no sign of abating and I hold it tight with my hand as the blood runs through my fingers and drips onto the ground below. It's she who should be bleeding or suffering; not me, yet I'll carry the pain if I can, bear her shame. The pain feels good in some way – it marks the moment. I wonder if I'll always carry a scar.

I should head back now for the light is starting to fade but I could stay out here all night. Another prayer vigil in the olive grove, though mother will only worry. I glance up into the tree as I get to my feet, my gaze lost in its deep canopy. The stars are out already; I catch them flickering between the leaves like weak flames, but as I step out into the open I have to take a moment to just look and wonder. In an hour or so they'll be all ablaze, not faint glimmers in the evening gloaming. Why can't you guide me Lord as clearly as you make these stars shine in all their brilliance? May your direction for me be like the brightest star, burning in the deepest night sky: unmistakable, for I so fear getting it wrong.

I break a young, pliable off-shoot from the small olive tree and clutch it in my hand. So... If I can't have Mary, I don't want anyone. I had managed before I'd found her; I'm sure I'll manage again without. I'd been feeling the pressure from the community. Mother is aging and has taken some looking after lately

17

– 'Why don't you find yourself a wife?' was the phrase I'd heard a lot of from well-meaning friends. 'A wife would look after her.' I'd never been in a hurry for this though – I mean, I always was very self-sufficient and I knew she'd need a strong faith for me to want to share my time with her. There are so many vacuous girls out there now, all concerned with how impressive their houses might be – I see it all in my profession. What mind-numbing conversations I would've been subjected to – 'Joseph, would you mind building me an archway... Joseph, could you just make us a more impressive set of steps up to the roof?' Dare I say it, I've even noticed how they stare at me when I'm on a job – I suppose a strong physique is inevitable in my line of work, but it's never been something I've set out to achieve.

But anyway, I'd noticed Mary – who could not? ... It wasn't her beauty that attracted me, though very beautiful she is, with those big, dark eyes of hers that open so wide. If ever eyes could look honest, hers do. Everyone thinks she is beautiful. She seems unaware of it herself, or, at least, refuses to give it any thought...perhaps that's why. It's her beauty of spirit that always made me look in her direction long after she'd gone. Long after. I'd see her crouching down to talk to children or listening to the old folk in the temple when everyone else had gone home. She'd engage with them like no one else was more important to her in the whole world.

Well, perhaps I was wrong. Perhaps this dear, fragile Mary is not all she seems. For a while I worried about how unsuited we looked, just on a physical level – me with my height, my big hands that look so clumsy, my long stride, her with such a small delicate frame that she looks as if she might break. I should have listened. Or am I wrong? I need to give God space to invade my thoughts. I'll have an early night I think and will try to lie still with a mind that's open to him. I will sleep alone on the roof beneath the stars. He always steps in when we're real with him. At least *he* never lets me down.

***

So then—Mary. Of course she was telling the truth. That was the clearest, most memorable dream I've ever had, and I know what I must do now. I wonder if it's too early to drop by. What must she have thought of me? I can't quite see why God has allowed me to be a part of this grand scheme – I mean, why didn't he choose someone a bit less fickle to support her? This must have felt hard enough, without me doubting her. The first thing I'm going to say is how sorry I am. 'Mary, I'm so sorry I didn't believe you.' Then I'll take her hand and she can play with my fingers as much as she likes. Dear Mary. What must her father think of me? ... Perhaps he even thinks it's my child; no, I doubt that.

He's going to want her married in her predicament, anyway; at least that's a given. Well, life certainly won't be dull from here. My existence has never been exceptional really; I have worked hard, kept my commitment to my customers, and, of course, kept up my commitment to God. But until recently he had never asked much of me. All that seems to be changing.

So I'm going to make it up to Mary as best I can. I'll be the most devoted husband she can ever imagine, and I'll never doubt her again. There's that olive branch in the cup on the table; I'll bring that as a peace offering. I'm sure she'll get it. A rainbow in the sky would be nice too, a sign that I'll never break *my* promise. But I don't think that will be needed. There's a reason why God has chosen her for this task and I know his decision is so right…. So then, what do I need to tell her, I mean, where do I even begin? I'll explain the dream as best I can, and how the child's name is to be Jesus. I wonder if she knows that yet?

See Matthew chapter 1, verses 18 – 25 for the biblical account of Joseph's first dream.

Welcome, little king

Five days ago she was in Nazareth, bags and baskets packed for the journey, saying those lingering farewells. Her mother clung to her and asked one last time if it was really safe for her to travel. Joseph could do it alone, she'd reminded her; but no, he was faithful and kind and she wanted to be by his side. Dear Joseph. The way he looked at her and smiled – such commitment in his face, such depth of love. God really knew what he was doing in choosing him, though she wondered if *she* was up to the task herself. Why exactly had she 'found favour' with God, as the angel had said?[4]

It really hadn't been easy though. Joseph had told her his fears when they were alone together, that the neighbours couldn't be trusted, especially with him out of the way. He'd protected her so well and tried to shield her from the unkind comments, but she knew what they said about her: 'Damaged goods', 'Harlot', and, the worst one of all, 'Stone-worthy. He should stone her; why didn't he?' Did they really think she couldn't hear them, or spot the hands in front of their mouths as they whispered? She saw the looks they gave her when she walked on by. She'd found there was nothing she could do but keep her head down and pass quickly. What kept her strong was the knowledge it would change – she knew, even then, that the shame would all be gone when this little one was born… To have him in their midst, the most awesome thing, what her people had dreamt of for so long. And now here he was. Incredible. Praise God, the King of kings. His tender mercies would know no end, and it started right here, with this precious little one in her lap.

Five days! How much had changed since then. She dipped her fingers in the shallow dish of olive oil beside her and ran them over the baby's smooth skin, massaged the oil into his dark strong hair, over his cheeks and his little nose with the gentlest of touches. Did he look like her? It was hard to tell so early on; she wondered if there would be any likeness at all. He certainly wouldn't look like Joseph, but he had the purest, deepest love of all and would be the best earthly father she could imagine.

She picked up one of the baby's small hands and felt it wrap around her finger. He held on with all of his little might. What a beautiful boy he was and how she loved him already! What an incredible gift! Her heart felt so full of love for him that she could even feel it beating; she felt more alive than ever

---

[4] Luke 1:30.

before. What purpose he had given her, what hope! How wonderful God was, that he should have dreamt this up and thought of *her*.

She wiped the tears from her face that had started to fall onto the baby, and felt Joseph lay his big strong arm across her shoulders. He swept the remaining tear from her cheek. 'It's going to be alright, you know,' he said. He paused and hummed while he filtered his thoughts. Then, 'We've got this far,' he continued, 'and one fine day we'll take him home, show the family. You need to get some rest now, you must be so tired.'

'I could stay here forever, just us three,' she said as she rubbed the oil over the baby's legs and feet, her fingers lingering on his tiny toes. 'I'm in no hurry to go back anyway – it won't be easy, the gossip won't stop.' She paused. 'Can you pass me those strips of cloth?'

'One day at a time,' said Joseph, handing them to her. 'I...I wanted to provide you with some place better than this but we'll find a proper room soon.'

'I'm comfy here,' she said. 'And look how settled he is.' They gazed at the baby, transfixed by him. She tenderly wrapped him in the swaddling bands then kissed him on the forehead. Joseph arranged some straw in the feeding trough next to where he was sitting, then rose, took him in his arms and placed him inside, very slowly though so as not to wake him.

It was getting quite dark now, but the moon was large and casting enough light for them.

There was the noise of a stampede outside and raucous shouts, the heavy feet of young men racing down the track.

'I'll go and see what's happening,' he said. But as he spoke, there was a gentle cough from outside.

'Shalom!' came a voice. 'We're looking for a baby.'

Joseph stepped over to the mouth of the cave[5] and there stood an old wizened shepherd who, on catching sight of mother and child, stepped back and bowed his head. 'We saw some angels out in the fields; they invited us down, *us*,' he said, looking at his old woollen tunic and brushing off the debris from the field. A cluster of shepherd faces joined him in the entrance, their eyes wide and shining bright.

---

[5] See note at the end of the story for why a cave features in this account.

'Come in,' said Joseph. 'All of you.'

'He's the Saviour of the world,' said the old shepherd. 'Ach, it's the Lord, he's here and the angels chose to tell *us*.' He shook his head in wonderment and, in a moment of boldness, went right up to the manger and knelt before him. 'Welcome, little king,' he said, and shook his head again.

A young, vital shepherd put a hand on his shoulder and knelt down beside him, and the others followed.

'Well, well, what a night indeed! I'm glad to see you've found our manger,' said a tall shepherd with a long beard who stood up now and leant on his staff. He placed it against the wall and began rotating a twig in the centre of a limestone slab, at the entrance to the cave.

'*Your* manger?' said Mary. But was the Lord in this as well?

'It's where we birth them – in here,' the shepherd replied. 'Otherwise they're out on the hillside, every day of the year.'

Soon the shepherd had a small fire going and brought over the oil lamps from the craggy shelves, before placing them back, one by one.

'I did wonder how you found us so easily,' said Joseph. 'The angels—they didn't give you directions then?' said Joseph with a smile.

'Ach, we knew where to come, alright,' said the oldest shepherd, the wonder in his eyes now even more visible. 'We've known for a very long time.'

There was a silence now – a holy silence, and it felt like no one should break it. It was a moment that would stay with Mary for eternity. These were certainly respectful men, she pondered. But they were more than that, it seemed. For they'd been called to witness the dear child's arrival. Oh, what a moment was this! And what a God they served.

'Those...those angels...so what *did* they say to you?' asked Joseph, sitting down again and resting a hand on Mary's shoulder.

'It was just one who spoke, but soon there was a great crowd of them, singing their praises to God. I'm surprised you didn't hear them from here.'

And the old shepherd told them what the angel had said and the hearts of all were warmed.

'So...What've you done with your sheep?' said Joseph and they laughed together.

22

'Ach, they'll cope without us for a short time,' said the oldest shepherd at last. 'You know, my sheep don't roam far.'

'We really shouldn't stop long,' said a nervous looking young shepherd, and he pulled on the leather belt around his waist. 'If they end up blemished, they're no good.'

'Just this once, lad, just this once,' replied a shepherd with a greying bushy beard. 'Tonight is an exceptional night.'

'So the Bethlehem sheep are special, I've heard,' said Joseph, 'very special.'

'That's right, young man. King David tended these sheep as a lad,' said the old leader.

'And I wrapped the most recent one,' said the young shepherd, now appearing to gain confidence as he realized how warmly they'd been received. 'I put him in that self-same manger. It's our tradition,' he said, with a proud smile.

'Well, ours is a holy calling,' said the tall shepherd. 'We declare which will be Passover lambs at birth, then wrap them, like the boy said.'

'And the only journey they'll ever do is to Jerusalem to be sacrificed,' continued the oldest shepherd, picking up the story. 'Course, not all of them will be good enough. They have to be without blemish, no broken bones either. We walk them in on a Friday to be slain. Only when their last drop of blood is spilt will the temple priest declare, 'It is finished.''

'Grandfather, they don't want to hear such detail, not on such a joyful night,' said the youngest shepherd to the eldest.

'Oh I think they do,' the old man replied. 'I think they understand.'

'There's bleating, it's getting louder,' said the young shepherd. 'I think they've nearly caught up with us!' 'Come on lads, we'd better go. Pleased to meet you, little king.'

See Luke chapter 2, verses 1 – 20 for the narrative of Jesus's birth.

There is an old tradition that Jesus was born in a cave. While we cannot be certain, some researchers think this was the Tower of the Flock, Migdal Edgar, the cave used by the temple shepherds in which the Passover lambs were birthed. Researchers like to cite Micah 4:8.

The sacrificial temple lambs had to be one-year-old males, and living outside for 365 days. The fields around Bethlehem are known to be where they were raised. (See 'Bad for Business' story and accompanying notes later in the narrative.)

There is the thought that Luke 2:7 states 'in the manger' rather than 'a manger' (Cambridge Bible for Schools and Colleges and the Thayer Greek Dictionary). Commentators do raise the question of how the shepherds knew where to go otherwise, for the angels didn't tell them, and they were not led by a star. I wonder how many mangers there would have been in Bethlehem.

Simeon's tale

Ah, I always knew I'd recognize him, never doubted that. In fact, I've built my whole life on this day actually happening. It's a humbling thing, living on a promise from God – I think he has these blessings for us all if we ask – you see, I'm nothing special. I've just grasped something incredible: I've understood something of the abundance of his love and clung to it all my days.

That assurance he gave me, that I'd see the Messiah, it changed my life really. See, I've been able to take wonderful risks, as I've known it's impossible for me to be in mortal danger. I guess that's pretty unique. 'Abba, you've got to stop exploring those caves by yourself,' they'd say. 'Abba, you should come back with us now, it's getting dark.' And 'You can't walk all that way, not on your own. What if your legs should give way?' The latest concern is this: 'Abba, you mustn't toil out in the sun all day. You're exhausting yourself, then you sleep so deeply we worry you'll never wake.' I raised my eyebrows at her and sighed yet still she went on, that grown-up daughter of mine. You see, she makes out the rest of the family worry like she does, but I'm not convinced. 'Yesterday you slept through all the chatter of the morning as we got up around you,' she said. 'I wove half a child's tunic before you even stirred, then there were seven of us outside in the courtyard as we finished making up the order.' She was immune to my laughter and expression of good fortune, being able to sleep through all of that. She's only staying with us as her husband is away; is it wrong to wish him back so soon? 'All the usual girls' banter and the others wouldn't tone it down,' she went on. 'You were out cold the whole time. You really mustn't overdo it – you do worry us so.'

'Oh, I'm not going anywhere just yet,' I told her. 'The Lord hasn't come.' I wasn't about to explain I'd been up most of the night praying. It's the only time I get any peace around here. Ah, I love looking up at the stars from the rooftop, knowing that he hung each one in time and space, and feeling the reassurance it brings – that he holds me here too, for his great purpose.

I must admit, at times I have tried to hasten his coming. You see, these old bones really do ache, I cannot grip things anymore and my sight is not what it was. It gets a little wearing, too, when the family start to doubt you and ask you to explain yourself again: 'How can you be so sure?' they'd ask. 'What if you got it wrong?' That last phrase is the wife's. It's tiresome and has made me long for him even more. I'd been having another of these spells recently; as always I turned it into prayer. 'Send him soon,' has been my cry; I would utter it under my breath. Often I'd fast and protest in groans, begging him to fulfil his promise soon. 'You need to eat properly,' the family would say, 'you've been fasting for days.' That grown-up daughter of mine, she really is the biggest worrier. I don't know how she'll cope when I tell her my news of the day – she'll find a way to make it negative, adding some fresh anxiety of her own. She twists that long dark plait of hers and tries not to look at me as she comes out with her fears.

'I'm alright,' I'd say to the fasting nag.

'Look how thin you are,' she'd tell me. 'You're wasting away. We think you're a bit fixated, Abba.' Then she'd kneel in front of me to implore me, like I really don't know my own mind, like I need advice from the young.

'I'm just fine. I'll eat again tomorrow. I can hear from him better this way. Besides, I'm not going anywhere until I see him,' I'd say.

They'd smile at me as if I'm old and daft, thinking they know best. Ah, how funny is that? I long for them to have God as close as I do. But perhaps now they'll believe me – you see, that's what I've been building towards telling you – it happened today. I was out in the sun, whittling my old staff as I leant against the whitewashed wall of the house, when my heart started to burn and my legs started to tingle. I could feel my face flushing and it wasn't just the warmth of the day – it was still early. It was as if my spirit leapt inside me and said to my body, 'Come on, get a move on, it's time!'

Don't you just love these moments when the Lord prompts you? I hope you have experienced them too. Sometimes your heart is beating fast and you're thinking, I must speak out, I must say something or go some place. If you're not quick, you can lose the moment, then you find somebody else is doing that thing, or saying what you knew you were meant to. Other times you only know in retrospect that something happened by his prompting; you stand back amazed, as if you're admiring a beautiful painting that's in progress and seeing it all come together.

I had been on the alert for this moment for quite some time, so conscious that the day must be coming that I was worried... See, it meant I'd wander up to the temple and wait on the Lord very often, thinking, *Could today be the day? I must be ready.* It was never time wasted, sitting quietly before him in prayer. But today's prompting really had to be of him, and I could see a baby in my mind's eye: his head of thick dark curls was poking out of the top of a striped woollen shawl. Ah, the energy I felt in these old bones, it was like being a young lad all over again, and the excitement! I left my stick at home and practically ran the whole way up there; I just knew the day had arrived.

26

They entered the temple just minutes after me, and I think I startled the poor mother. I raced up to them the moment they walked through the door and threw my arms open wide, both in praise to God and in welcome to them; it's all the same really, for God himself had arrived in human form.

There he was, that same little head of curls emerging from the striped blanket, though I'd have known it was them without this. I'm sure tears fell from my eyes and perhaps I looked a little wild, for she stepped backwards and looked questioningly at her husband, but he only smiled back at her, as if this kind of thing happened to them all the time. His eyes smiled too. 'Shalom,' he said to me, and a feeling of warmth encompassed me, a sense of good will from all in this little party. The man introduced himself as Joseph, took the baby from her and placed him in my arms – *the living God, in my arms* – and I burst forth in praise, acknowledging his fulfilment of that old promise to me, that I would see his salvation. I blessed the mother, such a gentle soul, such tender love she has for her child but she will have to be strong, for I see it all. I know he will be pierced, and I told her that she would be, too. For though he will bear it physically, taking the weight of the world's sin on himself, she will bear it inwardly, her very soul pierced through seeing him suffer and letting him go. Today it was hard to imagine that would be possible. The baby whimpered as my voice boomed over him, and threw out his arms as he began to cry. His mother placed a hand on his little chest and soothed him with her motherese. She is the Lord's choice and he knows what he is doing. There's plenty of time for him to prepare her for what lies ahead.

And now I am back, sitting against the wall of my house again in the sunshine. As I run my thumb over my old gnarled staff I know that I won't need it for long. It has served its purpose and so have I, though I say this without fear and without regret. You see, my life is complete now, my Lord is faithful and I am ready. What a privilege it was to look down on that little face, God's love made visible to us. To think, that little baby will grow into a man, the very best man ever to live. Ah, it is the most significant event in human history. How this old world will be different, how many lives he will touch, as he dwells here and then beyond, as he weaves salvation into the hearts of men. That God looked on me and revealed his plan has been the biggest blessing of my life. We're all significant to him though – as I said earlier to you, I'm nothing special. Would you like him to speak to you as he did to me? I dare you to ask him, 'What do you have for me, Lord? Is there a promise you want me to hold onto?' I must admit, I'm glad I did. It changed my life for good.

See Luke chapter 2, verses 25 – 35 for Simeon's testimony.

Uncle Joseph

'Uncle Joseph, you awake?'

'Huh?' He was now, though he'd rather not be.

'Uncle Jo-seepph.'

He paused before replying this time, as was his way. 'It's very early,' he said at last.

'I know, I kn-know.'

'What's troubling you, Jacob?' Joseph rolled over to face the lad and blinked in the half-light. So this was the reality of parenting a teenager, though he was only looking after him for a couple of days. He'd thought it would get easier, for babies and toddlers were definitely challenging, even when they'd been heaven-sent. Could he have prayed for Jacob a little too much? Joseph smiled to himself – too much of God was never a problem. Too much of God? What a ludicrous thought! But for some reason the boy was different to his peers – he was so intense, and well ahead of his years.

'U-uncle Joseph,' he hissed. 'H-how h-how will I know God's will? Last n-n-night you made following him sound so easy but really it's not. H-how can I be sure of what he wh-wants from me?'

'I'm still learning myself,' he whispered in reply. 'Go back to sleep... We'll talk later.' Mary needed her sleep; it had been another disturbed night for her, and even in the quiet she had been restless. He wondered if she might be pregnant again, or if it were simply the fact they had travelled so much and now even home didn't feel permanent any more. She was one to feel things keenly.

'I want to hear from him. I w-want to know all about your dreams. Abba says you always were a dreamer, even when you were li-little boys, but there's m-more to it, isn't there?'

Joseph laughed his deep laugh so that a sheltering bird flew from the windowsill outside.

'Sshush, little Jesus is stirring,' said Jacob. 'And it's rude to laugh at me.'

'Trust your father, always a put down at the ready,' he said in his quietest voice, laying his hand on the toddler to settle him. 'That's why I was laughing. This little man needs some peace with his mother, though he can sleep though anything. Come on, roll up your bed. Let's go for a walk before we wake the others.'

'T-t-tell me it's not just a character thing,' said Jacob when they were out on the road. 'I want to hear from God like you. I want him to give me d-dreams, to share his thoughts with me. Is that unreasonable?' The boy continued mouthing his words after he had spoken, as if his speech had been rehearsed.

'Not at all,' said Joseph, landing a heavy hand on the boy's shoulder. 'The Scriptures speak of God wanting to share his secrets with us.'

'Wooh, that would be so great. Wh-where does it say that?' asked Jacob, pulling at a branch of eucalyptus as he walked on past. 'Hmn, smells good,' he said, holding the leaf to his nose.

'In several places. I like this phrase, though: "Friendship with the Lord is reserved for those who fear him. With them, he shares the secrets of his covenant." It's from the Psalms.'[6]

'I fear him. That's good isn't it? B-but I am only fourteeen,' and he scrunched his eyes so they were tightly closed. Joseph waited for the lad to recover and watched him blink several times.

'You're never too young to hear the voice of God.'

Jacob looked up at him and smiled a broad smile that made deep dimples appear in the centre of his cheeks. 'Where are we walking to? Wh-what path do we take? It's been a while since I was here.'

'We'll go on up to the olive grove, we can talk there.'

'I don't know the way, you-you are making me anxious.'

Nothing new there, then. 'Just follow me,' he replied.

Joseph could hear Jacob muttering to himself as he walked behind him along the now steep and narrow track, but soon the path opened into the olive grove and they sat side by side beneath a shady tree. The fruit collection had finished a week ago, but still some less-than-perfect olives lay discarded on the ground. Though the sun hadn't yet risen there was enough light for them to appreciate the view of the settlement below.

'So, Jacob. We're here because you're longing for God. You've grasped that a relationship is a two-way thing I see, you're wanting something real. As your uncle that makes me very proud. But it's a risky thing, hearing from God,

---

[6] Psalm 25:14.

Jacob. Are you up for that?' Joseph threw a shrivelled olive that lay beside him on the ground as others might skim stones beside the sea, causing it to bounce several times before landing.

'Course I am. I think so. H-how do you mean?' Joseph watched him as he blinked excessively, then rubbed his eyes. If only he could reassure the lad, for the Lord could heal him of all his fears. At least he was searching in the right place. Searching way beyond what was comfortable for him, that was clear. There was no point trying to make a life of faith sound any easier, though it would be the most freeing thing for him.

'You find yourself having to go with what you think God's saying. Even at the risk of making yourself look ridiculous.'

'I'm used to people laughing at me. You know how… tongue-tied I get.' Joseph saw the boy's eyes well up before he took a small twig and drew circles in the dirt with an intentness that was hardly required.

'I was like that too once, but I'm getting better. Perhaps it runs in the family.'

'H-how did you stop?'

'I don't know. It just happened. I think it has something to do with recognizing the trust God has in me.' He paused as he tried to work it out in his mind and shook his head. 'I still don't get it, but if he believes in me I guess I should, too.'

Jacob blinked hard again and Joseph ruffled his hair.

'So tell me how to hear.'

'You have to get to the point where what God says matters more to you. What he thinks of you is more important than whatever your so-called friends might say.'

'How did it all start for y-you, Uncle Joseph?'

'It was with Mary's pregnancy.' He stopped talking for a moment and wondered just how much to say. But the lad was old enough to be frank with, he decided. 'You heard me talking about it last night. That first dream was easy enough to handle – so, it made sense of everything. For Mary to have been unfaithful to me was not something I could even begin to understand. When a person you trust turns out to be not as they seemed it's deeply troubling. It's like… like trying to light your lamp and the wick just won't take. You wonder if some joker has filled the lamp with water… if you have filled your friend or loved one with qualities from your imagination. That first dream just confirmed what my heart told me; it all fitted.'

'She is lovely. She's always b-een kind to me.'

Joseph smiled at the interruption, but now the lad had him started, there was just so much to tell. 'And even the challenges that I've thought preposterous have had a purpose,' he said. 'To start with it didn't seem fair, having to take Mary one hundred miles to Bethlehem with her being so heavily pregnant.'

'That's a long way, a long long way,' said Jacob, 'and you were gone for ages. We thought you were never coming back to Galilee.'

'Of course, she wouldn't have to walk it, I found a good steady mule for the job, but I did wonder if God's timing could have been better. Then I heard a verse I had long forgotten when we visited the temple. That place will always hold special memories, with old Simeon's joy when we walked in, his utter certainty.'

'Simeon?'

'He's an old prophet there. He may be with our Father now, he was holding out to see Jesus before he died.'

Jacob's eyes widened a little.

'If I'd still needed convincing by then that Jesus was special, my doubts would have all gone after having seen him. What a treasure he is.'

'What was the verse?'

'It's from the book of Micah, and speaks of how out of Bethlehem "will come for me one who will be ruler over Israel, whose origins are from old, from ancient times."[7] I shook my head in wonderment when I heard it and I steadied myself on a pillar, for it made me feel quite lightheaded. I don't know why it hadn't occurred to me before – it certainly would have made that long journey seem less tedious. Hindsight is a wonderful thing.'

Jacob was silent and Joseph didn't want to break it. God was doing business with him. Being treated like an adult probably helped, and he could see this was a significant time for him. But that the lad looked up to him so much worried him. 'You know, even with all that, I still find it hard to hear him sometimes. Perhaps that's why he gives me dreams, just to get through to me,

---

[7] Micah 5:2. NIV translation here.

but then I question if I've made them up, if they are really of God. It seems there's always so much at stake, but to miss his purpose would be even worse, so I keep pressing in, praying with each step, that he will make things right if there's an error of judgement on my part.'

'Tell me the n-next dream, Uncle Joseph.'

'The sun is coming up, we should be getting back.'

'Ju-just one more, one more.'

'That would be what happened after the unusual visitors.'

'Visitors?'

'Wise men. It's a miracle we could even understand them, they had travelled so far. If anyone can give you the perfect example of going out of your way for God, then it's these fellows. When you do what you think God's telling you to, then you can massively boost the faith of others.'

'So where had they come from, what were they like?'

'The whole thing sounds like a made-up dream, you'll think it so far-fetched.'

'No!'

'It all started when I heard a camel outside – have you ever heard their low moaning, it's very distinctive?'

'I don't think I have.'

'Considering how expensive they are, you'd expect an animal with a little more dignity. Anyway, dignity was not something lacking in those riding them.'

'Go on.'

'They looked like they were from another world – their clothes were of sumptuous colours, like the midnight sky, and the ripest fruit, bright reds and oranges fresh from a tree, pomegranates, loquats, plums. When I first saw them I couldn't look away. It was their conduct that was so amazing, though. It turns out they'd travelled for hundreds of miles, but instead of requesting a drink, they tied up their camels, and on seeing Mary come outside with Jesus, they knelt down, right there on the street. I couldn't help noticing the star – it was phenomenal, I'd never seen the like before and I could see people gazing at it from their rooftops right across the valley. I never drink heavily, but it felt as if I had – as if my mind wasn't in control, for none of this was logical or followed expected norms.'

Jacob stared at Joseph again, his eyes now even wider and unblinking.

'I encouraged them inside while some of the local lads came up to pet their camels, like these kind of visitors came every day of the week.'

'Wooh, wooh, that's amazing. Could you understand them?'

'We could. They said they'd had no special preparation in language study, but I think the Lord enabled them to communicate with us. They told us how they saw a magnificent star back in Persia, yet it appeared to them at dawn, shining as brightly as the sun.'

The pair looked towards the sun rising across the valley then, the trees and buildings mere outlines as dawn took hold, and they had to look away, such was the strength of the early rays. 'They knew they were to follow it,' Joseph continued, 'but they didn't leave immediately, for somehow they understood it was to be a very long journey and they would be away for months. They had to explain to their families, make some provision for them. I think they set out around the time Jesus was born. Such devotion, such determination. If ever you want a godly example, look to these men.'

'Bu-but Uncle Joseph, I-I don't have *them*. I have you. God has given me you.'

Joseph ruffled his hair again. He was so fond of the lad; it was such a privilege to have him stay with them. He wondered if he might be able to teach him his trade and keep him for months at a time. He was of the right age.

'Anyway, we wanted them to stay, but once they had given us their gifts they didn't stop long. They had a simple meal with us and then went. It had been a very emotional time. One of them cried when I lifted Jesus up to him and put him in his arms. He doubled over as if in pain, but he said he wasn't ill – quite the opposite, he told me. He was the one who gave the myrrh.'

'Sounds a b-bit morbid.'

'I don't think so. You don't know what an honour this was, and how strange it all felt. It somehow reassured me that we're securely in God's plan. Things aren't happening randomly; he's unrolling his purposes and nothing's going to stop that.' Joseph paused and looked at the boy. 'We just need to remain close to him and he'll do the rest.'

'And what happened next?'

'I had the second dream. It was that same night and I think it had to be. So God was to tell me something big, and their example was at the forefront of my mind. It was the journey to Egypt. It was the weirdest thing. "Get up," he told me, "take the child and his mother and escape to Egypt. Stay there until I tell you, for Herod is going to search for the child to kill him."'[8]

'Imagine if you-you'd got that wrong.'

'We just had to get on with it. I roused Mary and she packed up quickly and did as I asked without question. I almost wondered if she already knew, she was so obliging. "I've had the strangest dream," I told her, but she was beyond being surprised by God. And she trusts him implicitly. Always a good thing in a wife, it makes life so much easier.'

'Amazing though.'

'Sometimes it can take a while for the truth to sink in – when we wake we remember life as it was before a momentous change, but other times God really motivates us and we wake with such clarity. This was one such time.'

'I really want to hear from God like you do. Do you th-think I will?'

'I don't doubt it. When your desires are for the things of God he always follows through. But there's a learning curve. There'll be times when your conscious mind tells you God's plans are ludicrous. You believe God has told you something, but no matter how much trouble he's taken to make it clear to you, there is still wariness lurking, telling you how foolish you are.'

Jacob nodded with an intentness that showed he'd listened hard and learnt well. His squinting was forgotten; perhaps he'd let it go now.

'Come on, we need to get back. Mary will wonder where we've got to. Would you like to come to work with me today? Have a taste of it while your father's away?'

'I-I'd love to but I'm n-not so very strong.'

'That's no matter. I'm just glad to have you around.'

Jacob walked ahead on the steep track and stopped to pick up a large stick from beneath an olive tree.

'Hey, Jacob.'

'Yes?' he replied, thwacking the trees overhead with the stick as he went.

---

[8] Matthew 2:13, NIV.

'Pray about the work God wants you to do. That can be your first challenge. I'll be praying too, let's see how he guides you.'

Jacob gave him a nod and smiled. Perhaps he already knew.

See Matthew 2, verses 1–12 for the visit of the Magi, and verses 13–21 for more on Joseph's dreams and obedience.

Jacob is an imagined character, but I like to think of how Mary and Joseph's story would have influenced others, and perhaps there were young nieces and nephews who wanted to know more. To my mind, there must have been those who were impressed, who wanted to know why they did such outlandish things. I feel sure God would have used them to help others understand how he leads and guides.

Young James

Jesus is going to be in such trouble, wandering off like that. I'm glad Imma and Abba let the rest of us stay with the group, though Imma did take some convincing – 'I can't lose another one – oh, what a trip this has turned into.'

'They'll be perfectly safe,' said Abba.

Of course we are.

It did take a while for them to notice, and I didn't realize he was up to anything, either. Abba thought he was walking with the women and children, Imma thought he was walking with the men. It wasn't until we stopped for the night that they began to realize something was up.

It makes a change for Jesus to get into trouble and I'm quite enjoying it. 'I wish you could be more like your brother,' they say to me. That's so unfair, as I'm not naughty – just a bit lively. We are close in age, which doesn't help, I think. It was sure to make them compare us. Now he's being a little like me and I can't help smiling. The brother who is hard to live up to, the child every parent wants, behaving like a normal boy for once. But he is the best big brother I could imagine. I can trust him with anything, he always has time for me and always has exactly the words I need to hear. He's at least as wise as Imma and Abba. He's funny too though – his timing is perfect. People do look at us oddly when we laugh so hard, but to explain our jokes to them wouldn't be easy. He's my best friend and brother all in one.

I hope he's having a big adventure. I'm looking forward to hearing all about it. Now I'm the big one, looking after Joses, Jude and Simon. I've carried little Simon on my back for miles, but Imma did say not to take my eyes off him. Now he's snoozing on my auntie's back; I think she could see how I was struggling under the weight of him.

I heard Imma and Abba getting ready to leave this morning, felt Imma's kiss on my cheek, but pretended not to notice. She's too emotional right now and it was much easier that way. Jesus has made a lot of work for them and he'll get a telling off like he's never known before. In fact, I don't think he ever has been told off. I do hope they find him.

See Luke 2, verses 41–51 for the biblical account of Jesus's boyhood trip to the temple. For references to his siblings, see Mark 6:3 and Matthew 13:55–56.

Finding Jesus

'We're looking for our boy,' said Mary, approaching a party of elderly women on the outskirts of the city. They were only just leaving and probably didn't have so far to go before they reached home, for the light was already beginning to fade. 'He's lost the group,' she continued, using her hands as she spoke, her voice animated and urgent. We haven't seen him in –'

'In this crowd?' replied the oldest looking member of the party, a pilgrim who was bent double and had to lean with both hands on her stick as she uncoiled her back to give eye-contact. Her condescending glare made Mary realize just how hopeless their situation was. But they were wasting their time with her – she could only have seen her feet the whole way out of Jerusalem.

'We see it all the time,' the old woman continued. 'We live quite close to the city and there are lost children every time there's a pilgrimage.' She rolled her eyes before resuming hunched position over her stick.

'He's got to be somewhere, Mary,' said Joseph, apparently sensing her despair. 'He's a sensible boy.'

'Clearly not sensible enough,' Mary replied. Joseph raised an eyebrow at her and she stared back at him, defiant. 'Oh, I can't believe this. We wouldn't be hunting for him if he was everything we thought he was, would we?'

'Come on, Mary, you know that's not true.'

'Give us something to go on,' joined a slim, sprightly woman who looked as if she walked the pilgrimage route for fun. She was softly spoken and seemed keen to help. Perhaps she came out of her way to help the pilgrims who wandered so close to her home.

'Jesus, twelve, he's a tho–'

'Well that's half the boys his age with that name,' said the first woman. 'So *common*.'

'No, go on,' said her friend.

'Jesus, twelve, he's a thoughtful looking lad,' said Mary. 'He often seeks out quiet locations on his own; either that or he's in the thick of things, friends all around him. That's why this is so surprising – most of his friends were walking back with him, or so we thought; there's nothing for him around here with them all gone.'

'Sorry we can't help,' said the considerate woman. 'We'll keep an eye out as we walk.'

'Thank you,' said Mary, her gaze already down the track, scanning the walkers for young lads, in groups or on their own, but there was no one who even remotely reminded her of him. 'We must go on,' she said to Joseph, her eyes wide and imploring. 'I wonder if he's lost and waiting for us. Perhaps he's gone to our gathering point, that would be the obvious place, wouldn't it?'

Joseph only hummed a quiet agreement then thanked the group, taking her hand when the women had passed on. He held it long enough for her to remember his past good judgement, and her own in choosing him. He was always so reassuring, but was she wrong to take comfort in him? It seemed he was never ruffled – oh, he was so *unflappable*. Surely now he should seem just a little bit bothered?

They were on their way again, covering ground at an even faster pace, slowing only when groups came into view. This really couldn't be happening – but what was the boy thinking? He had never been selfish before – in fact, he'd always been so *considerate*, assisting her in the house, being a big brother to the other children, helping Joseph with odd little jobs. Had they taken him for granted, put too much on him, was that it? Sometimes it was easy to forget he was only twelve. He was the loveliest boy – she knew she shouldn't have favourites and she didn't, but her heart connected with his. He was intuitive and had been like adult company for her even when he was very small; in short, he was such a God-send. Had God now taken him away – but why? Did he want him for himself now? Or had the boy injured himself somewhere, or come to harm? But how? Hadn't he been there when they all gathered together to set off for home? Now she came to think of it, she couldn't locate in her mind exactly when she had seen him last. She never had to worry about him, that was the thing.

They had done this trip for years. Every Passover they would make their way to Jerusalem and the week always passed uneventfully. Why should this year be any different? She needn't have gone anyway, she could have stayed home with the children, but she liked to go, and had never thought there was a risk before. Jesus loved it too, and next year he would be obliged to go, in his newfound 'man' status.[9] The boy had some growing up to do before then.

---

[9] V. 43 *pais*, (Greek noun) "boy, youth, child, a young person normally below the age of puberty." Walter Bauer and Frederick W. Danker, *A Greek-English Lexicon of the New Testament and Other Early Christian Literature* (1957, 1979, 2000).

The olive trees were in bloom and she was reminded of the olive tree that grew beside their courtyard doorway, that Joseph had given her as a cutting all those years ago. She had seen the greeny-white buds on the tree when they set out. Oh, how could losing Jesus fit into God's big plan? It made no sense at all.

The day was drawing to a close and it was almost twenty-four hours since they had realized he was missing. She had felt frantic from the first moment, but it had taken a while for them to understand the seriousness of it all. The party from Nazareth had stopped for the night and were busy pitching tents and preparing family meals. She and Joseph then assumed Jesus had dived into a friend's tent or had wandered the short distance to the river, and no one even took her concerns seriously to begin with, for he was such a good lad and everyone knew just how responsible he was. Of course, she quizzed her children. It was when James said he was the one looking after the younger two that she had started to worry. James and Joses helped with the search; Joses seemed to think it was a game, family hide-and-seek around the campsite, but James understood and stayed close by her side. Then they asked Jesus's friends, and they hadn't seen him either. There was no sense of a cover-up – of course not, for he was not that sort of boy – but something clearly wasn't right.

Joseph said they would have to retrace their steps, but that it would have to wait until morning. It was a dangerous road, and they had all heard tales of bandits jumping on unsuspecting tourists, of muggings and even of one man being left for dead. There were wild animals too; oh Mary didn't want to think on it. But there were bears, weren't there? And lions, imagine if one were feeling particularly hungry, though even a wild ox could be pretty scary. Could he have been alone on that road? She barely slept on that first night without him, and lay in the crook of Joseph's arm while he stroked her hair and whispered reassuring things in her ear and muttered half-prayers to God – keep him safe, Lord, protect him, I pray, be with him Lord, let us find him – she didn't think he slept much either, truth be told.

They had set off as soon as dawn was breaking, leaving their friends to clear up their tent and carry it on with them, for they could only think of finding their son. Now they had reached Jerusalem and Joseph said they must bed down for the night before resuming their search in the morning.

***

All Mary's fears seemed to have been realized, for he could not be found there after a full day of trying, and her voice was hoarse from asking so many people, her eyes stinging from the constant flow of tears. The truth was, he didn't look any different from all the other lads his age, there was nothing distinctive about his appearance. She could hear the negative answers to her questions before she'd even finished asking each time. Oh, she just felt so desperate. They found themselves lost on several occasions, having walked down the old streets and somehow looped back to where they had already been. Now it was three days since they had seen him. Three days, and her heart felt so burdened, so full of sorrow. Joseph said they should go to the temple and pray, make an offering, to show God their unwavering commitment to him and implore him for his help, to re-consecrate themselves and Jesus to him.

They were on their way there now. They hadn't decided on a sacrifice for the time being, but they were going there to pray and make their peace with God. She knew that in her own heart some hostility towards him had crept in – she had blamed him, blamed Joseph, had blamed herself too, certainly, but her spirit hadn't been right, and she wanted to collapse into God's grace again and seek his face.

The temple didn't look the most inviting of places. She wondered if they wanted anyone to really feel at home there in God's house; they had installed golden spikes along the roof line to keep the birds from settling and adding their own 'decoration'. She couldn't look at the outer walls in the brightness of the day – the marble shone with great flashes, like lightning, or a sword-blade in the sun. The bronze doors were blinding too, and the scale of the place was intimidating.

Walking into the temple from the glare outside made them blink and stand still for a moment, and the cool stone beneath their feet was halting. There was a heady smell of incense and they could hear chanting coming from a far-off chamber, but something else had caught Joseph's attention, for he nudged Mary in the ribs – 'Over there,' he said, 'Look. Does that not look like our son, sitting at the feet of the rabbi?'

Mary didn't need convincing and started to run towards her son. That he was here, looking like such a good boy, listening so intently, but without a thought for his mother and father! Were not earthly responsibilities important, too? Oh, what she would like to say to him but she could not, for they would judge her most severely. She could hear him asking a question about the Passover as they approached, though they had discussed it often enough at home. He wanted to know if things would ever change, if that system would have to go on forever. If anything could ever take place, if a person might intervene somehow, or if they were locked into the routine perpetually.

Had he not even noticed them standing over him now? One teacher looked a little aghast, perhaps even afraid of him. His posture was defensive and he was staring at her boy with contempt, his brows rutted, his hostility evident in the way his staring eyes bulged, a vein pulsating in his temple. What else had Jesus been saying? But another of the group looked particularly impressed by him, he was transfixed by the boy and stroking his chin, looking thoughtful. It was *astonishment* in his face, that was clear to see. He was looking on him as one looks on a child of whom they are especially proud, when they do or say something that warms your heart and makes you feel glad they are yours. If he only knew.

'Son, why have you treated us like this?' she said to him, for she had had enough. 'Your father and I have been anxiously searching for you.' It was hard to keep the rebuke from her voice, to keep the pain from being audible, for that should all be expressed in private once they were alone together, but the anguish of the last few days caught up with her. It was overwhelming, to find him here like this, and she couldn't help the tears from falling, tears of relief that he was at last found. Why did he look so surprised? She wiped her eyes with the bottom of her shawl and drank him in, drank in the peculiarity of it all, everything.

'Why were you searching for me?' he said to them, and it was the same old Jesus. She could not remain cross with him, though she was bewildered and confused. There was such an innocence in his question, such a lack of understanding. Of course, this was perhaps the most obvious place to have found him and they should have come straight here. 'Didn't you know I had to be in my Father's house?' he went on. Well, quite honestly she thought he had to be on route back to Nazareth with his family. They had been together in Jerusalem for eight whole days and really, why on earth did he need yet more time listening to those men? His Scriptural understanding clearly could match theirs anyway. In fact, there were things he could probably teach them.

He seemed to grasp a little of his parents' pain for he stood and said his farewells. The teacher who had appeared genuinely impressed by him put his hands on his shoulders and said a blessing over him. He asked him to come back again soon, said he would like to continue their conversation. One or two of the others certainly looked glad to see the back of him. Had they thought them neglectful parents, felt obliged to look after him in their absence?

He surely was an unusual lad, one of a kind and they *were* blessed they'd been chosen to be his parents. It had been without challenge until that day, all straightforward. But then there had been those strange circumstances surrounding his birth, hadn't there? Now, what was all that about? When would it come into play? Oh, but it was so incredible and there was much to think on. She would hold these events in her heart and try to make sense of them. She was just so glad to have him back, and now the long walk home. Perhaps it would all become clear once they were out on the open road, looking back on the city. She had so much to ask him. Could they even begin to understand him, this strange but wonderful child?

See Luke chapter 2, verses 41 – 51 again.

Wedding guest

Shalom, shalom! Would you like to come and sit with me? You look like you need some refreshment. I guess you've come a long way. My name is Nathaniel and I'd be glad if you'd join me. This wasn't a wedding I expected to be at, but then the events of the last few days have been pretty unexpected all round. I suppose you know the young couple well? I've known of the groom for years but he's not in my close circle, for he is younger than me, though this is my home town and not much escapes me. I had no idea he was betrothed to such a pretty girl. Her broad hips and sturdy frame suggest to me she will bear children well, but enough of that. I can tell from your unusual accent and your even more unusual style of dress you are not from round here – know that you are very welcome.

I clear my throat, sensing some unease on your part. Sorry, I am a little loud. The events of the last few days? Yes, of course, I really should explain. Forgive me, I've left you hanging rather, I do find these social occasions a little awkward. Can I pour you some more wine first? You are fine for now, you say. Then let me begin. I'm here because I am a friend of Jesus. He's over there, that man at the end of the table who has the group around him enthralled. They are laughing so loudly, heartily, but have you noticed how then they listen intently and turn very quiet, as if what he has to say is just for them? You would probably rather be listening to him, too, but for now we find ourselves just out of earshot. I will introduce you when I get the chance.

I have only known him for a few days myself but it's been the most significant friendship of my life. You're surprised? – believe me, I was more than surprised when I first met him. You see, he has a habit of turning people's lives around, of saying what's needed with such perception, as a fisherman unties a jumble of ropes that's had you baffled – those two over there are fisherman and I've seen their fingers at work. Jesus can do that with your soul, with your problems, if you let him. Don't smirk – you must hear me out. I had been sitting under the large fig tree beside my house, contemplating life as is my habit, but my thoughts made me restless, depressed even, for the uncertainties of this world and life beyond have troubled me. I wandered down the hill with the intention of roaming the valley for an hour or two. It's the Beit Netofa valley – you see over there, in the direction of those trees, beyond that low wall – when my friend Philip – he's the chap in green sitting opposite Jesus – came to find me. 'We have found the very person Moses and

43

the prophets wrote about! His name is Jesus, the son of Joseph from Nazareth.'[10]

To my shame, I was pretty scathing in my reply, and made some rude comment about nothing good ever coming out of Nazareth. I cringe to think of it, but I've never been known for my tact! Anyway, Jesus was with him and heard everything I said, but he didn't hold that against me, for there was no visible reaction at all. He even suggested I am 'a genuine son of Israel – a man of complete integrity', those were his words. A polite way of saying I'm blunt, but I appreciated that. I mean, people are usually quick to write me off and I do understand; I'm not sure *I* would have much time for me if I were the sensitive type. His words did seem to cut to the very core of who I am. I was being told who I was by a complete stranger, but then came the real shock! He explained that he'd seen me beneath the fig tree before Philip found me. I knew he hadn't *actually* seen me, I'd never encountered him before in my life and I can be sure of this, for once you've met with him he's impossible to forget – everyone I've spoken to about him has said the same thing. I had been praying under that fig tree though, asking God to reveal more of himself to me. Something flickered inside me when he said those words and took hold – it was like lighting a lamp in a very dark room, and my whole life was illuminated. A momentary quiver then my soul was ablaze. There was a witness in my spirit like I've never known before, and in my usual direct way I came out with it: 'Rabbi, you are the Son of God – the King of Israel.'

So here I am, one of his students, or 'disciples' as he calls us. Looks like I've got myself a job at last. You smile and ask if he's going to pay me and we chat about purpose and vocation. I tell you that he has kingdom values, and with the Son of God walking the earth I have found the most valuable thing to do with my life.

You tell me you might just have that drink now, and as I wave my hand at the girl serving wine I can see she's looking bothered, as so many people want her. Some of the guests have had more than enough already, which is not exactly fair. She shrugs her shoulders at me and gestures at all the people between us and her. If we get up we can go and ask her, for she's in such demand. Then we can sit nearer Jesus – would you like that? You agree, for I suspect you are a little tired of my voice. I think I've sold him to you – or, at least, you want to check him out for yourself.

---

[10] John 1:45.

Now we are on our feet you say reaching the servers is impossible, for others are trying to do the same as us. No matter, we decide we'll wait our turn. The other disciples let us squeeze into the group and as I'm about to sit I have to move out of the way for Mary, Jesus's mother. She tells him the wine supply has run out! I thought so. And the party hasn't even been going for long. The shame of it – this is going to follow the young couple around for a very long time. But hold on… she *is* telling *Jesus*, and she must believe he'll be able to help. There seems to be some happy banter between them: 'Dear woman, that's not our problem,' he tells her, and she looks at him and throws her head back aghast, hands on her hips, and he laughs. 'My time has not yet come,' he says, and she clearly thinks it a feeble excuse. She rolls her eyes at him then smiles back. There is an understanding between the pair, and it's obvious she knows his kind heart well. We all hear what she says to the servant in a very loud voice: 'Do whatever he tells you,' and he doesn't look at all surprised.

As Jesus walks over to the canopy under which the servants have grouped, we're glad of the chance to chat about him, for none of us have been around him long. They are all clustering now around the large limestone water jars and we can no longer hear what he's saying, but he can't hear us either, not that he'd mind our speculations. 'This will be good,' I say. 'I'm looking forward to this.' 'How can he possibly help,' you ask, and we start to talk of those Scriptural prophecies about the Son of God. As the phrases are uttered around the table the outlook is good for this wedding: 'And when he comes, he will open the eyes of the blind and unplug the ears of the deaf,'[11] finishes Philip. We're agreed he's going to do something special here, but didn't he say his time had not yet come? Now we're not sure. The conversation then moves on – what has his mother been witness to as he grew up, what wonders had she seen? That's the line of discussion. For her to be this convinced he's able to help, she must have some specific knowledge, I say.

If Jesus's sibling broke a pottery bowl would he have put it back together, you ask, just so they didn't get into trouble? Probably not, says one of the others, and I don't have the chance to introduce you, for the conversation is running on. This goes much deeper, says an older voice belonging to one who's not a part of our group, who suggests the stigma would be lifelong. We talk about whether he might have prayed for family members to get well,

---

[11] A reference to Isaiah 35:5. The disciples would have been watching Jesus closely, trying to understand if he really could be the promised Messiah. Throughout the Gospels they seem to believe he is, yet can't quite grasp it.

practicing his method, all the while depending on God. The fishermen seem to know him best of all as he called them first. They explain that his faith wasn't immediate but had to be worked on, as we all experience ourselves. That he'd learnt from the teachers in the synagogue, from his parents too. We all agree that is pretty phenomenal, that he'd somehow surrendered his omniscience to be with us. Yet here he is, thirty years of age and with more godly wisdom than we've ever encountered. These two brothers keep interrupting each other and can't wait to share more, but I don't stop to engage as I want to see what Jesus does. I nod at you and you smile back as I go. I can see you have been incorporated into the conversation well enough so I leave you with them.

Jesus is having the servants fill these enormous jars with water, right up to the brim. Four of the team have gone to the well, as much of the water they contained had already been used to wash our hands on arrival. The servants didn't stint as they poured it out for each of us. We loitered as we took turns to hold our hands under its flow, for the day has been unseasonably warm. I can hear those left behind muttering to themselves – Does he really think they are going to drink this much water? Is he mentally troubled? – but they are fearful of their master so they comply. It seems illogical to them, yet Jesus is so calm that he instills a sense of confidence, and soon the whispers of complaint turn into a hubbub of excitement. He is looking on and smiling, nodding at them with approval. I love Jesus's confidence. It's clear something good *has* come out of Nazareth, and life is a whole lot more interesting. The whole process is taking a while though, and the three servants present stop and wait for the others, swapping over with them when they return.

The wind has dropped since the first group left and this is likely to take some time – the small portable jars only hold a couple of gallons. Jesus is now chatting with the servants while they wait and seems to have won their trust. The gang returns with full jars again and the others make one last trip to the well. Meanwhile, some of the guests have grown disgruntled – probably because they drank more than their share of the first lot of wine the bridegroom had provided. Some people do get carried away when there's alcohol around. 'Deluded fool,' they say. 'Just look at him! He's presiding like he owns the place.' I can hear the old me in them. I want him to shame them all.

It's interesting to see that Jesus isn't against people partying, though I'm not sure what he makes of that crowd – he simply has the bigger picture in mind. Now the first of the group is back and he pours in his two jars' worth, then stands back to wipe his brow. Jesus thanks him. The rowdy crowd have started to bang their fists on the table and words of ridicule must have been heard by the bride and groom, for they are only metres away. They are so besotted with each other that they don't seem to have noticed, which is just as well. They don't really need us, but we are here and the celebrations have to continue. If things don't hurry up they'll be off to consummate their marriage, for it's that time fast approaching and clearly the groom has intimacy on his mind. The lusty fellow, but I don't blame him. He hasn't touched his food. They should have gone when the jar-filling started, they would have had time. Always such a strange old custom, to bring the blushing bride back to the party after all that.

But here come the other servants at last and two of their group let out a quiet cheer, then laugh amongst themselves. I walk around the back of the huge stone jars to take a look and see the last one is very nearly full, but Jesus still isn't satisfied. The group empty their containers in turn, until the last servant girl pours in the water and it reaches the brim of the sixth jar. She bows her head to Jesus, then does a small curtsey and walks away. Jesus steps up to the jars, stretches out his arms to heaven and prays. I can't hear the words for he is praying quietly, but that he is praying is very clear to see. It is as if the rest of us are not even here, such is his concentration. There is an intensity about it and a beautiful calm, as if he's pronouncing God's favour, not just beseeching it. And then it happens. Oh, it happens! He tells the servants to dip in their jugs and take it to their master. As the first jug is plunged into the jar the liquid splashes down the sides, then falls in a slow trickle. It is a dark crimson, the deepest claret red and drips onto the floor like blood – I can see there is value in every drop. He's done it! Now jug after jug is being dipped in and goblets filled, an endless supply of God-given wine. I can't wait to taste it. The master of ceremonies pronounces it a success, saying 'you have kept the best until now!' yet knowing full well the wine has come from the hands of Jesus, that it has been drawn from those water jars filled from the old Cana well. He has said it to save face as much as anything.

Jesus isn't glorying in this but has sat down with his disciples again and is trying not to be the centre of attention. That seems to be his way. I haven't known him long, but I sense that he doesn't do things for the acclaim, but he genuinely wants to help people, to get to know them, to draw alongside and demonstrate something more of God's character. He certainly sussed me out quickly.

I can't help thinking there is more than just a blessing to be grasped from today's events. For sure, he knows the impact on the couple if they run out of wine at this celebration. I think he's making a larger point too, though I'm not sure what just yet. So those jars are normally for water, for ceremonial cleansing. He's filled them with something better – with wine that's limitless. What does that represent? I think we'll know in time.

I ask how you're doing as I squeeze in beside you. You say you plan to stick around for a few days, if that's allowed. Jesus tells you he's glad of your company and says there's an open invitation for you, wherever he happens to be. I know he has things he'd like to say to you, insights to bring, words of blessing and encouragement. You seem to have forgotten about me now, your attention being held by Jesus as he speaks. That's fine with me. We'll catch up later no doubt. I'm looking forward to hearing your story, how he works in your life and helps you onwards. There's plenty of time for that.

See John's Gospel, chapter 2, verses 1–12 for the biblical account.

Woman at the well

Same old walk, same routine, the water jar cold on her hip and not too weighty on the walk up to the mountain pass, though on her return it was always a burden. She could see the women staring from their doorways as she followed the path out of town. *So what* if she chose not to carry the jar on her head? *So what* if she were different? *So what* that she chose to come out at this time of day? The pain of being ostracized when she was there with the other women just wasn't worth it. She wouldn't give them the satisfaction any longer. At least she would have the house to herself for the next few days. *He* was with his 'real' wife, though she really couldn't see the difference. So what, indeed. She had lost her ability to fight over the last few months, that courage – or stupidity – that she had become known for. Her mother often told her that her 'spark' was dangerous, that it would start fires she could never put out. Now it occasionally glinted, some encounter or other would cause her to speak out when she shouldn't, say what needed saying, but she knew it was a dying ember and that was fine with her, for it had brought her nothing but trouble.

The 'real' wife, then. She was *welcome* to him, now she knew what an abusive, pig-of-a-man he was, feeling entitled to whatever he wanted because of his wealth and position, stopping at nothing to get his way… She didn't want to stay with him, but for the time being there was little choice. She'd been taken in by his money, the fact he could 'keep' her in a house of her own, away from his family. It was the same old story. His promises of marriage came to nothing, but she was worthless and he had no one to answer to, for her parents were long gone.

The years hadn't been kind to her, and each of her failed marriages had written their way into her appearance, scoring deep lines about her hands and face – she could even feel them, especially on her broad forehead, like she was some old forgotten wineskin, all withered and cracked. So what to that too. How awful she must look but it wasn't her problem; in fact, even that was a rebellion of sorts. If she looked less desirable perhaps he'd stop harassing her, so she left the expensive lotions he brought her untouched, and the brass mirror had stayed in its wrapping. Why should women be held responsible for *their* lust anyway? Rules made by *men* for their *own convenience*. Her hair felt warm on the back of her neck and she put down her jar for a moment to twist it into a rope, then tied a short cord around it to keep it in place. She could see the white hairs easily enough, that threaded their way through her thick tresses. She was fine with them, she was reclaiming herself, one hair at a time: let no man want her, let her be free.

The well was in sight now, and there at its edge sat a man on his own. She picked up her earthen jar and carried on walking, all the while feeling more curious about him as she drew closer. It was, after all, a strange place to wait, with no shade to speak of. As she got nearer she could see the fringe on his shawl blowing in the breeze. She put down the jar and wiped her brow and he looked at her and smiled. 'Please give me a drink,' he said. His accent was strong and there was the sense of a rule-breaker about him – he was cheerful towards her, friendly even, though of course it wasn't allowed. She could feel her own spark rekindling slightly – but why shouldn't she speak to him? So what that people would gossip? For once it was her thinking of the boundaries, though – '*You* are a Jew,' she reminded him, 'and *I* am a Samaritan woman.' Some lines should never be crossed. And it was about time that she protected herself a bit more, thought ahead to where things could lead. She wiped her hands down her apron and felt heat flood to her cheeks. 'Why are you asking *me* for a drink?'

He gestured at the cloudless, seemingly endless blue sky and smiled again with that defiant gleam in his eye. Then he laughed as she hesitated, yet she still felt so unsure of what to do. It was, after all, a fair enough request, and to her so many of their customs were outmoded, preposterous even. But then what he said surprised her. 'If you only knew the gift God has for you and who you are speaking to, you would ask me, and I would give you living water.'

She stood a little awkwardly, folded her arms and looked down at her clay jar. So what should she do? If it had been anyone else she would have suspected a come-on, seen it as one of the worst chat up lines in history – *the gift God has for you* – but he seemed so genuine, and the fact he was in no hurry to go, even wanted to be in her company, drew her to him. He wasn't after anything untoward, she knew that at least. He was far younger than her, for one thing. And she hadn't had a real debate for ages – arguments, yes, but grappling with life issues, she hadn't had that since she lived with her one decent husband, the one that she truly loved.

She pushed to one side the rotten old wooden cover of the well and picked up her jar which she attached to the rope. Lowering the jar with both hands, she hoped he wouldn't go when she had fulfilled his request. As she retrieved her jar and gestured to him with a slight tipping motion she was relieved to see he looked as relaxed as ever. He held out his cupped hands – she poured water into them and he drank. No one had seen, but so what if they had? She lowered the jar to the floor again and sat down next to it now, for he was in no hurry to move on, still leaning against the edge of the well in the blazing sun. She shielded her eyes with one hand as she looked up at him, her shawl providing little protection in this exposed spot.

So he started talking to her about this 'living water', how it was quenching, life-giving, and how she'd 'never be thirsty again'. Once he said this, she knew that she wanted it so very much. She'd spent her life being indomitable – she'd had to be, with the lot she'd been given, and she realized at that moment how worn down she was, how tired from it all. She thought about never needing to come out there again, how amazing that would be, and she asked him to give it to her. She surprised herself that she had made a decision so quickly. So what that she had? Didn't her life need to change? Didn't she deserve some good luck? Yet this was more than just luck, and she had given up on that concept long ago. He seemed so trustworthy, and well, so *likeable*, in a way all the other men never had been. There was something pure about him, something so good. She had never encountered such genuine respect and kindness before and she couldn't help but believe him. Yet deep down she suspected there'd be a catch. It was the same old world, after all. Since when did life suddenly become full of hope like this? Yes, it was the same old life and she really must protect herself. Hadn't she let her guard down often enough? Then out it came:

'Go and get your husband,' he said to her.

He said it kindly, knowingly, for the sad expression he wore wasn't full of judgement but warmth, sympathy even. She half got to her feet but she hesitated and sat down again, for she couldn't oblige him anyway. She felt sure his request wasn't just down to social etiquette, for they really shouldn't have been talking alone, but there was more to it. She knew she didn't have anything to lose with her reputation then – perhaps he did, but he didn't seem to care. *So what*, his manner seemed to say, *so what*? She decided that was why she liked him – he was a free-thinker, like her, not one for being bound by the rules everyone else thought were so important. So here he was, a Jew talking to a Samaritan woman, and not just any old Samaritan, but an outcast from that already outcast group. He was looking at her with a steady, unblinking gaze, with the attention someone gives you when you tell them bad news, like a loved one has just died, or you've got some terrible, life-shortening illness. It was as if he knew already. And clearly he had time for her, felt she was worth investing his energies in, worthy of a meaningful conversation. She hadn't been used to that for a long, long while.

She chose her words carefully. But did he really know, or was it just a façade? Would he reject her, just like everyone else had, once she'd told him? Come what may, she knew it was worth the risk; he was showing her respect and she at least owed it to him to be honest. She recognized something unusual in him and thought perhaps he'd be able to help. He sounded like a great philosopher, or certainly a very deep thinker anyway, and quite honestly she was bored of her life, of the same old routine.

So she told him. 'I don't have a husband,' she said.

'You're right!' he replied. But his words weren't acerbic in any way. She felt secure somehow, that he wasn't about to denounce her. She knew that he knew anyway – no, that idea was ludicrous – oh, where was this leading? He paused, nodded his head as if thinking and kind of hummed to himself. It was enough of a gap for her to know he was still good-natured. *So what*, his manner seemed to say… or at least, *so we can get beyond this*, I can help you get beyond this. Was she reading too much into his silence? Then he went on. 'You don't have a husband,' and he paused again. She was conscious of there being so much kindness in his deep, far-off eyes, that looked fixed on a place way beyond where they were seated. She couldn't help staring into them, though she felt it must look brazen. He just intrigued her so. Again, she was struck by the lack of judgement in them – it wasn't like he was condemning her and she felt able to trust him. It was like he wanted to help her, move her on. His eyes told of an inner freedom, and someone so sorted, so whole. Could he see her future, where he wanted her to be? Then he came out with it, and she really wasn't expecting what he had to say, well, not all of it: '…you have had five husbands, and you aren't even married to the man you're living with now.' But did he understand she didn't *like* living as she was, did he know the stress she was under, being with *that man*, and that she had *no choice*?

She tried to change the subject quickly, she felt she could be as quick with the come-backs as him, but he kept bringing the conversation back to her. She felt he'd sought her out, that she was special, even though she stood before him in all her filth the very moment she arrived there. Now he was talking about 'true worship', about how the Father was seeking people who'd worship him 'in spirit and in truth.' He knew all about her and still wanted to chat with her, suggested that God himself would have time for her. That was the most amazing thing to her – that he had none of the accusation of the locals. There was a kindness in the way he spoke to her, as if he really cared. He wasn't out for gossip – rather, to show her he understood and could help her turn her life around.

She knew she was in a very privileged position, to be having that conversation. *Could he be?* No, she decided it was an outlandish thought. She might drop it in, tease it out of him, see what he would say –

'I know the *Messiah* is coming,' ...there, she'd said it... 'the one who is called Christ. When he comes, he will explain everything to us.'

'I AM the Messiah!' he said.

She knew it. She just knew it. She had so much to ask him, though how should she phrase it? She looked away at his words, and briefly covered her face with her shawl. But she could hear voices, and glancing over her shoulder she could see his followers approaching them, and they were getting close enough to call out. They wouldn't understand – how could they? She got to her feet and ran back down the track towards her small town, for it was all too much, and they didn't look impressed. At least this way she didn't have to face them, and this was a safer path back down the hill. It really was *him*, sitting right there beside her like that, talking to her as if she was worth something. She felt overwhelmed by his goodness. Her father used to speak of the waves he'd seen and she imagined a wild, crashing wave tumbling over her, unbounded, drenching, subsuming. She could feel it – a wild, reckless, wholesome love – *at last* – the kind that engulfs you but doesn't rob you, doesn't violate, take yourself from you. No, it wasn't out to dominate but to bring release, a wave that wants to pick you up and carry you along, sustain you until you reach the shore on the other side.

Her feet were running fast and free and she could see people staring as she reached the road to the outlying houses. So what? So what! She didn't *care*, her dignity was long gone, and now she had found something far more precious. 'Come,' she said, trying to catch her breath and feeling a sharp, hard pain in her chest. 'Come,' she shouted, looking round for a response. 'Come and see a man who told me everything I ever did!' She shouted it again to anyone who would listen, her feet pounding on the spot for the moment of entreaty, her arms open wide.

'That'd be interesting,' said a man of about her age to his son. 'I'm glad you weren't there to hear it.'

She kept running and people came out of their houses, some to laugh and gawp, but soon they started to follow her as she ran through the settlement and took the track back towards the well. Nothing interesting ever happened in Sychar after all, they had to see what all the fuss was about. She called it out a final time, 'Come and see a man who told me everything I ever did! Could he be the Messiah?' What other explanation was there? But they must decide for themselves. It was no longer the same old Sychar – this place could be different; they all could. He was the Messiah and he was here to transform lives.

***

She wanted to get closer to him but the crowd had grown so big around her that there was no chance. They all started to sit down, and as she stood at the back of the group he glanced across at her and smiled, exchanged a knowing glance with her. He looked pleased with her, *he* looked pleased with *her*, was it really possible? Everything that had happened, all that he'd said to her, and now, here was her community, or most of them, ready to hear him. They would have to accept her again, though whether her circumstances were to change and how she couldn't be sure.

As the Messiah spoke her eyes caught sight of her abandoned water jar that lay at his feet. She hadn't even remembered to take it, such was her joy and her need to get away. And then 'I've missed you,' came a voice from behind her.

She turned and there was her sister who had passed her so many times, without even an acknowledgement. *So what*, she had thought back then, and she'd hardened her heart against her. She guessed now that it hadn't been her choice; it was what was expected of her, after all. The same old smile beamed at her, and the same dancing eyes, a younger version of her own.

'Did you hear? How do you know?' she whispered to her in snatches.

'I heard you alright, saw the spectacle you made of yourself,' she replied. Then she paused and that broad smile broke across her face. She slipped her arm through her sister's and led her away from the crowd to a space where they could sit, yet still see what was going on.

'So what do I do now?' she whispered. 'I've been used, badly used. I can't go back to him. And I know now I shouldn't be living with him. *He* wants better for me,' she said, nodding at the Messiah. 'I just don't know how I'm supposed to get there.'

The younger woman looked at this apparently devout stranger as he was speaking. 'Come and live with us,' she said, without hesitation, snatching a glance at her sister. 'We've got space, it will be just fine,' and she squeezed her hand.

An answer to her prayer so soon? How else could she explain it? 'He's called Jesus, you know,' she said in her sister's ear. 'You must listen.' He was finishing his address, but what was this? He told the crowd that he would be staying on for a couple of days. That an entire community seeking him out like this was unprecedented, and he wanted to set them up well. He said he was tired, and for now he needed to rest.

It really was the best day in her life so far, and she looked again at her sister – she was crying now, just quiet tears, but she saw them. She pulled her tunic sleeve down so that it concealed her wrist a little better – the bruise was fading but she'd ask her how it got there. It was too much for both of them, for now.

They followed two of his disciples down the hill and couldn't help but overhear their conversation. They were talking about how Jesus wanted to see more towns and villages turn to him, as Sychar had. That with the faithful prayers of his people it could happen, again and again. This was what her life had been waiting for, but she had never known. She walked quicker than usual, just to keep up and hear all that she could and her sister seemed to understand.

Without discussion the two women walked straight to the house where the older of the two had been living. 'Oh, it's beautiful,' said the younger, coming in behind her.

'So what?' she replied. Her reaction was tedious. The same old worldliness… but then she was no different herself not long ago.

'But it's so big! And this drape, it must have cost –' and her voice trailed off as she dropped the deep green fabric from her hand. She walked around a central pillar, her hand resting on it as she went. 'You will need many bags for all your things. This vase,' she said, stopping by a low table, 'you'll want this, it's exquisite,' and her finger traced the grey slip-work that coiled its way from top to bottom.

'No, I'm leaving it all behind. I want no reminders of him, or this life. It doesn't satisfy, it never can, though you always reach for more, think this next time it might. I've been drinking from the wrong well for a long time.'

Her sister raised a questioning brow at her.

'*He's* the living water. Did you hear him say that? It's true, my soul isn't thirsty any more. God values me. Isn't that incredible?'

'You sure it's not another man obsession?'

'How can you think that? You cannot be serious!' She looked offended at the suggestion and crossed her arms in front of her. 'You'll see. I didn't know I needed him but now I do. It makes sense of everything.'

'Can you just slow down a little? He's not going to walk in on you, is he?'

'I just can't wait to get out of here. It's the same old house, the same old memories. Come on, we need to go,' and she placed the few basic items she'd gathered into her wicker basket that she held on her arm: a couple of tunics, her sewing kit and her own pestle and mortar that her one true husband had once given her. Her sister looked at her and stared –

'What?' she replied.

'Of all the belongings here and you chose that?'

'Aaron gave it to me.'

'I don't think I ever knew him.'

'He was the only one who didn't divorce me.' She wished he was still around. The frustrations she had ground into that little bowl, the anger – it did mark an era that had passed though, and it was all she had left of him. 'Come on,' she said, and they walked out of the house together.

'When does *he* get back?'

'I've no idea, but no matter. I could leave a message with a neighbour, but they'll know to tell him. Word may even have reached him already. Perhaps one day the love of God will change him, too.'

See John's Gospel, chapter 4, verses 1–42 for the biblical account.

The servant's tale

'It's been so 'ard, watching young Jason, the master's son, his illness progressing so fast these last few days. You must be aware of 'ow serious this is, or you'll land yourself in it, I'll be bound. Just be glad you've got yourself a job and keep y'r head down. Come on this way, our quarters are down at the end. Bring your bag with you, lad, that's it. My name's Jonas and I'm in charge of you young uns.'

You say you'd gathered there was a problem but 'ad been too afraid to ask the master.

'That's probably just as well,' I tell you. 'Let me fill you in. You see, Jase has grown so weak, and no one's been able to 'elp. The master has sent for all the local doctors, and even sought out the best from Perea – that region belongs to his own boss, Herod Antipas, so he knows it well.'

You gasp at the mention of Herod and surely cannot have failed to have 'eard of his reputation, so I draw a line across my lips and mime at you to be quiet. You cannot seriously want to lose your job before you've even started. I think you must've wondered what he does for a living with a home like this but I won't patronize you. That's really not my responsibility. I walk in silence now, leaving you to follow on behind.

'The master's son, though,' you whisper. 'You were saying?'

'Yes, I've had my own ideas on who could help,' I tell you in a hushed voice, and we arrive at the servant's quarters and I pull the door quietly behind me before I continue. 'But it's not easy convincing a master like ours, I'll warn you now. I was serving at a wedding over in Cana a few weeks ago –'

'Cana?' says the boy.

'It's not far on horseback and the master owns several mounts. He has good friends over there who were seeking extra servants for a cousin's wedding. They'd had trouble finding enough people, as you know 'ow many days the celebrations can drag on for. Our master has more staff than he knows what to do with, and he finds such opportunities are good for his reputation, or dare I say it, his ego!' I try to contain my rather deep, some-say corrupting laugh that catches my chesty cough and struggle to recover myself. I can see you are not sure whether to be amused. 'So many staff come and go here that I haven't even asked you your name. I think the master likes the opportunity to flaunt his manpower,' I say. 'He has no need for you and I wonder at your employment here, though the mistress probably took you on out of kindness, like she did me.'

You look down at your soiled, threadbare tunic and apparently empty knapsack and I can see realization settle in with you in its humbling way, for your easy smile disappears. 'My name is Reuben, by the way, just so you know.'

'Anyway, at the wedding I met Jesus. You could say he saved the day.'

'Jesus?' you ask.

'Yes, Jesus. Have you been living under a rock?'

You give me an uneasy smile and tell me you had heard a rumour about the wine supply at a nearby wedding last month.

'Well let me inform you properly. The wine *did* run out and things were looking pretty embarrassing. Jesus had us fill up the six ceremonial washing jars with water, prayed over 'em, and the next thing we knew was we were dipping jugs into the very best wine. It was incredible.'

You look as if you don't believe me and are searching my face for signs of honesty, but then we have only just met. 'It's true,' I say. 'Of course, the master got to hear about Jesus soon enough, for the whole household were interested in what occurred, but *he* wasn't convinced. He was away on business when it happened, and told everyone the story was outlandish, and there must be a perfectly reasonable explanation. It was all spelled out to him, but he said Jesus must be some miracle worker and was not to be trusted. "Who knows what power he's drawing on," was his response. "He's certainly not acting out the will of God. It's quite preposterous. People should live with the consequences of their own actions – who ever heard of a miracle to provide more alcohol? Where is the wisdom in that?" Those were his words.'

You nod to show your understanding, though I can see a question in your eyes, as if you are only agreeing with me to be polite.

'Only I saw this Jesus pray. I stood near him and it was abundantly clear he was drawin' on the God of heaven.'

You sit down on the floor now and I join you, leaning back against the wall as I continue my story. 'He was not functioning on his own, you know, and he certainly wasn't calling on anything bad. To watch him pray...Well it was inspirational and I knew I was witnessing something very profound. You could see he had a real connection with God 'imself; he radiated warmth and peace and there was an honesty about him that I'm not used to. Have you served before?' I ask.

You tell me this is your first job.

'Well, young Reuben, isn't it? It'll come as no surprise that we usually 'ave to look on from a distance, or eavesdrop from the kitchen, perhaps snatch the odd overheard phrase whilst serving the food. I could have stayed in his company all day and all night, but of course once the wine was ready we were in big demand, needing to distribute it again to the guests, for they'd 'ad to wait for a long time. Jesus treated us with such respect – you wouldn't have thought we were second-rate citizens at all; it was as if we were partnering him in an important task, and it was better to have our role than theirs.'

You nod slowly as you picture the scene, rubbing your not-yet-there beard that forms a faint shadow on your chin.

'A goblet of wine was passed around us servers at the end of the evening; I would like to say Jesus started it but I can't be sure, as I walked back to the group last of all. It would be just like him. He seemed to be energized by serving people, which was certainly a lesson for me, but I would have thrown my present life away and followed him right there if I could – I did 'ear a group of men talking about doing just that – but I'm bound in by this family, so 'ere I must stay.'

I watch as you take in your surroundings and I can see you feel you've had a lucky break, for even the servants' quarters are clean and bright, with fresh reed matting and oil lamps on the walls. There is always that jug there ready with oil, and couches in every room. I won't tell you how you'll bore of this.

'The mistress had suggested we call on Jesus to pray for little Jase, but the master won't hear of it – "Have this peddler of miracles in my house?" he said. He's worried he'll inflict some evil force on Jase, says we don't know what we'd be opening ourselves up to.' I can 'ear her weeping again now and it's much louder than usual. 'I should go,' I tell you. 'You go back to the entrance lobby, young Reuben, and try to make yourself busy in case the master comes along.'

***

Jason is lying on the cold mosaic floor and being fanned by the mistress's chief maid but he is quite delirious. As he writhes this way and that every muscle spasm is mirrored in the mistress's face. He is sweating and moaning, quite unconscious of himself and where he is and it pains me too. I love this young lad but that 'as never been understood here – I've seen more of his milestones than his father. I've witnessed 'is first steps, I could even tell of his favourite foods and when 'e started to like them. The children mean more to me than the parents could ever realize – or perhaps they do know, for we're constantly told that although we live close to the family, we're not a part of it. Yet we are the ones the children come to when they graze a knee or sting themselves. And with Jase being the oldest, there is more of a connection – I've been the one to invent stories for 'im at bedtime, taking 'im on adventures as we soar like birds over mountains and deserts, and explore the deepest, darkest caves. He's already pointed out to me how our lives are similar – having to be obedient to them, being courteous at all times, speaking when spoken to, and the similarities have never been lost on me. But I cling to my 'ope – if this Jesus cares enough about the wine running out at a wedding, he'd care about the 'ealth of this little boy, I'll be bound.

Dear God in heaven, please will you help young Jase here, I pray. May they allow Jesus to pay 'im a visit. Give me courage to raise it again, Lord, as he's far worse than when I last saw 'im and I'm worried he won't pull through –

The mistress is distracting me and growing quite hysterical, her wailing echoing along the long empty corridors and rebounding back to us here. 'I hear Jesus is back in Galilee,' I offer in a quiet voice, all formal like, unsure of how she will react, for she is very temperamental.

'Where?' she says.

'I really can't be sure.'

'Find him! Make it your business if you value your privileges here,' she replies.

What sort of veiled threat is this? But it is progress, for if she is commanding such action her husband will hardly stand in her way. Her wailing has started up again and I'll be glad to be out of 'ere. 'I'll go,' I tell her. 'I'll find him, you can be sure of that.'

It didn't take long to 'ear of his whereabouts on the local grapevine. A quick sprint through town, and my ear is drawn to the voice of a woman, bragging at the lakeside while she plaits her young granddaughter's hair. I keep catching the name 'Jesus' above the hubbub and I stand nearby, feigning an interest in a tablecloth that I have no intention of buying. She claims she has it on good authority that he's in Cana with his disciples, staying next door to her eldest daughter. That's good enough for me.

I run back till I'm breathless and shout out, 'He's in Cana, I think he's in Cana,' for everyone to 'ear. I do hope this is right or I will be in great trouble, even out of a job. I bend over double and cough hard, struggling to catch my breath.

The master is outside now, not waiting for help and is removing from Myrtle her bucket of barley, throwing the bridle on her if that were possible, forcing the bit into the poor bewildered 'orse's mouth and fastening the throat straps. I would go myself if he would let me. 'Out of here, man,' he shouts at me, 'don't get in my way.'

Back in the house there are whispers that the boy is dying and I make my way back to his chamber, where the mistress allows me inside. I worry the master will be rude to Jesus and the opportunity will be lost. He's never lacked anything, he can buy whatever he needs, and no doubt he wants to take this one intervention from Jesus and do away with him – I mean send him on his way with no sense of connection gained, no realization of his own need. I 'ope I get to meet Jesus again, that he does manage to bring him back home. I wonder if 'e'll remember me.

I take the boy's hand and pray for him and soon the mistress leaves, for she is exhausted from worry and tears. The hours pass and I hum our favourite tunes to him, and tell 'im of all the things we'll do when he's better. I tell 'im how loved he is. How wanted in this home. I tell him to hold on, because his father will bring someone very special home to meet 'im. I tell him life is going to be better than it was before. I don't know if he's heard any of it, and I realize that I am feeling very tired, for I was up much of the previous night with him and find myself struggling to stay awake. I shut my eyes and pray for him.

I awake with a start. 'Where am I?' I hear, 'can I have a drink? I want to get up and play, I feel a bit stiff.' I think I'm dreaming, but my eyes are open and... It's young Jase! 'You're with us,' I say. 'But this is incredible. Young fellow, you've been very sick.'

'I know,' he says. 'I want to get up.'

I should call his mother but I'd like to keep this moment for myself, just for a short while. That's unfair, though I'm glad *I* was the one to be with 'im when it happened.

'Just stay there for a little bit,' I tell 'im. 'We should get you looked over first. And your mother will want to see this –'

'Oh, must she? I just want to go and play. I've had this idea of making a toy boat out of wood and taking it to the water, if you can –'

'Halloo!' I shout, opening his door wide and calling down the steps. 'Good news! You must come quickly. The boy is well.'

Jase sighs at me then laughs. 'Why d'you always have to do things properly?' he says.

'I wish to keep my job,' I reply. 'We'll see about that boat later.'

His mother bursts into the room and throws 'er arms wide in greeting, a giant smile on 'er face, 'er bangles clattering as she rushes towards him. 'That will be all, thank you, Jonas,' she says over her shoulder. 'Notify the household please, come on now, don't delay. This is a private, family time. We do not wish to be watched,' and I nod courteously and make my way out. 'Oh, and it is supper time,'[12] she says as I am closing the door. 'Please arrange a light meal for the boy.'

The next morning the master still hasn't returned and I 'ear Jase has been asking for me. Yet before I can go to him, word reaches me that I have been selected to lead a group on horseback to find the master and take the news to 'im. I suppose this means Jesus won't be coming back with 'im, but I don't mind really. It's just wonderful to have the boy on the mend, and 'opefully there will be another opportunity to see Jesus.

Out in the stables I find *you* again, leading out my preferred horse and tightening the bridle. 'Young Reuben, isn't?'

'It is.'

'I'm getting' good! What time was it, when the boy woke? Do you have any idea, for I had nodded off and had lost track of all time.'

'It was the seventh hour,' you say with certainty.

'Are you coming with us? Are you a horseman?'

'Well I'm not really,' you say, and I worry you might slow us down, but I'm glad to have your company.

We set out at an easy trot and your horse falls in behind mine. We pass the lake and are 'eading towards Tiberias at an even pace when we can see a couple of horses up ahead.

---

[12] See note at the end of the story on how time functions in the biblical account.

'That's him,' you say, your eyesight clearly better than mine.

'You sure?'

'Of course,' you say, and I nudge my horse into a gallop.

'He's better,' I shout, breathless and proud. 'The boy is better!' I stop the horse with the reins and hear the hooves of the others drumming up behind us.

The master looks profoundly relieved and yet a question has occurred to him. He's waiting for the others to gather round us before he asks. 'When did the boy to recover? Exactly what time was it?'

'Yesterday at the seventh hour,' you say, with a youthful boldness that quite becomes you.

'I was with the boy,' I add, hoping this won't count against me in my future duties, for I am aware he has noticed our special bond. 'His fever suddenly disappeared!' I tell 'im, and I explain his amazing recovery.

He turns to you again. 'How can you be so sure of the time?'

'The mistress sent through an order for his supper and we had everything ready for the rest of the family to dine, the platters were all arranged and the wine on the table.'

The master nods his gratitude and leads the party back to Capernaum. Later he calls a special meeting of the entire household, servants included. He explains what had happened to all who've assembled, and how he met with Jesus at Cana: 'Go back home,' he told me. 'Your son is living.'[13] He looks around the assembled crowd, then speaks very slowly and clearly. 'This happened at the seventh hour. The seventh hour, which, I believe, is when the boy's fever passed?'

We all nod in agreement and the sense of euphoria is palpable. 'I can't thank you all enough for your involvement,' he says. 'Are we agreed that something incredibly profound has happened here? Dare I say it is the intervention of God himself?'

Of course, we all smile and nod and assenting noises are made. 'There will be changes in this household,' the master continues. 'Good changes. This Jesus has done something wonderful here, and I take back all the negative things

---

[13] Present tense in the Greek – 'Your son is living; he lives.' Jesus has already performed the miracle before sending the man away.

you may have heard me say about him. I was only trying to protect my own son. Ours is a believing household now. I hope you will work with us in this.'

Not that he needs to ask.

See John's Gospel, chapter 4, verses 46–54 for the biblical account.

There is some discussion in commentaries about whether John's Gospel might run on 'Roman time', unlike the other three gospels that use 'Jewish time'. This would make the 7th hour 7 p.m. and not 1 p.m. as some translations have it. It's worth considering whether this might make more sense of the master's slow return. Could he have stayed a night away from home, fearing the dangers of night travel?

Could John's account be based on the same events as the healing of the Centurion's servant in Matthew 8:5–13 and Luke 7:2–10? My own conclusion is probably not, but see what you make of it:

The Centurion is concerned for his slave, the Royal Official for his son.

The Centurion's faith is acknowledged by Jesus, whereas the Royal Official seems to have exasperated Jesus and has to plead with him.

The Centurion believes Jesus can heal from a distance but the Royal Official feels Jesus must accompany him to his home.

Rejection in Nazareth

'Abba, you should get that ankle looked at. I'm not sure you'll get down these steps again on your own.'

'Not sure I'll manage, eh? I'm fine, Zach, and now I'm up here I've no reason to go down.' He stopped to turn and look him in the eye. 'I've nearly made it.'

'Go carefully, then.'

'Darkness falls quickly over the vineyard,' he said, hobbling onwards, then leaning forwards and resting his hands on his knee. 'It's just me and the skies. I'll sleep well up here tonight, whether the family choose to join me or not.'

'You know Imma would join you if she could, and I think the girls are keen to look after her. You must let me stay tonight,' said the young man. 'And I can see from here you need some more branches on the roof.'

His father took the last of the watchtower's steps backwards on his behind, and let out a satisfied groan as he shuffled into the cabin itself. There was always a draft coming through the stone walls, which the old man said was refreshing. 'Shouldn't you be with your wife, eh? The baby could come any day. How will you get help if you're up here?'

'I can't leave you here, Abba,' Zach replied, entering the hut himself. 'You've done yourself a right injury,' he said, kneeling in front of the old man and touching his swollen ankle that had all but doubled in size. 'That was some performance this afternoon, I didn't know you still had it in you.'

'Still had it in me? How decrepit do you think I am, eh? *Still had it in me.* Pah.'

'Sorry, Abba. You should look where you are going then.'

'Oh, enough sarcasm! That proclamation of his was a scandal and it needed dealing with. Somebody had to take the lead.'

'I suppose so.'

'Suppose so? Where's your sense of outrage, eh? I feel like I'm watchman over our synagogue, too. If I wasn't guarding the old ways, who would? We have to get hold of this Jesus again, and give him no opportunity to get away.'

'Do you think?'

'You're soft. I knew we had to talk about this without the women present, but you're just like one of them. I can't believe he managed to escape us the first time – it was us against him, all the men who were in the synagogue, and we dragged him up to the cliff edge with such force. I was proud of everyone – we didn't even wait for him to finish but had him by the hair, the tunic, his arms, le–'

'Shush, I can hear someone's on the steps,' interrupted the son, getting to his feet. 'Yes, it's young Joel,' he said, looking out over the top of the crumbling wall.

'So what? Let him hear! We need to learn from today.'

'I tore his robe! Did you see?' came his voice from the stairway. The lad must have overheard his grandfather's loud pronouncements from outside and rushed up the steps, not wanting to miss out on the adult conversation. 'Grandfather,' came his breathless voice again, 'did you see?'

'I'm afraid not, boy. Come in, come in, sit down here with me,' he said, patting the rush matting. 'I was too busy giving him a bruising he'll never forget.' Zach winced but it was lost on his father and son. 'You'd have thought he'd have put up more of a fight, though. No one comes into our place of worship and starts proclaiming dangerous untruths like that: "The Spirit of the Lord is upon me," he started – upon *him*? Since when? He stood at the desk in the centre like he owned the place with that commanding presence of his. The way he looked out on us all and said, "The Scripture you've just heard has been fulfilled this very day!" He needed a beating, an encounter he wouldn't forget...'

'Some of them were impressed to start with, Abba, didn't you notice?'

The old man looked thoughtful for a moment before he replied. 'I really don't know why. Just who does he think he is?'

'I must admit, it was him saying Scripture had been 'fulfilled' that had me most rattled. *Jesus* saying that. *Jesus* of all people,' and he shook his head several times. 'I'm just not so sure as you about how he should be dealt with, that's all.'

'I think I need some wine to take the edge off this pain,' said his father, pouring the deep red liquid from the earthenware jug. He smelt it before taking it to his lips and inhaled with his eyes closed tight.

'I think I need some, too,' said Zach.

'From our grapes, son. Nazareth's best.'

'Who ever said nothing good ever comes out of Nazareth?' he replied.

'What?'

'Oh, it's a recent saying that's been doing the rounds. I blame the neighbouring villages.'

'Yes, well. There's plenty to hang onto in Nazareth, you need to appreciate what you have here.'

'You don't need to tell me, Abba.'

'Did I not look frightening enough, Grandfather?' came the lad's voice, for he was keen to feel included again. 'Some of the other boys laughed at me for joining in.'

'Of course you did. I like to think we all looked pretty intimidating.'

'I've never heard you shout like that, Grandfather. Some of those words were new to me, you really went for it,' said the boy.

'Those words are not to be repeated, my son,' said Zach, giving him a long look, then staring deep into his wine. 'Your grandfather can get a little carried away.'

The old man ignored the comment, or perhaps he didn't hear it, with his mind racing on. 'Why the hell did he look that calm, eh?' he asked them, but didn't wait for an answer. 'It troubles me – the man is most bothersome, the worst, most irksome type of rebel. He had that infuriating façade, as if he was completely untouched by our hostility, as if we couldn't get through to him, as if he still wanted to reason with us. Perhaps he lacks intelligence. He should have felt fear, understood our *rage*, he can't get away with this, it's not going to happen, it's not –'

'Calm down, Abba, you're shaking, you should see yourself. You're all red in the face, like you've been treading grapes in a fury. He's not here now, you know.'

'That's as may be, but we'll be ready for him next time.'

'Would you have pushed him off the cliff, Grandfather, if you'd been closest?'

'What do you think? All it took was one or two of our group to doubt their actions for a brief moment. We had every right to hurl him off the cliff – stoning for blasphemy, it is written,' he said, in his most commanding voice, pronouncing his words slowly. It contained echoes of antiquity, as if he were doing his best to sound like an old prophet. 'We would have thrown him like a stone – it's no different.' His sleeves shook as he spoke, waving his arms around for dramatic effect. 'The law is precisely to prevent the sort of scenario we're facing now: the 'Jesus' following. Glory glory Jesus. A forty-foot drop – that would've done it. He needs to wake up, remember his roots.'

'Perhaps a simple conversation would do it,' said the old man's son. 'I'd like to reason with him. Remind him of his background, it shouldn't be hard.'

'It sounds much worse than it is anyway. Our town is half-way up the mountain as it is. It's not wrong to let nature give us a little helping hand,' said the boy.

His father studied him hard – he hadn't taught young Joel this hostility – had the grandfather often engaged in fighting talk when he'd been out of the way?

'I can't believe he escaped us – he was surrounded,' continued the old man. 'It makes no sense, and rumours are circulating that he's *healing* people and *delivering* them. He thinks he's God himself, thinks he's the Messiah. Plain old Joseph's son has returned to give us signs and wonders.'

'Oh, I'm so frightened, he's going to cast a spell on me, or call out all my evil,' said the lad. 'Perhaps that's how he got away – a spell.'

'I'm more worried that he's going to cause a rift in our congregation,' he replied, 'that's why I'm so angry. No doubt some fools would start following him, given half a chance. Pah. But what happens when he's revealed to be the imposter that he is? He's brainwashing people. You joke of spells, young Joel, but I don't think you're far off. I wonder how he does it – does he put them in a kind of trance and speak mumbo-jumbo into their ears? Just how? Eh?'

'He always was clever, compared to me anyway,' said the young man, who had been content to let the conversation run on without him for a while.

'Is that why you don't like him, Abba? Is that why you hate him so much?'

'Hate is too strong a word, really,' he replied, 'or it was, before today. Now I'm not so sure. I don't know what to make of him any more.'

'You really should fill us in,' said his father.

'Well, it goes back a long way,' Zach answered, topping up his own tumbler of wine until he could see its surface glimmer in the sunlight that flooded through the cracks. 'He should've been one of us but he really wasn't.'

'I know boys like that,' said Joel.

'He really used to wind me up in lessons,' went on Zach. 'The learning was tedious but he loved it. He always had some profound, unfathomable question to ask, or a comment that would stun all of us, tutor and students alike. We used to whisper, 'Who cares? Does it really matter? Why is he so bothered? It's not going to change anything.'

'That'd be right,' said his father.

'His Hebrew was always so perfect, he must have spent hours memorizing Scripture at home. And all for what? So he can lord it over us now and claim he's God's chosen one.'

The old man stroked his beard and grew thoughtful now, the alcohol apparently making him sleepy and numbing the pain. 'I don't think he'll be coming back,' he said. 'No nostalgic visits to see his mother and siblings,' he went on, his imagination stirring once more. He was quiet for a minute, but his anxieties were getting the better of him. He sat up straight with a start and looked at his son. 'Perhaps we could send him a message via them – use some intimidation tactics, you know?'

'No, that's not fair. She's widowed now, of course. I think she's got enough to contend with, all those children at her feet.'

'Yes, well, he'd better watch it. If he comes anywhere near our synagogue again he won't make it away alive. History won't remember him but it might remember us – defenders of the synagogue against blasphemers. We're upholders of the truth. Yes, indeed, upholders of the truth. That has a certain ring to it, eh, boys, don't you think?'

See Luke's Gospel, chapter 4, verses 14–30.

Following Jesus

Cephas remembered the strangeness of it at first. Waking to wonder, 'but was it the Sabbath? No – but of course!' Next door's cockerel had been pronouncing itself lord of the neighbourhood, causing Cephas to be wide awake. That he was not used to hearing. For his group had fished regularly at night on the lake. In those early days he had rolled onto his side and looked at his wife, sleeping beside him in the half-light. He knew he must not disturb her. That change in circumstance then: no longer the lead fisherman – she had reminded him of that, with a haul of anxious thoughts. *But the loss of livelihood, the dangers... who knew where it might lead,* she said. The error of his impetuous nature – that was the gist. *Cephas, you act, then you think. Cephas, you are in your own little world sometimes. Cephas, just think of me for a change.*

But he knew then that there was no other way.

Cephas was again restless and awake in the dawning light. He rolled onto his back this time. Indeed, he had much to think on for his life had been transformed. He thought he *was* a follower, of sorts, right from the very start. His brother Andrew and a friend had followed Jesus without being asked initially – their group had been with John[14] for a while and they'd all considered themselves *his* disciples. But when John pointed him out and said 'Look! There is the Lamb of God,' all it took was a nod and they tagged on behind. This was what John had been preparing them for and there was no need to explain – no time even. How he wished he had been there! John had smiled a blessing on them, and when Jesus realized he was being followed he'd asked them, 'What do you want?'

They should have come out with a profound spiritual question, like 'Are you the Christ?' or 'How can I please God?' But all they could ask was 'Rabbi, where are you staying?'

Jesus didn't seem to mind though. He didn't know them from Adam (or so they thought) but took them home and allowed them to be with him for the remainder of the day, as if he had nothing better to do. That's the thing about him – relationships are his priority. Had they ever seen him rush anyone away, in all the weeks that had passed since then? No, they hadn't – well not anyone genuine, for he always could assess people's intentions. When it occurred to Andrew to include his brother, he came to get him – 'We have found the

---

[14] John the Baptist. See John 1, v. 35 onwards for this initial response to Jesus.

Messiah,' he said, and they ran back to the house together to find him. Never again would Cephas be outrun – he'd missed out on that first moment but it wasn't going to happen in the future, he decided. Not if he could help it.

When they got there it was as if Jesus knew him already: 'Your name is Simon, son of John – but you will be called Cephas,' he'd said. Had Andrew been singing his praises to Jesus, was that it? He did wonder, but quickly he realized that somehow he'd been chosen, that Jesus had recognized something in him. That had made him feel good inside. It was like when someone gives you the most incredible gift – their best cloak that they feel is too good to wear themselves, or a ring they take from their own finger and place on yours. You don't feel worthy, but they insist you are. He wanted to run somewhere and proclaim it! For it was so significant he wanted to share it with anyone he could find. More than that, though, he wanted to stay there and listen to him. He had thought on his old name then: *Simon*, 'he has heard', and even that had taken on a new meaning, though it was second-hand news. His new name was far better – Cephas had wondered then if the others would start to use it too?

So Jesus acknowledged them as his followers from the very outset. Glory to God – what a mercy! But there was a sense that he was expecting more from them – they could see that being a follower of his was more costly than being a follower of John, but ultimately much more rewarding. They went to a wedding with him a while ago – that amazing wedding, and just being with him was wonderful. It was what they'd been waiting for all their lives and finally it was happening, but with them included. They had dared hope that perhaps, just maybe, they would live during the coming of the Messiah. But in those just-waking dreams, when faith and reality most often collide, he would be far off, not in their close circle. It had never occurred to them that they might *know* him, that their reality could be lived in his very presence! Jesus's mother knew what she was doing when she told him the wine was running out. Since that time they'd taken a trip to Samaria with him, but they had their jobs to do, family members to support, and it was accepted that they had their own lives as well. Jesus had never pushed them into doing more for him. But he had a way of getting through to them without even saying a word. Jesus had won their trust – that was how, he decided. It was the care he showed people, the time he took with them, that was so appealing and reassured them. For he was living out all that he talked about.

Jesus didn't even need to be asked to visit when Cephas's own mother-in-law was dangerously sick. There is a feeling we all have when concerned for a loved one – like something's being crumpled inside of us, scrunched into a smaller and smaller ball that then bounds around within and won't let us relax. For it is hard and it hurts. It's all we can think of. Jesus just walked into the room with such calm, stood beside her bed and commanded the fever to leave her. How simple he made it seem, and how pointless the fretting. It was as if she'd woken from the most restful night's sleep and she set to work straight away, preparing a meal for everyone, lifting her old ceramic pot onto the fire and beginning the stew, sending for more pomegranates and figs for dessert. He didn't know how to thank Jesus for that, so he didn't even try. There was just quiet appreciation and respect. Sometimes you can't find the words for what someone does for you, it means so much, they mean so much. So they had sat there together in silence and the bond grew stronger. It had been phenomenal to see Jesus at work in in their town – it would be difficult to list all the lives he'd touched, and a list wouldn't be sufficient anyway. But it was enough to know the place was transformed, people were healed, delivered and changed.

All of that was astonishing. Glory to him, now and always! But as fishermen, what happened most recently was more exceptional. Cephas was still living it out in his mind. Jesus knew exactly what would reach them, and events in that little boat changed everything. It can be hard to get someone's attention when they think they know all there is to know about you, or when they think the relationship is established, everything's as it should be and with no need for more. And so they were clueless as to what Jesus really *needed* from them. They hadn't realized how all-consuming it would have to become. It was important to them that they fulfilled their duties to their loved ones. Therefore, on that particular day, they were busy washing their nets while Jesus preached to the crowds. To have a family member healed like that does a lot to win their approval at home; it did mean his wife and mother were more positive about Jesus. But it wouldn't have helped his cause at home if they'd stopped to listen to Jesus and drifted the day away with him. Not after having been out all night long on the lake. It was a hard job, putting food on the table and they knew they'd have to go out again soon, as the previous night's catch was non-existent. They were exhausted then. They wished they could do more for Jesus, but the demands of life somehow got in the way.

It was good to still feel a part of things, and when Jesus asked to borrow Cephas's boat to get some space between himself and the crowd, it felt a privilege. Jesus wanted to address that huge group of people from the lake and just requested that he loan it to him, like he was his best friend. He liked that easy way of his – it was clear he was so much better than they were, and yet that sense that he needed them, that he wanted to be around them when there were so many other people pressing in, trying to get a look in – that was amazing. So, back to the point. Jesus stepped into his boat and asked him to push it out into the water. He talked to the crowd for a while, and when he'd finished they expected that to be that. He had returned the boat and the day was done. But Jesus called him over and said to him, 'Now go out where it is deeper, and let down your nets to catch some fish.'

That felt like he was taking things a little too far though, even for Jesus. The nets were all stretched out on the rocks to dry at last and they were feeling famished. Tiredness had really taken hold by that point and he couldn't help himself. So he told him: 'Master, we worked hard all last night and didn't catch a thing.' What did he know about fishing, after all? That was what they were all thinking. It was their thing, they did it week in, week out, but what experience did Jesus have of *fishing*? Everyone knew nighttime was the best time to fish, anyway. Well, everyone except Jesus, or so it seemed then. Quite frankly they were annoyed with him. But Cephas agreed to it – he wouldn't have for anyone else but he could make an exception for Jesus.

'Get the nets, lads,' he called to the others as he stepped into the water. 'For our master commanded it.' He tried to keep the irony in his thoughts alone.

And then it happened. The people on the shore looked as small as their hands and the breeze was picking up and catching their hair, while on the beach it had felt still and sultry. They were most certainly in the deep waters, so he and Andrew dropped the nets. They barely had time to sink when they felt the boat rock with the weight in them! It was a catch like they'd never known, a catch to define them as fishermen. It would be the talk of the town, such a glut of fish would feed several towns and villages for days, maybe even weeks. How exactly could they store it, they wondered? Would they be able to sell it all? But it was remarkable –

'Over here!' they shouted. ''Bring the other boat, we need you!'

No doubt Jesus was smiling and had expected it. Cephas loved to dwell on this. For certain he always would. If their crew hadn't heard, he knew Jesus would be on the alert and would send them over. He had seen it all already, they felt sure.

'The nets are tearing,' they had said to each other in the boat. 'Just hold on,' Cephas had said, 'don't haul it yet, wait for the others to reach us.' Birds were circling above them and the nets moved with a life of their own, writhing and turning, tugging away from the boat.

When the second boat arrived it took the strength of all the men to haul in the nets, and even that wasn't enough. As the nets came up into the air and the water poured away they were still no lighter. The boats were soon full to overflowing, like they had caught all the fish that were in the lake, that would ever live in the lake. 'We're sinking,' they said to each other. 'Row faster, come on fellows, keep it moving!'

Seeing Jesus on the shore after that was the most humbling and terrifying thing. Cephas climbed out of the boat and sank onto his knees as the water slapped around him, then swept over his back as he knelt. He coughed and gasped, but not so much from the mouthful of water but the equivalent slap his spirit had felt as he realized how significant Jesus was, how profound, and how pathetic his own self. The thought of it still gave him shivers. 'Oh, Lord, please leave me,' he said. 'I'm too much of a sinner to be around you.' Of all the people he could have chosen, he thought, couldn't he see, didn't he know? That was how he felt. For he really wasn't up to the task. He was no rock, he knew that for sure. He was crumbling and couldn't stand, let alone support anyone else, let alone support *him*.

But Jesus was having none of it. 'Don't be afraid! From now on you'll be fishing for people!' That was really what he said, and it was to the whole group.

Well, that did it for all of them. Cephas, James, John, it was enough for them – more than enough. For they knew that if Jesus could do such a thing then he was aware of their greatest fears and their material needs. And what was the point in fishing if they had *him* with them and he had a greater purpose – if he felt they could be useful to him in some way? The abundance was amazing, but it was simply that. It had been the means of convincing them, just a sign to show them he was altogether trustworthy. He had been their master, but from then on, he was their Lord, as Cephas had said. And now they'd had this dream catch, no fishing trip could ever come close, anyway. It was the ultimate catch, the high point on which to walk away from it all.

As Cephas had stepped up out of the water, his beard dripping, his tunic heavy as he made it onto the shore, he wondered if there could there ever be a time when he'd feel more certain about anything. The moment the rest of them landed they had all looked at each other and knew it was time to follow Jesus full-time. Outright commitment could be the only response, no matter where it led them. No matter what happened as a result. They were grateful that Jesus had been patient with them, but they wondered at how slow they had been to grasp what was really required. A crowd had gathered and some of them were still around from when Jesus spoke to them on the lake. A cheer went up as they helped the first boat in.

'Sell the fish,' they said to them. 'But take what you need yourselves. This will provide for our families for a bit, but you can keep the boat.'

'Are you crazy?' said one of the young lads who helped bring in the haul, the rope tied firmly around his waist. 'We want to fish with you, not your boat!'

'How did you do it?' said his friend to them. 'Teach us and you'll set us up for life.'

They knew there was no point in trying to explain to them. The more perceptive amongst them would have witnessed their rapport with Jesus and seen his purposes in what had happened. It didn't take long for the rumours to start – that the boats were lucky, blessed in some way, but such a catch was never seen there again. The gossip was always so ridiculous – could they not see it was all to demonstrate Jesus's lordship? That miracles would be pointless without his purpose?

As for them, it was all for Jesus from that moment on. It was a given that their loved ones would quickly understand after that, if they hadn't already. They would be sure to be included by Jesus – when they felt ready, of course.[15] At times Cephas wondered if his wife had forgotten what Jesus had done for them. Yet there was progress – though it was at times slow. But how much proof did she need? Her mother healed, that miraculous catch, and more. She was human, like him, he thought, as he gazed on her as she slept. For himself, he would never doubt Jesus. For his own faith was solid at last, like the rock after which he was named. Of that he was sure. The cockerel was crowing now and she was stirring. It would always remind him of his new routine with Jesus, his new life. Strange how the smallest things point to his glory.

See Luke chapter 5, verses 1–11 for the most detailed biblical account of when the disciples gave up everything to follow Jesus more fully.

Is God calling us out into deeper waters? Does he have more to give us than we are prepared to receive? Is it possible that our fear or ignorance causes us to stay his hand? Do we sometimes put our trust in the boat or the calm waters? While God is patient with us, wouldn't it be good if we could cause him to smile as he waits for us on the shore? No commitment to him is too deep and we cannot outrun his ability to sustain us.

---

[15] In 1 Corinthians 9 verse 5 we read about the inclusion of the apostles' family members.

Making good

You've come to see how I'm getting on with that hole, you say, with patching up my *wanton vandalism*. You put a little too much emphasis on those last two words and I inspect my nibbled fingernails before looking back at the job in hand.

'I'm more than happy to do the repair,' I tell you, and I stare at it like it really requires some thought. 'I promised I would and I'm always true to my word. I only wish I'd had time to fix it last night. I really am very sorry about it, if there'd been any other way –'

Relax, you say, you're only joking. Then you tell me we did the right thing. That we could do it again a thousand times if it brought salvation and healing as it did yesterday. What a relief – you had me worried for a moment. Now I dare look at you and I stop what I'm doing. There is a genuineness about you, a warmth in your smile and such a fire in your eyes – being around Jesus so much means his kindness has found its way into you.

I press the new cane matting into the outer crevices, then add another layer before starting on the plaster mix. My ingredients were measured out earlier – it was the first thing I did when I arrived. I enjoy mixing the straw and lime into the mud; there's something very satisfying about a job well done.

'Could you pass me that pot of lime?' I say. 'I just want to strengthen the compound.'

'This ceiling is going to be far more secure than before,' you respond. 'For if I'm honest with you, it had developed a bit of a leak anyway.'

'It's the least I can do.'

'How's Gabe now?' you ask.

'You wouldn't recognize him,' I say, as I beat the mixture till it gloops in a slick paste. 'He's been running around with James – my son, that is – and throwing a ball for him, chasing him through the village; you know, non-stop craziness. I'm surprised you haven't seen him. You'll hear him hooting with laughter if you listen for long enough – that outrageous laugh of his that we had all but forgotten. I can safely say he's back to his old self; back to how I remember him as a boy, before the paralysis took hold.'

I put the paste on the floor to give myself a break – 'It's coming on, wouldn't you say?'

'It's looking good.'

I splash myself with it as I pick it up and you laugh at me. It's cold and it dries quickly on my skin. 'Save me some of that,' you say. 'It's like a potion my wife would use!'

The laughter fades, and as I start to spread the paste over the cane matting, I can't help but dwell on how God has used me. It's just so exciting when he includes you in his plans – this whole thing with Gabe has brought me so much closer to God and has really enlivened my faith. 'Never again will I doubt my value in plugging gaps,' I say, leaning back on my haunches to admire my handiwork. 'Usually it's not this literal – more often than not I'm wrestling in prayer for people and before now I thought, what's the value in me apologizing to God on behalf of them... Isn't that pointless? That was what the nagging voice told me.'

You nod in agreement and I sense you really understand.

'But now I feel totally sure of this: God hears every prayer and not one of them is wasted, not a single one. We might forget what we've said to him, but he never does.'

'You're so right,' you say, and you sit down next to me. 'You know, I've seen Jesus bring the answer to many a prayer. He really is astonishing. For I'm sure he's from God himself – he's not performing miracles for his own sake, for his own glory. I really believe he's the promised Messiah. Every day I spend with him he's reordering my world – this hole in the roof – it's nothing. You should see what he's done inside me.'

We're both silent now, our eyes fixed on my repair as we enjoy the heat on our backs and time to think. You seem content to sit and wait with me as the mixture hardens in the warm midday sunshine. There is an earthy smell that takes me back to childhood, days of stirring mud and telling Imma I'd made a mix to fix the leaks, but my concoctions were never trusted by her. I've a lot to thank Gabe for, as it turns out, because I'm going to seek out Jesus again, but for my own benefit next time. Good old Gabe.

'So tell me about your friend,' you say. 'What's your background with him?'

'We've always done things together. We've been friends right from when we were small. I think I was a bit in awe of him. He always was quite wild and I liked that.'

'I was getting that yesterday. Even in the way he leapt up from his bed, picked up his mat and walked out. For he clearly enjoyed the moment, and not just because he'd been healed.'

'It was a back-at-you to all the judgy people.'

'For sure.'

'I'd had enough of seeing him suffer in recent years, but had quietly prayed for him from the moment his condition came about. To have never walked is one thing, but to have gone from being able-bodied to as debilitated as that is quite another. When we were kids we'd build the best dens together, and run across roof-tops when everyone else was out late at some festival. I even remember filching grapes from the vineyards, and dares around the winepress in the dead of night, then having to explain to our mothers the stains on our clothes.'

You smile and something tells me you were no different.

'We got into some scrapes, but I kind of grew out of all that. Gabe didn't. He'd made some very bad choices as an adult, and some say that's why he got sick – struck down they said.'

There's no time for me to hear your opinion on that for we hear a thump on the door and then a whistle. 'Hey, Ceph,' comes a voice from the ground. 'You home?'

You get up and lean over the parapet to chat to your friend.

'Oh shalom. Cephas, can I borrow your boat?'

'By all means,' you call back, 'take it out, I'm not using it.'

You feel the need to explain something to me, as this conversation has been pretty one-sided, it must be said. 'That boat of mine – well, mine and my brother's –'

'Go on. It can't be any more curious than what I've seen here.'

'It'll sound strange but I'd tried to give it away a few weeks ago, in a moment of euphoria.'

'To be honest, nothing surprises me now.'

'Well, this might. I finally realized I needed to give up my livelihood for Jesus, which will sound peculiar. But I reached the point where I wanted to throw my lot in with him. Opportunities like this one don't come along every day. For I figured that he could use me, bizarrely, and I'd been trusting in my own capabilities, not his. Anyway, my boat – none of the locals felt they could take it from me. Jesus had given us this miraculous catch, you see. Instead they would all take turns to borrow it, hoping beyond hope that our success that day might rub off on them.'

I nod my understanding at you. It is fascinating to meet someone who is further down the line in this than me. I'm glad it's not just me that's drawn by him, because if you try to explain it to someone who's never met him they just think you plain odd.

'I still go out in it from time to time,' you say. 'But more for the fun of it, and to catch the occasional supper for our group. I enjoy it much more that way. I'm glad Jesus doesn't demand from us everything we enjoy. Instead he seems to transform our abilities and give us an even greater purpose. I must admit, I found it draining, fishing for a living. He values our uniqueness you know. For our skills and interests are more often than not God-given. Longings that he's put inside of us. It's pointless us clinging selfishly to them – we're not going to be any more fulfilled.'

'That was still a bold move though,' I say.

'No bolder than what you've done, bringing your friend to Jesus as you did. Faith comes with small and steady steps. Then at some point you look back and are amazed at how far he's brought you.'

The plaster is going off now and I'm preparing my next compound, a concoction of chalk, ashes and dry soil. I stand up to stir it, and you shuffle back as I begin to scatter it on top of the last layer, waving a hand in front of your face.

'I must be careful with you around,' you say with a laugh. 'For we all had soil in our eyes yesterday when your friend made his dramatic entrance, dead leaves in our hair. Don't suppose it occurred to you that the debris was going to fall on us folk below, Jesus included!'

I brush down my tunic and feel heat come into my cheeks. 'Oh, I'm very sorry for that. I had no idea – we were just struck by all the astonished faces, and Jesus actually smiling up at us.'

'Not a problem,' you say, and you throw a friendly hand against my arm. 'You're one of us, I can see that. I'm very proud of you. But not everyone was so impressed.'

'That was clear enough from our view up here. Some of them looked pretty angry.'

'You mustn't worry about them. The politically correct crowd will always try to trip Jesus up – he's just so unconventional and not bound by rules for rules' sake.'

'Gabe's going to love him.'

'Some of the officials have been following Jesus round. And so it was with reluctance I let them into my house yesterday. I think they're taking notes, trying to gather evidence against him.'

'That's a bit much. They've nothing to go on though, have they? It's just a nonsense.'

'When they can't find fault they invent one. But he is *Jesus*. I think it's going to be resolved somehow. I couldn't be as tolerant as him, but he looks at us when we're about to turn them away and we know not to. I wish I could be as charitable.'

'This stuff reminds me of the treatments they used to smear on Gabe,' I say, perfecting the surface with a precision-smooth plank of wood, though it's not necessary at this stage.

'Such as? How do they even attempt to cure paralysis?'

'Oh, he's had salves daubed all over him, potions to take. He's swallowed borage that did nothing but release his bowels, and turmeric that turned his skin orange. He's smelt of garlic juice, and of hyssop that made him smell like a girl. His family ran out of money to spare, which is when I got involved. I took him to see a 'specialist' once and regretted it from the moment we carried him in. He clung to his sheepskin bed like the man was there to torture him.'

You let out a sigh and your intent concentration encourages me to say more. 'We saw other, more general physicians, too. Gabe's condition came on gradually and to start with they were dealing with numbness, which seemed fair enough. There was muscle weakness and balance problems and I expected they'd be able to treat these. But it just got worse and worse. It was seeing him pulled around so badly that did it for me – that made me decide to give Jesus a try. He had no sense of embarrassment left anyway, his self-worth had all but drained out of him.'

'I want to know what these 'pain doctors' do,' you say. 'Some of the Pharisees say that's just what Jesus is – what a nonsense. So how does it work?'

'We carried him in like we did yesterday – except through the door on those occasions!'

'Good,' says Cephas with a smile.

'Then the doctor would try to manipulate his joints. They say there's no pain in paralysed joints but that's rubbish. "This won't hurt," they'd say, but every time I saw pain written into each line on his face – lines that didn't used to be there before – and he'd screw his eyes up tight and look away. I'm sure some of the 'doctors' delighted in it. They looked like unnatural manoeuvres to me – it was as if they wanted to prove there was still life left in the joint, that it could return to normal. I found myself clenching my own fists, digging my nails into my palms as I saw Gabe wince. He'd jerk and shake uncontrollably. I hate seeing anyone in pain – let alone my best friend.'

Concern is written into your own face now and tears have gathered in the corners of your eyes. I can see you are a good man and your kindness convinces me of Jesus's genuineness all the more. 'Go on,' you say. 'We need to know about these things.'

'There was pain in his face even when no one was trying to fix him: his lips were set tight over clenched teeth, his brow permanently creased. I knew when he was having a bad day – they weren't hard to spot. He was short with everyone, cross with us even for caring. It was fair enough – anyone would have felt miserable in his position. If I could have taken even half of his pain it would have made me happy.'

'And yesterday? How did it happen?'

'I'd been hearing more and more about Jesus. As his friends, we told him we really should visit him, but the crowds were always so massive that it looked impossible. But I was determined – I'd heard they were coming with toothache, deafness, withered limbs.'

'They do,' you say. 'The slightest whim sometimes. "Jesus, bless my children, Jesus, touch me, please" – it's like he's some good luck charm, like they want amazing physiques and perfect bodies. *You* are the type of people I long to see – those that want his enduring touch on your lives to change you, to bring complete wholeness. For people are all too quick to forget the soul – that's where they really need him.'

I smile.

'The roof is looking good. Thank you.'

'We'll just sprinkle some water over it, then tread it down. One more layer and we're done. It will dry and shrink in overnight, then we'll see if it needs touching up tomorrow.'

'I appreciate it, it needed doing. Perhaps I should get you back to do the whole thing sometime.'

'I'd be very happy to, but there's something you could do for me – introduce me to Jesus properly some time? My spirit is restless, like it's flapping around inside me, all of a jitter. Like it needs to commit to following him. Do you think he'll let me?'

'God be praised!' I think that's a yes. 'He's coming for supper. Why don't you come at the seventh hour and eat with us? He won't have forgotten you. For he was impressed by your faith yesterday, you know. Any act of kindness is never lost on him, and he can see into your soul; he knows when you're keen to follow. He's going to be delighted with you – just you wait and see.'

See Matthew (9:1–8), Mark (2:1–12), and Luke (5:17–26) for the story of the paralytic lowered through the roof.

Many commentaries suggest this incident happened at Peter's house. This idea appeals to me and so it is the setting for my tale. I am sure that many people who were healed by Jesus and the disciples would have encountered them again, at the very least. These were small communities, and I believe the intention would have been there to encourage them in the faith.

Widow at Nain

Where was her God now? Why hadn't he answered her cries for help? She wondered what the point was in going on; no one needed her and she had no one. Why couldn't their God take her, too? She stood up and folded the rough woven blanket that had covered her in the early part of the night, before she'd kicked it to one side.

She had 'slept' there on the roof as *he* was laid out downstairs. But he had a name, of course – Eli, or Elisha, as his father would always say in full. That almost superstitious name choice felt ironic now. Again, she asked herself, where was her God? But that story only happened on the other side of their hill, and what is eight-hundred years to the God of Heaven?[16] Surely that counted for something – wasn't he reminded of his mercy of old whenever he saw her boy? He had been a living, breathing person yesterday; he was her son, her very own, and they had been so close. 'I'll always protect you, Imma,' that's what he'd said when disaster struck the first time. What had she done, why had she been singled out to receive this double-dose of tragedy?

The stubby wicker broom lay propped against the wall and she began sweeping the already clean roof, gathering an imaginary pile of dirt and pine needles in the middle of the floor, for she had to do something. She would go down later – not now. But she should dress, for surely people would start to gather outside her house very soon. Oh, she must face it, then.

As she turned to descend the steps a small, cloth-wrapped parcel caught her eye, tucked underneath her cane basket. She took it in both hands and sat down on the floor with her legs crossed, removing the brown patterned fabric as if something highly breakable lay inside. She lifted out Eli's prized flute, feeling its weight in her hand. How he loved that old bit of hollowed out bone, and the tunes he could make on it! It was given to him when he was very small and he'd always loved it. He played his tunes on it when with his friends – they were a faith-filled little group and worshipped together, some playing on drums, others belting out the songs they'd written, or psalms they'd set to music. How his death was going to affect that close-knit group. Soon the community would see her and pick up their own instruments to play their dreadful tunes, pronouncing his passing with sounds too painful to hear.

---

[16] Nain sits two miles north of Shunem. See 2 Kings 4 for the story in which Elisha is used by God to resuscitate a loved son in Shunem, and 1 Kings 17 for a similar story of how God used Elijah to bring a widow's son back to life at Zarephath.

Would any of his friends join in? Somehow she doubted it. She let out a long sigh. She couldn't afford professional mourners but that wouldn't stop them all turning out. It was as if they enjoyed it, some of them, thought it a 'spectacle', whether or not they were being paid.

***

Father, bless Eli's mother, I pray. Who is there to help her? Who's going to provide for her now? Quite frankly I can't believe you've allowed this to happen. To have lost her only son? We had prayed, we had sought you, but this thing just went from bad to worse. I wish I could go to her, but socially that's all wrong. I don't even think I can join the procession; to see her on her own like that – I cannot bear it, for I'm not allowed to support her. Oh Father, the gossip that's doing the rounds! "God takes her husband from her, and then her son. She must be a terrible sinner! What things has she thought? What things has she done?" Oh Lord, she's no worse than the rest of us. And Lord. I miss my friend already. Please do something to help. It's beyond me to know what can be done. Amen.

***

Her son had passed away so late last night that she had to wait till dawn before they could take him for burial. The doctor who had come sent for a man to wash and anoint him there and then, for he had seen how beside herself she was. She could barely stand. It had felt strange, allowing someone else to touch him, so she had let him in and made her way to the roof on her knees, where she'd remained ever since. She had stood on occasions, paced, then tried to sleep, but she had felt most comfortable on her knees and resumed that position to intercede for him – she knew it was pointless but she had to do something. To think of that man washing Eli down and wrapping him; the lad meant nothing to him and may as well have been an object. She felt awful about it but she had no physical strength. Should she anoint him now? She had asked that the ointment be left behind. A last personal farewell with no one looking.

She took the stairs down from the roof slowly, pausing on each one, her hand placed on the cold white wall to steady herself. Her thoughts meant she was unaware of how long it was taking to reach him. She wanted to touch him but she knew it wouldn't feel like him. His flesh wouldn't give but would feel hard, solid… If only the doctor had come when she had asked. He told her it was short notice, that he had more pressing cases; more likely he had richer patients, those whose illnesses could be more lucrative for him. She had been let down all round – were her prayers not fervent enough? Did God even know what he was doing?

As she stood in the doorway she closed her eyes, for it was all too much. All she had seen was his outline wrapped in linen cloths, his face covered with a sudarium, his hands and feet tied, but that was enough. There was no way she'd be able to remove the wrappings. A sob rose up from within and she crouched down on the floor, letting the tears fall.

She had expected some support from friends, even her deceased husband's family in the circumstances, but the house had remained empty. Surely her 'brother-in-law' would come soon – not that he had any obligations by her now. Many people would have turned in for the night when it happened, but word did travel quickly in Nain. Why should this be any different? Perhaps they didn't know what to say to her. Perhaps they even felt his illness still lurked in the building. She knew what they'd all be saying. She'd had enough of their judgements; she'd heard them when she had struggled to conceive and all her friends had a quiver-full. Eli's arrival had silenced their gossip for a while, but now the stigma would be back, only ten times worse.

She remembered the time when her husband had passed away. She stopped eating and if it hadn't been for Eli she would have grown very sick and weak. He had held food to her lips and implored her to eat. That old feeling was back, for she had no appetite now and did not anticipate it returning. It was no matter, for she would have to get used to living on very little anyway. Eli had given her something to live for and he had provided for them both, in time.

***

Father, I want to remind you of Eli's mother again. Lord, who will support her? How will she cope? Will you please show her she is valued and loved. Go with her, as I would, if I could. Give her some people that care – may they get alongside her. She must be broken-hearted. Remember your concern for the widows; we read of it so often. You say you will plead for them, establish their borders. That you provide for them at harvest time. Look on this poor widow now and be merciful, dear God.

***

It was happening, then. Her worst nightmare was continuing to unroll, but it felt strange – as if she wasn't really present. As if she were spectating herself. She should be tearing her clothes, but for now she felt a certain numbness. Perhaps it was her mind's way of protecting her. She was meant to be wailing, setting an example at the head of the procession but she just couldn't do it, and it was causing a mild panic to sweep through her. She felt like God had blanked her and it was just easier to blank herself. Hadn't her prayer been perfectly reasonable?

The community had shown up, but she suspected it was more out of a sense of obligation, and to see how she was coping, too. It was a scandal of sorts. She was a scandal. To have lost her family, to be all alone – what must God think of her?

Along the road they went, the crowd swelling as they neared the edge of the town. She could see the view across to the Nazareth hills, and she wondered if that was Mount Hermon in the distance, or just a cloud. It was a view she had always loved before, but now it made her heart beat faster, for soon they would be out of the town and down the road to that place where the dead were banished…

At once she heard the sound of footsteps pounding the ground as someone young rushed up to the front of the crowd. She turned to look over her shoulder, and there behind her walked Eli's best friend Nathan, struggling to catch his breath. What a dear young fellow. He caught her eye and she started to cry then. The two of them had grown so alike over the years; they had the same expressions, the same mannerisms and it was really too much. That hard stare of theirs that wouldn't let go, that was usually awaiting at least a smile, or laughter when she was in the mood – it was like looking at her own son. Today it conveyed his concern. She couldn't expect his support after today, but for now she was glad of it.

She could hear a rabble on the road ahead, making light of the steep path leading into the town, laughing together, shouting. It was surely a big crowd. And then they began to emerge through the gate, and at the front was their leader, a calm looking man of about thirty with a joy about him, a happiness that was surely inappropriate; could they not see what they'd stumbled into? But what was this? He was coming over to her, for he must have seen the most distraught face amongst them, though of course she walked with the bier. 'Don't cry!' he said.

Some of the musicians had stopped playing and the wailing had died down. She could hear the mutters from those around her – 'Who does he think he is?', 'I've heard things about him!', 'Doesn't he realize what's going on here?', *'Don't cry* – what else does he expect her to do?' Yet they were all wrong, for there was such a concern when he spoke, such a warmth, and she felt a connection with him. It was the first time she'd really felt anything vaguely resembling love since her son had grown sick. It even looked to her as if he might cry himself, though of course they had never met before. She could feel her cheeks flush and give way to the makings of a smile. How bizarre that was, and she couldn't account for it. It was a moment that seemed far longer than it actually was, for pain was met with kindness, and though the deep hurt still remained it gave her some irrational, doom-defying hope.

But it didn't end there. For then he strode right up to their procession and grabbed a side of the bier with his hand.[17] Now the bearers halted, the remaining musicians who were still playing stopped, and everyone was silent. Well, he'd defiled himself now, that was for certain. All the noise and clamour had faded away and people were staring at him – even the women. He leaned over her son, as if he was about to speak to him, but then he did! This whole encounter was getting stranger and stranger. 'Young man,' he said, his kind gaze now fixed on her boy, 'I tell you, get up.'

Straight away her son sat bolt upright and there were gasps from the crowd. She felt strong arms on either side of her that prevented her from falling, for she was in a state of shock. Was it even her son under those bandages, was this some cruel joke?

That thought was silenced by another voice, one so familiar to her and dearer to her than life itself. 'Where am I?' he said. His arms fought their way out of the linen cloths and he felt his face with frantic hands, pulling off the sudarium so that he could see. His face had colour again and his big, dark eyes were searching, darting around the crowd. 'But these are my neighbours! I thought I'd left this place for good. Oh, I can see it now – it was you!' he said, looking straight at the stranger who had been standing beside him all along. 'Thank you so much! Oh praise God! This is beyond belief. But... I had... died,' he said to his healer, the crowd forgotten by him for now. 'But I know I had. I was so unwell – my last earthly memory is of my mother crying tears over me and I didn't have the strength even to reach out to her, to embrace her, to reassure her.' The stranger heard him out and smiled at him. 'She told me not to leave her but I felt so weak,' he continued, 'I just couldn't hold on. Where is she?'

At this moment she stepped forward to where he could see her, guided by the newcomer's hand that rested on her back. She embraced her son and felt his strong arms around her, as strong as they had always been, before that awful illness had taken hold.

How long they stayed there like that she had no idea, but after a while she became conscious of the voices around her again. 'Who was he?' 'He's Jesus,

---

[17] Greek for touch here – 'lay hold'. This was a very decisive and deliberate act of Jesus's.

he's been performing wonders over in Capernaum, don't tell me you haven't heard of him?'

Of course, she must thank him, but as she turned to talk to him she discovered he had already gone.

'God has been here,' said a young man in the crowd – another friend of her son's whose face was familiar to her. He looked around for someone who would agree with him and his eyes settled on Eli, who smiled back at him. Had there ever been such joy as was then written on their faces, such pure and overwhelming joy?

'God has visited his people today,' replied an old man who she knew from the temple, leaning forward on his stick, trying to add dignity to the occasion with his somber tone.

'A mighty prophet has risen among us,' said another of his generation, a man who had been a loyal customer of her husband's. He looked far off into the distance as he spoke, as if his perceptive powers were matched with visual accuracy.

The woman's neighbour who was holding a corner of the bier cleared his throat. 'This is getting somewhat heavy,' he said with a laugh that rippled through his large belly. 'I didn't think I'd be holding onto it for this long!'

'Come on lad,' said the woman's brother-in-law. 'Swing your legs over the side, we'll help you pull off the wrappings when you are down.'

'We don't want this thing to touch the floor, it's unlucky,' said the neighbour. 'I nearly dropped you when you sat up – we had it balanced perfectly, but we weren't expecting you to start moving!'

'Well, I'm sorry,' he said with a grin.

***

The house hardly looked familiar to her when she was home. The events of the last few days – it was as if she had imagined them, but there on the window sill lay a pile of linen strips, a few nuggets of myrrh and a pot of salve from the preparations. She gathered it all together to sort through.

'I still smell of that stuff,' he said to her as they sat down together. 'Smell my hair, it's gross, Imma.'

She bent her head over his and laughed as she took in the fragrance – it caught in the back of her throat. Then she held his face in her hands and kissed him as she had longed to earlier that day, when the fear of how he would look beneath the coverings had prevented her. 'Don't ever do that to me again, will you?' she said. 'I thought I'd lost you.'

'I'll try not to. I wish that Jesus lived closer to home,' he replied, rolling a dried piece of myrrh resin between his finger and thumb. 'I want to find him, perhaps I'll go out with Nathan, camp out for a few nights so we can tag along once we've tracked him down.'

'I wouldn't mind coming too, but I don't want to get in your way.'

'You'd be very welcome, Imma, though you can't rough it with us. We'd have to find you somewhere to stay.'

She smiled at him. 'We really should find out more about him. I owe him everything,' she said, smoothing a linen strip across her lap and pulling a thread from its fraying edge, before folding it with meticulous care. 'He gave me my life back,' she told him, after a long pause. 'You know, I hadn't imagined I could ever live again.' She stopped to look her son in the face. 'That a stranger can care that much is just incredible. When he looked at me I could see that he was sharing my pain; I saw my own anguish looking back at me. What kindness it that? I don't think it's human. I think it's godly. And what he did to you – for you. He has to be something special.'

'You don't think he's the Messiah?'

'Well, who else is he? No one has power like that. He wasn't reveling in it, either. He didn't seem to want to be noticed. I even wonder if you'll be able to find him.'

Eli shook his head at her. 'Did you see the size of that crowd? With the following he has, I think it'll be easy enough.'

'But what would be the point? What more do you expect to gain?'

'If he's the Messiah, I want to hear all he has to say. I think he brought me back for a reason.'

'He'd taken pity on me. Wasn't that reason enough?' she replied, folding up the last of the linen strips. 'We must return these, by the way.'

'On one level, for sure. But I want to learn all I can from him. Opportunities like this one don't come along every day.'

See Luke's Gospel, chapter 7, verses 11–17 for the biblical account of this story.

Not my name

'Ya-oo, joom, joom… He's coming, Jesus is coming here and I'm going to meet him! Look, the boat is moving towards us again! Ya-ooo, get down, shut up, I can't meet him. He hates me, he threw me out of heaven! Shut up!'

'Woo-uld you just listen to yourself, you strange, unnatural fool. And you're drooling, your bulgy eyes staring. Whaaat makes you think he'll come anywhere neeear us? I'm cringing inside, and can you see, I'm doubling over the neeearer he gets; my God, I'm struggling to stand. I'm out of here. Brother, you be careful. You're on your own, if you wa-want to try and approach him. Ya-eee, yow, stum, stum!'

His screeching and protesting echoes through the caves, returning to me with twice the volume than went in.

'Come back!' I call but he's off, out in the light again and running with a sideways limp. He lollops towards the deepest cave at the far end of the burial site. He's still screaming and I have to leave him alone. He'll be himself again shortly – he may still come out when Jesus lands, for the pull will be too much for him. It always was – you what? You've never known him, he doesn't want to know you, know me. You're in too deep, you've sold yourself now. I've sold myself. Some people are just in too deep to ever get out alive and I'm dangerous, I'm evil, I'm 'ee-yaaah, boom, sheeerow, yaaah,' I'm screaming with all I've got and I want to kill something, someone… Perhaps I'll kill Jesus, 'yaahhh!'

Seabirds are circling and mimicking my cries, mopping them up and absorbing them in their own vile screeches. I'm exhausted and I hate myself – my selves. That's a sharp stone, it looks perfect – I stoop to pick it up and swipe its jagged point across my neck. 'Yaahh!' That's better… But it's not really, for the relief is only short-lived. I don't want to be like this; it's not who I really am, who I used to be. That we'd trusted the old fool with his dark arts, believed him when he told us we would be powerful and control events! I suppose we do have power for I am strong enough to break the chains they've attached to me when I've slept. But it's not the sort of power that's good for anything.

The boat has landed and I'm running towards him now, feeling the rocks jabbing the soles of my feet. Nearly there. Oh, I'm nearly there. He won't be able to turn me away, and I can subdue him if I need to. So why am I so afraid? 'Yaaah,' I scream at his face and I'm spitting who knows what. He looks startled as he steps out of the boat and I fall face-first onto the beach but I really don't care. I can't actually stand in his presence and I'm tasting grit between my teeth.

'Come out of the man, you evil spirit,' he says over me and I shiver – oh but I'm burning up, then in a moment so cold again. I can't breathe, I can hardly catch my breath to speak.

'Why are you interfering with me, Jesus, Son of the Most High God,' I say to him. 'Please, I beg you, don't torture me!' Am I dying? Perhaps my life ends here. Perhaps there's none of the real me left…

I dare to look up and he's extending a hand to me! No one has dared to do that in years. I see my brother running for the cave again. I wonder how much of that he has just experienced but he's not likely to be able to tell me for a while. He'll probably deny being here at all, like he usually does. I often doubt my sanity, he disputes what I see so often.

'What is your name?' Jesus says to me.

'Legion,' I reply, and the voices are coming out of me again, voices that never were mine but have owned me and tried to possess me all these years. 'Don't send us out, Son of the Most High,' they say. 'Don't do it, leave us alone!' 'Yaaah! Not the abyss.' 'Leave us here!', 'Please don't send us there!'

Jesus looks at me and says something I don't understand, and the next thing I know I'm on the ground again and feeling winded. I could have been out cold for a while, for when I come round he is talking to a crowd that have gathered around me – a huge gawping crowd. He puts out a hand for me again and gestures for them to back off and give us some space. When I'm on my feet he puts an arm around me and leads me to one side, then gestures for me to sit down next to him on a large rock. He hands me a large cake of bread and one of his followers steps over to bring me a tunic that I slip over my head, with the clean, yeasty smelling bread still in my hand.

I thank Jesus for sorting me out and he smiles and nods at me, with such an understanding in his eyes. I'm not imagining it. It's all the kindness I could ever wish to be in the world, and it's all directed at me. He looks into me and doesn't turn away. There's nothing in me that repulses him now – nothing that could repulse anyone. It is only a short moment but somehow it lasts a long time; I feel it will last me forever. He assures me that he's freed me once and for all, and gives me some instructions on keeping clean from here – not externally, though I hope that too will be a possibility now, but on the inside. I learn of how he's sent those demons – I won't use the word 'my' in connection with them any more – over the cliff in a herd of pigs. I don't think that's going to do anything for my popularity round here, but never mind. I don't think the locals are very popular with him anyway – he seems to know somehow that they'd banished us and tormented us, chained us up and hated us with every inch of their beings.

I can't sit beside him any more. I'm just in awe of the man, and I slide off the rock and sit at his feet, my head in my hands. The tears come now – tears of relief, for I'm just so overwhelmed. His disciples have joined us and I learn of how determined Jesus was to come and find me here – that he'd already singled me out and had crossed the lake for my benefit alone. 'It made no sense to us,' says the outspoken one. 'We thought we were going to lose our lives in that storm, and when we arrived we realized that it was because of *you* that we'd come.'

Jesus raises an eyebrow at him.

'Shut up Nate,' says one of the others, poking him in the side.

'What?' he replies. 'I'm sorry young man,' he says to me. 'I'm still learning. I'm coming to understand that God values everyone. That not one of us is outside of his reach.' He scratches his black beard and allows his hand to linger there, as if lost in thought.

The crowd around us has grown very large now and I can hear whispers and gasps, and some louder voices, sharing their disgruntlement, though I daren't look at them – 'We've got to get him away from here!' 'How dare he?' 'Who does he think he is? How am I supposed to feed my family now?' Soon they butt into our conversation. 'I hope you plan to reimburse us?' and 'Don't you think it's time you were going?' 'Yeah, it's about time you were off.'

Jesus stands to leave, for those negative voices are taking over now, and I have to look up. 'We don't...want... you...here,' says one old, shaggy-haired man who steps towards him, pausing for effect between each word. A group of men behind him step closer too and stand with a wide stance, their arms folded in front of them. 'Take your dodgy magic tricks somewhere else,' calls a voice from the back of the crowd. 'We were fine here until you showed up,' says a young fellow who's at the elbow of the old man and here to support him, for he's actually quite frail, despite his venom. 'Now look!'

Many of them actually seem afraid of him. Small children are clinging to their mothers' legs and some have been scooped up by their fathers and are held in their arms. It's as if they think Jesus is dangerous – it's quite preposterous. They simply don't want their safe ground shaken, irrespective of any members of the community who might actually need his help. They all need help, the lot of them, if they could but see it. They all need delivering from their ridiculous fears.

Jesus looks unshockable, though I can see he's not going to stick around where he's not wanted. I stand up now for it's possible they will chase him from here. 'Jesus, let me come with you! I need to be around you,' I say, but he's not having any of it.

'No, go back to your family and tell them everything God has done for you,' he replies.

You can't argue with Jesus and there's really no point. He seems to know best anyway, from what I can see. I sit down on the rock again and watch him go, wondering if he'll look back at me.

I can see it's not a rejection but what I really need to do. My family? I had one once, though it's been years since we lived together, since I had any positive contact with them. Of course, there's my brother and I know I should find him, too. I wonder if the demons have left him now, if he was a part of that whole thing or if he's still tormented?

And so Jesus sits down in the boat, and as I look on, he grows smaller and smaller on the lake, until at last he is taken from sight. Will I ever see him again? I think I will, and I plan to live my life now in such a way that he might be proud of me, see his efforts were worthwhile. I'd love it if he got to hear news of me somehow because I'm doing such a good job... though it's difficult to know where to begin. I'll have to seek out my family again, as he said. I don't know if they will trust me or want me back... I shall stick around for a week or two, and if I'm still rejected, I'll set off for the Ten Towns. I could earn a livelihood as I travel and preach, perhaps putting my strength to good use.

I stand and attempt to lift this rock that Jesus and I sat on together – it's not shifting and I try again, but it's no use. I can feel myself going red in the face and a muscle in my neck straining. Then I hear a voice behind me –

'Now let's see you cope, strong man.'

I turn to see the head pigman at my shoulder. He's been my chief tormenter. He always was a pain, even when we were children. Come to think of it, he was perhaps the reason I bought into the idea of being powerful in the first place.

'Oh, good morning,' I say. 'Sorry about your pigs but if you'll just let me–'

'You'll do what exactly?' he says, his face now up close to mine. 'How exactly am I going to feed my family now, Legion?'

'That's not my name,' I reply. 'I'm happy to help you, but you must understand, that's not my nam–'

I start to run and he's chasing me along the path I've not been allowed to tread for years. Jesus knew what he was doing when he healed me – he must've thought it'd be possible for me to start over again or he wouldn't have bothered.

I'm feeling my frailty once more but actually I quite like it. I'd rather this than all the strength I had before, yet no peace inside.

I dive through a gap and into a burial cave, where I wait for the man to pass, or we'll come to blows – I have no fear of them after what I've been through, and no fear of death either. It does stink in here, now I come to think of it. I don't think I'd smelt anything in years, though it hadn't occurred to me. I can hear my blood pumping though my ears and I just feel so alive! I crouch down in the quiet and listen to hear if he's waiting out there for me. I can even *hear* my thoughts now. I never believed it possible! It's like being made over anew, like I've got my old self back, but better. If it were possible to be reborn, then I think I have. I haven't been my own person for such a long time, so this is kind of bizarre – but in a good way. When I relax as I am now there are no words going through my head, no sounds. It's what they call silence, I suppose. I'd forgotten it was even a thing.

I hear someone clear their throat quietly and I sit upright. 'Shaa-lom,' comes a soft voice that echoes through the chamber. That old word, so pure and so poignant. 'Josiah,' it says, and I hear my name said in my brother's familiar way twenty times, but not in his wild screech of old. There is warmth there, good sense and normality. 'Josiah,' it comes again, and now he's standing beside me in the dark.

'You were there, then,' I say to him.

'Hello, brother,' he says with a smile I can just make out, and he puts a hand on my shoulder. 'You always did have the best name,' he tells me.

'Looks like he healed us both, though,' I say. 'What happened to you?'

'I ran off when it all got too much. I stood further back than you, and I saw you fall in front of him. I th-think he'd delivered me before I ran off, as it turned out. I couldn't approach him though. It felt almost like I'd s-stolen your blessing.'

'Don't be stupid. He wants wholeness for everyone – that's one thing I've worked out. Wholeness for you too. Do you know, he crossed the lake for us, even in that storm. I can't get over it.' I shake my head to myself and let out a deep breath in a sigh.

'Can I... Can I still be one of his?'

'Of course you can. I'm sure he knows about you already.'

I head over to the mouth of the cave to see if the pigman has gone. 'We need to go into town and find out if Imma is still alive,' I say.

'I don't think she is. It looked like the whole town had turned out. I was watching from here. I think our waywardness... it probably killed her.'

'I doubt it.'

'I really do. She wouldn't have stood for us being chained up otherwise.'

I sigh again. 'We can't keep looking backwards or it'll kill us too. I'll check things out here, then I'm going on to spread the word about Jesus in the surrounding towns. I don't think they'll want us around here now anyway, not after the encounter I've just had.'

'I'm starving. Do you think there's any food in this one?'

'Are you kidding? I've had enough dead ancestor offerings to last me for this kingdom and the next. It's time to head on from here and see what life throws at us.'

'I'll come, I suppose, so long as no one f-follows us.'

'Hang on, not like that,' I say as we come out into the light.

'What?'

'You're still naked, Dov.' I think you look relieved that you're not coming, and it's not just about your lack of clothes. 'I'll bring something back from town for you, but you'll have to move on from here. You know that, don't you?'

'I guess so, but I've never felt fear like this before.'

'Come back into the cave,' I say. 'I think we should pray.'

For the biblical accounts of this story, visit Matthew 8:28–34, Mark 5:1–20 and Luke 8:26–39.

The daughter

'I think you've come to the wrong house.'

That's how it all started. Those were my first words to you that day and I'm still reliving the moment, trying to make sense of what happened.

'I'm lost,' you said, 'and would be glad of something to drink, if that's alright.'

'You must be a stranger here. Can you try elsewhere? I'm not allowed to be a part of this community any more. Let me explain –'

'No one knows me here,' you said. 'I'd be glad of your hospitality, if you don't mind.'

And so in you came. Darkness was falling and as I glanced out of the door I couldn't see anyone looking. It was a relief to have some human contact again, though I felt sure once I'd told of my predicament you would want to leave. But it didn't seem to be so; you wouldn't hear any of it.

'You really don't look well,' you said. 'You must let me prepare you a meal.'

'I don't have much in,' I said, and I hoped you wouldn't notice that I was struggling for breath. I gathered the rags, drying in a row on a line across the back of the room, and put them in a small heap in the corner.

'You lie down,' you said and I had to oblige, I was feeling faint and my palpitations had started up again. I fully expected you to quietly let yourself out at that point, and as I shut my eyes I didn't have the strength to worry. I pulled my mantle over my head and slept.

I don't know where you found all the ingredients, but when I awoke you presented me with the most delicious meal I've ever known. There was fish that you'd cooked so perfectly that it fell apart in my fingers; it tasted sweet, like honey. You gave me bread that contained moist olives and served me with more respect than I had ever been shown. I started to cry and you told me that it would all be alright in the end. You told me that I needed to find Jesus. I said that I had heard of him, but that even he wouldn't be able to help me. You said that I was wrong. Oh, can I remember it all? You talked to me about wholeness, about complete well-being and the shalom of God. You asked me to promise that I would find him, and not to go back on my word. And then you were gone. It was as if I had dreamed it all up, but my bowl was still warm from the food that I had just finished eating. I took the last of the bread and wiped it clean. I thought of Abraham and Sarah and how they too were a laughing stock once, but three special visitors changed all that. I knew I absolutely had to do what you had said.

I wish it were possible to thank you but it's not. Instead I must think it all through and hope that one day I get to meet you again. Perhaps I was indeed entertaining an angel – though you were the one serving me. I didn't even get to ask your name.

***

So today I must be true to my word. I will disguise myself by wearing my grandmother's old mantle and tunic, and take special care to wrap a deep hood from my shawl. I'm used to walking quickly with my head down, though usually I go about my business when it is dark. I have a few food items left for me on my doorstep by a kindly neighbour, so I don't have cause to go out much during the day. But I suspect people will know who I am; I know that my issue makes me smell, for it is impossible to keep myself clean, washing myself as often as I need is so problematic… No matter. I have been instructed to do this and for good reason. My faith hasn't left me through all these long twelve years, and I know my Lord loves me as much as anyone. Yesterday I watched the most perfect blue and white butterfly, painted with the same colour as a brilliant sky, a rare, exquisite and expensive hue. It rested on the flowering thyme that grows in a pot beside my door, then it landed on my neighbour's wall. I watched as it flitted through the neighbourhood with no discrimination; that's how I feel God is with us. I may be termed 'unclean' by the law, but I was taught by my mother that the rules are in place to protect us women: 'You'll be pregnant or breastfeeding for much of your adult life,' she told me, 'and when you are not, the laws are for your good. You have to rest, let others prepare the food, and your husband isn't even allowed to sleep with you. You get some long-awaited personal space time, and, believe me, you've earned it.' Well if it was meant as a blessing it most certainly doesn't feel like that now.

Something is urging me to get ready now so I may as well. I haven't anything to lose – with my health as it is, I don't expect to live much longer anyway, and there's nothing anyone can say to me today that they haven't said before. If I don't see him this time it will be a practice run.

I will have to brush past other people in my quest to get close to Jesus, and the prospect bothers me. Once I'm dressed fully I fill a bowl from the pitcher and wash my hands one last time before stepping out – perhaps this way I won't make anyone else unclean when I inevitably touch them. I take my father's old stick from behind the door – it's been a while since I've walked very far, and I might need to run to keep up with the crowd.

I shall be whole, I shall be whole, I say under my breath as I step out into the bright sunshine. I am really not used to this, but then I have some catching up to do. When I *am* whole I will wander outside every day, linger over every flower that he has made, bask in the beauty of it all. I have enjoyed the Creator's skies for a long time now – I can't touch them but they still touch me. There is something very satisfying in that. I have known his touch on the inside for a long time too, and his fingerprints are all around me. I remember verses from his word; 'God stretches the northern sky over empty space and hangs the earth on nothing.' I haven't been allowed in the temple for years, but I haven't forgotten. It is in his strength I go right now. I shall be whole. Job endured far worse than me, and my God is giving me a way out.

I follow the old dusty path and watch a small pot-bellied gecko as it darts in front of me and makes for the bushes. I have a gecko that comes close to me at home; I believe it's always the same one that's hanging around on my ceiling. I am sure it watches me and makes its way down deliberately. It clambers onto me and I enjoy the sensation of its cold feet padding along as I transfer it from one hand to the other. I love a trail of ants too and have been known to encourage them into my house by leaving out some sweet dates on the floor. They will walk over my hands one at a time if I place them in their path; they accept me without question, one after the other, it's a very reassuring thing. I know God accepts me, too. I am no different from anyone else on the inside, and I shall be whole.

'Watch out,' says a man to me as I reach the thoroughfare; I really hadn't seen him coming as I do prefer to look at my feet. 'You should look where you are going,' he continues, but then he pauses. 'It's *you, you,* what are you doing out here? Do you mean to make me impotent? How dare you come close to me?'

'I'm sorry,' I mutter and I keep walking but he hasn't finished with me. 'I suppose you think that was clever, brushing past me like that. You should be at home, go back and shut yourself away, you dirty rag, …'

His words are fading now but that feeling of worthlessness has filled me again. I increase the speed at which I am walking, *I shall be whole, I shall be whole,* I repeat, saying it inside my head this time. I need to get out of his sight before he makes a complete spectacle of me. Was this a bad idea? I would turn around and go straight home now if it were not for last night's visitor. I can hear tree frogs croaking and the cicadas humming, familiar sounds that I listen to from my house and remind me that my great creator God is with me – he's not angry with me or accusing. Who are these people to set themselves above God and judge me?

And then I see him, the one I set out to find, for ahead of me at the end of the road a big crowd has gathered. Garnering all of my strength I increase my pace, but my breathing is laboured and I just hope they will hold on.

The crowd are talking of a little girl who needs him – who am I to come between them? But I must catch up, get close. My chest hurts but I force myself on; if I collapse in his presence no doubt he'll come back to me after visiting this child... I at least want him to know I exist. I am in the crowd now, I will crouch down low and bustle my way through; they will think it's someone small, I doubt they will even bother to look. And there he is, I can see the fringe on his shawl... Dead they say, the child has *died*, oh how sad. And here am I, worrying about my small, petty life. To have lost a child; how awful. I will reach out my hand and touch his cloak; that will be enough for me. He needn't know I exist, it is enough that I know he does.

As my fingertips press into the soft robe I feel something quite miraculous; it's like the surge of lightning that I once saw travel from the top to the bottom of a tree without stopping and I just know that I've been healed, *I've been healed...*

'Who touched me?'

Oh, he knows. But there's no time to lose, he must go to the child.

His friends seem to laugh at him and remind him people are pressing in on all sides. But he's not going to let this go. 'Someone deliberately touched me,' he says, 'for I felt healing power go out from me.'

I must speak, then he can go to her, I must not hold him –

'It was me,' I say, and I cast myself at his feet and feel such anguish. I'm sure everyone is looking now – oh, it has all gone so horribly wrong. I dare to glance up, but as he turns and his eyes fall on me I realize there is no anger there, only love; has he misunderstood? Such kindness I have never known. 'Daughter,' he says. Daughter? What acceptance is this? 'Your faith has made you well. Go in peace,' and he touches my face, reaches out a hand to help me stand. Oh what love is this, what kindness. Has he really understood who I am, how unclean I was? Surely he meant this blessing for someone else, but no. I can see he truly knows me, knows everything about me. He has spoken wholeness over me and I am his. Truly this is the son of God.

This story is found in several biblical accounts. See Matthew chapter 9, verses 20–22, Mark chapter 5, verses 25–34 and Luke chapter 8, verses 43–48.

A bit left over

'We'll have to send them away,' says a man over my shoulder and I turn to look. He's one of the disciples I think; I've snuck up on them and have been trying to stand near them, all casual-like.

'They've no sign of going themselves and I'm starving.'

The man is serious, and as he looks out at the crowd I feel sure our time here is limited. He has a big black beard and a penetrating gaze that makes me feel very small; I look away in case he notices me, and fix my eyes on the one he's speaking to –

'Talk to Jesus, Nate,' replies the older man with a broad chest. He's the one the disciples all seem to consult. This man is a natural leader and he clearly has some authority over the rest. 'He must be exhausted anyway,' he continues, 'he hadn't recovered from the shock of John[18] when they all started to appear. He'll be glad to see the back of them.'

'I doubt it,' says the youngest-looking disciple. He scans the crowd in the same way that Jesus does, with the same concern – his brow wrinkles as he stares across into the setting sun, and seems moved to tears. 'And how can we get a word in edgeways?' he mutters, more to himself than the others. 'Look at him. And they're all mesmerized. They know he loves them, they just can't get enough of what he has to say.'

'Has it even occurred to him that he might be next?' says the man with the big black beard.

I edge closer to them to make sure I hear all of this. Some of them are talking in quiet voices, but not him.

'He never has a thought for himself,' says the oldest member of the group. I can feel my cheeks flush as I take a long look at the lunch Imma wrapped in a cloth and threw at me when I left the house. I want to tear off a corner of the bread and nibble it behind my hand but someone is bound to see. I really like this Jesus and I don't want them to take him away. Then I hear myself cutting into their conversation –

---

[18] Jesus' cousin, John the Baptist, is beheaded just before this scene. See Matthew 14:1–12, Mark 6:14–27 or Luke 9:9.

'I've got some lunch,' I say. 'It's not much but you can share it if you like. I really don't want Jesus to go just yet.'

The man with the big black beard laughs at me in a kind sort of way. He's really not so bad.

A man they call Philip comes over and starts talking to them – I don't think he's even noticed me. '"That isn't necessary," that's what Jesus said,' and two other men who came with him are nodding. '"*You* feed them," those were his words.'

They all smile at each other with exasperated expressions, laughter in their eyes.

'Even our father couldn't afford to feed this many,' adds the youngest one. He shrugs his shoulders and his brow wrinkles again.

'Well, it's this or nothing, John,' says Philip. Then the old fellow puts a hand on my back and directs me to a man who tells me his name is Andrew. 'Let's go and see what he says, shall we?' he suggests to me.

'Yes, please,' I answer. 'You mean you'll introduce me to him?'

Andrew nods at me and leads me to where Jesus is standing.

'This young lad says we can have his lunch: five barley loaves and two fish.'

He goes on talking to Jesus but I don't hear what he says. I am standing next to Jesus now and he's smiling at me, like this really was the right thing to do. Oh, wow. I'm squeezing my thumbs in my fists and trying not to let my smile show. I don't care if anyone teases me after this. *Jesus* is pleased with me. I can see it in his eyes, his face.

'Tell everyone to sit down,' Jesus says, but he doesn't seem to mean me – or at least he's not bothered that I'm still standing here and so I watch him pray. I'm going to pray like this from now on. It's very intense. You throw your head back and smile at God like he's really listening to you. You thank him with your whole being and speak to him as if he's hanging on your every word. I think he does, with Jesus. I wonder if he will with me.

If I was at home and Imma was preparing a meal, she would say I was getting under her feet, but not Jesus. He tells the disciples to share out my lunch now, as simple as that. They have found some baskets from somewhere and he tears up the bread and fish, putting a little in each. There's just so much of it! I can't understand how he's done it! I try to catch Jesus's eye as I really want to ask him, but he's too busy concentrating on what he's doing. Then the disciples take it out to the crowd who have all sat down, expectant looks on their faces, like they have just arrived at a friend's house and are awaiting a feast. Do any of them know it's *my* lunch? The young disciple stops by me and asks me to take some. The basket is full to the top and I could take what I had brought and more besides – I don't though, I just take one dried fish and one rather large piece of bread. At home I would have been told to share this with my sister; I think Imma was just glad to have me occupied today, that's why she gave me five loaves. And though she likes me to share, she really couldn't have expected my lunch to go this far.

Jesus! He's just so amazing. I want to follow him forever and I want this day to go on and on. Does Jesus accept part-time disciples? It's another year before I'll no longer be thought of as a child, and my tuition will go on for at least another three – but I'd rather have it from Jesus. Could I be with him in the holidays? I want to get baptized by him. I want him to know how serious I am. Imma and Abba really don't get it – they used to say I'd grow out of it, this obsession with God, but really I won't.

Mmn, this fish is actually rather good. It tastes much better than it usually does. We have more than our fair share of dried fish, living as we do near Bethsaida.[19] I've always wanted it to have a more exciting business going on than processing fish, but now I'm really proud of it. I think it's the best meal ever.

I've reached my group of friends now and sit down with them.

'Where've you been?' they say.

'I was just giving Jesus my lunch.'

'Yeah, right,' says Levi and they all copy him. Then they start to laugh at me.

'I did, it's true. You're eating it. Everyone is. It's another of his miracles.'

Michael rolls his eyes and pulls his gawky expression at me, like I'm really thick. 'My father knows Cephas, Andrew and Philip, he says they're no better than the rest of us. That they've been just ordinary men doing ordinary jobs.'

Michael never likes to be outdone.

---

[19] It is widely understood that Bethsaida was a fishing village that processed and preserved fish by drying and salting. Fish – ospon, 'cooked food eaten with bread', especially 'dried or preserved fish.' http://www.jesuswalk.com/john/13_feeding.htm

'I think Jesus has changed all that,' I tell them. 'They're really nice. Andrew took me to talk to Jesus and I actually met him. I can introduce you to him later, when things quieten down.'

'Yeah, right,' they say again, their mouths full of my lunch that they can't pile in fast enough.

'You were gone ages, anyway,' says Levi.

'I wanted to get closer to them, listen in to their conversation,' I tell them. 'I'm glad I did.'

'This is really nice bread,' says my best friend, Ben. He is at least always loyal. 'Did your mother make it?'

'She always does, but it tastes different now that Jesus has prayed over it.'

'Tell her it's really good.'

There is a real party atmosphere, like it's a wedding or something, and I can see Jesus relaxing with his friends now. He must be really tired, he's been with us for hours and it's getting late. I don't want to go home. Life will seem so ordinary again.

'Let's stick around to the very end,' I say to my friends.

'I need to get back to the village before it's dark,' says Ben. 'I had promised I'd be back in good time. I should be on my way.'

'Me too,' says Levi.

Soon I'm the last one sitting here so I get up and go and loiter near Jesus and his disciples again.

'Thanks again for your lunch, little lad,' says Andrew. 'It kind of went a long way!'

They are all laughing deep belly-laughs and I laugh too.

As the merriment fades the old guy begins to speak. He must be Cephas if Michael is right. 'I thought we'd had our biggest haul of fish ever, that day you told us to drop our nets,' he says, looking at Jesus. He looks bewildered as he ponders this and he's shaking his head, with one hand resting on the old olive tree, as if to stop himself falling over from the shock. Jesus simply smiles back at him, like it was no big deal and isn't even worth commenting on. Is there any end to his miracles? I want to know what he's going to do next.

'We've got a bit left over,' Andrew says to me, gesturing at a row of baskets that are still full to the top. 'Do you have any animals at home? Would you like to take one?'

I nod.

'Give it to your mother with our compliments,' he continues. 'Tell her we all had a delicious meal and she'd be very welcome to come with you next time.'

So I thank them and reluctantly take it as my cue to leave. I pick up the cord basket strap and place it on my shoulder. I want to stay with them but I know I can't. It's not worth getting into trouble over, and as this is going to be the first of many Jesus days for me, it really doesn't matter. It's already difficult to make out the path that leads down the hill so I take slow and steady steps. There are still pockets of people out here who seem reluctant to go home; in fact, their excitement seems to be increasing. I hear the titles 'king' and 'prophet' being said with every few paces. There seems to be some momentum building and I wonder where it will lead – how exactly *am* I going to get to sleep tonight?

I keep looking back at Jesus and his crowd, but soon I can only just make out their outlines. I expect they will still be there in the morning; I might just have to come out and check. Having said that, one of them is definitely climbing up the hill, as if to get away.

I'm so glad I came... This is not a day I'm going to forget.

This story is found in all four gospels: Matthew 14:13–21; Mark 6:32–44; Luke 9:12–17 and John 6:1–14.

So like Jesus

'He should really wait till the last of them have gone. What if someone follows him? It's downright dangerous.'

'You're such a worrier, Didymus,' I say, watching him as he scratches his scalp and pulls at his long willful hair. 'A little more faith would do you good.' He shrugs his shoulders at me and turns to watch Jesus as he climbs the hill. 'I can't agree with you, Andrew,' he says into the growing darkness. 'Life's not as simple as you like to make it.'

'That kid was an example to us all – no fear, just a focus on what's important,' I tell him. 'D' you think he'll come back?'

'I pray so. But Didy has a point,' says John, sitting down next to me and leaning back against the olive tree. 'Jesus is vulnerable now, and you heard the crowd.' He snaps a twig into several pieces as he talks, then scrapes at the bark with his fingernail. 'They could take him and push their own plans on him. Try to make him King, cause an uprising. That's really not what he wants. I had this dream the other night and –'

'He sent us out, and now we're back,' says Cephas, talking over the young disciple. 'It's just we haven't seen his following for a while, that's all. For it's easy to forget what things are like around him, what the demands are like.'

I lie back on the grass and shut my eyes as the debate continues. Waiting on thousands of people has taken its toll on me. Some of our group will always argue when they are tired, but it's not my way.

'Well it didn't use to be this bad. The crowds are huge, and they tell their friends… It's non-stop,' James tells him. 'We should pray about it. They can't all be genuine. Free food, a party atmosphere – what's not to like?'

'We barely had time to catch up,' says another; I hardly care who for it's all the same. 'He meant us all to get a rest together, that's what he said.'

'Well that wasn't going to happen,' comes Didymus's voice again. 'His fame is getting out of hand and it's about time he noticed. Sometimes I think he's a bit clueless; that's why I worry.'

'He doesn't need us to perform his miracles. He doesn't need us to protect him, either,' my brother tells them. 'The best thing we can do for him is give him some personal space.'

'So where is he now, Cephas?' says Nate. What's the big deal with getting space? We've only just regrouped. The crowd had him for all that time. Does he even get that we need to catch up?'

I sit up and watch them; trying to get rest here is futile. Is it worth waiting till Jesus comes back or should we just make our way home?

'He's praying, lads,' my brother says to us all. 'If he gets time alone with his Father he's restored, invigorated. We should stop challenging everything he says and get on with it. It always makes sense after a day or two have passed.'

'Well, I think we all need a break,' I say finally, for they have a point. 'But there's nowhere we can go to. He's recognized everywhere.' My hands smell of fish and I'd like to see my children tonight, my wife. Perhaps I should bring them out with me more often.

'He said to get into the boat,' Cephas reminds us. 'Come on, lads. He'll know where to find us if we just do as he instructed.'

'What are we going to do with all these baskets?' asks John.

'Just leave them here, they'll be useful to someone. At least we've tidied up, left the place as we found it.'

***

'I knew we should have waited at the shore, lads,' I say. 'I've never known a storm like it, in all my days. Cephas, are you even listening to me?'

No response. I can only see the back of his head as he sits in front of me and rows with a steady rhythm, just like he always does. Has he even noticed?

'It's getting worse,' says Nate who is sitting beside me.

'We should turn back,' add three voices at once.

'How exactly?' says Cephas. At last my brother has stopped ignoring us. 'For the storm is sending us across, and we're nearer Capernaum now anyway. Put your backs into it, lads! Let's get to where it's deeper; the waves will be weaker if we can just get a bit further.'

'What's the point?' says Didymus. We're going to drown!' The wind carries his words out across the sea and I try not to believe him. Ignoring him, we row for our lives. 'Where exactly is Jesus when we need him? Does he even know what's happening or is he still *praying*?'

'Hold it together, Dids. Now's not the time.'

'We're wasting our bloody time following him,' says Judas. 'If I get back to shore, that's it. I think I'll walk. I mean, what's in it for me, really?' A gust snatches his grumblings and leaves him gasping.

'Shut up lads and start bailing. Come on, faster!'

'Does he even care about our physical lives?' continues Didymus.

'Huh! Wake up Didymus,' says Cephas. 'Keep bailing lads, unless you want to go down!' He catches his breath as he chucks more water over the side. 'But why else would he heal, provide *bread*, do all that stuff? Of course he cares. Well, I like to think he does, anyway. We'll have to ask him why exactly he did that, though. I mean, w–'

'So where is he now?' Didy replies.

'We can manage without him,' I tell him. His moaning really wears me down.

'We did it before, we'll do it again,' says Nate, though I think he's mistaken what I was trying to say. 'Stop whining, let's keep this thing afloat. We don't need him.'

With that a giant wave sweeps over the boat – we're clinging to the sides, to each other, to whatever and whoever we can.

'What did you just say, Nate?'

'Oh, come on. Don't blame me. But he's not here, is he?'

It's hard to see who's speaking now… who's shouting over the waves. The rain's so heavy that I don't know where the sea ends and the rain begins.

'The boat's falling apart!' But that's Didy's moaning, for sure. 'I was holding onto that a moment ago, now it's gone – see that plank? See it on that wave!'

'How can you expect us to see in this darkn–'

'We can see because of *that*,' I yell to all of them. 'Look – on the waves, coming towards us! Is it a ghost?'

'Oi, over there! Get away!' says Judas, who has fallen and is now scrambling to his feet beside me in the boat.

'But think,' my brother replies, 'for could it be…?'

'Leave us alone!' continues Judas.

'Are we dead already?' I wonder, out loud and more to myself than the others.

'It's bright, brilliant, it's God himself and I am undone...' John sits on the floor of the boat, leaving the rest of us to try to steady it. 'Oh, great God of love and mercy...'

'It's Jesus,' says Cephas, as if finishing the thought that is too profound for him.

'Exactly,' says Nate.

'About ti...'

'What was that, Didy?'

'Nothing. Nothing at all.' He pauses. 'But he's walking on the sea! It can't be him, how can he?'

'Don't be afraid,' comes his voice across the lake. The very ordinary voice of Jesus that just a few hours ago told us to find the boat, that he'd be on his way. 'Take courage, I am here!'

'Lord, if it's really you, tell me to come to you, walking on the water,' says my stupid brother.

'Cephas, are you ma–'

'Yes, come,' says Jesus.

He climbs over the side of the boat and now he's doing it too – but how isn't he sinking? His eyes are on Jesus and he's walking as if on a level road, not even a mountain pass. It doesn't last; 'Save me, Lord,' he shouts, taking his eyes off Jesus and looking at the wave that has met him at eye-level. You can hardly blame him.

Jesus gives him one hand and grabs hold of him with the other. 'You have so little faith,' he says. 'Why did you doubt me?'

Well, his faith is better than ours. We wouldn't even have got out of the boat, but that doesn't seem to matter, as far as Jesus is concerned.

The moment they step back into the boat with us the sea is calm and the wind drops. It's as if nothing ever happened, but Cephas is still breathless and he's shaking. His eyes are wild. In fact, he's staring without blinking, like he's woken from the longest, deepest sleep.

Just the fringed hem of Jesus's tunic is wet and he's as unruffled as ever. He seems to find the whole thing quite funny.

'You really are the Son of God,' we tell him.

'That was amazing, Jesus.'

'We didn't think you were coming. Why did we doubt you?'

I still wish he'd come sooner. Nobody is brave enough to say this but it's what we're all thinking. I wonder what kept him? His time-keeping never matches my own, but we always learn something from it. It's his privilege, I guess.

I look around me – something very strange has happened here – shallow waters lap the side of the boat and we appear to have crossed over in an instant. This is so like Jesus – we fret, then allow him to take over and we feel belittled, though not in a bad way. We get some perspective and realize we should have trusted him all along.

As my thoughts wander the brightness fades and we talk in the darkness, just glad to have him with us again. He's completely ours until dawn, for the crowd won't appear until it is light. I look up at the moon; it's still there and just the occasional glint reflects on the water, with the shine of a new shekel. A mere crescent, the perfect outline of a thumbnail. It wasn't that which lit the sky so brightly just minutes ago; it was him. There is no other explanation and for a while I cannot speak – my thoughts cannot understand, cannot connect. What *has* just happened? What does it mean? Yet he is our friend and, despite his apparent godliness, he chooses to be one of us.

For the biblical account of Jesus walking on water see the following: Matthew chapter 14, verses 22–33; Mark chapter 6, verses 45–52 and John chapter 6, verses 15–21.

Hearing him out

I wonder if our visiting speaker knows who I am? My name is known around here and will be remembered: Elchanan no less. A proper Jewish name after one whose family wove the temple curtains in our holy city, Jerusalem. What heritage has this man, I wonder? Of what line or parentage? I look at you, Micha, my son. We're almost always in tune with each other, always know what the other is thinking. But when it comes to this Jesus you worry me, truly. I hope that by watching him you realize how a father's advice must always be followed, even into adulthood. It's easy for you young ones to get whipped up, caught on the latest wave of euphoria for whoever is doing the rounds. John, the fellow in a camel-skin tunic with obscure dietry tastes. Was he a sane man, truly? He looked like he lived in a cave. And now Jesus is showing himself to be somewhat peculiar. You nudge me in the ribs and give me a long look. I'm glad you are at least a little discerning around him... You don't need to say anything. *Eat* him? What *is* he on about now? Other less polite members of our community are laying into him; in fact, it's been a debate for a while, rather than a sermon. Only now it's getting heated.

'I tell you the truth, unless you eat the flesh of the Son of Man and drink his blood, you cannot have eternal life within you.'

I place my fingers on the floor to steady myself in preparation to leave but you put a hand on my arm. When we're around Jesus you make me feel like the child. You forget you are not long since one yourself. 'Stay a bit longer,' you whisper in your adolescent voice, that for a few words in every sentence is deeper than mine. 'We need to hear him out.'

I think I've heard enough. I am perspiring and I pull at my tunic to allow the air to circulate. I'd like to remove my head covering. I could do with a long cool drink, for sure. This bread he speaks of; "my flesh" he calls it. Gruesome, that's what it is. Truly abhorrent ... I can't listen to him any more. I will let this building distract me – it won't be the first time.

I settle on the floor again and survey the old mouldings that my eyes fix on whenever the preacher goes on too long. Ours *is* a beautiful synagogue. Above the doorway is carved a pot of manna, surrounded by vine leaves and a mighty bunch of grapes: symbols of God's protection and provision for our forefathers, for us.[20] But I can't block out what I'm hearing now. This Jesus claims that he is our Father's new substitute for the manna of old. That he is "the true bread of heaven". So we must consume him – how exactly? Whatever next? It's preposterous, outlandish and makes no sense. That's what I shall tell everyone. Only I do know what he's saying really; it's just easier to reject it, for what he's asking of us, it's just too much.

I could do with some real bread right now – we crossed the lake early in our attempt to track him down today. Chasing the whims of the young again. I wonder if we should have bothered, but at least we know now. I'm resigned to the fact this Jesus is a lunatic. Truly he is. I'm not angry now. I just feel let down. I need to make sense of all that's happened though – I owe it to myself, at least.

Following Jesus was amusing for a while – I think it made me feel adventurous, made me forget my age. I adjust my legs on the floor and wrap my hands around my swollen feet. That miraculous catch, when he first made a name for himself – that was pretty good. That fried musht tasted divine; I think every family for miles around ate well that night. I've enjoyed seeing all the healings, and the giant picnic yesterday, up on the hill towards home, well that was remarkable. Truly remarkable. Making life easier for people, filling their empty bellies – I like that. There's always room for more partying around here, more feasting and making jolly. His way of tackling illness is pretty unusual – the healing seems to hold too, it's not just attention-seeking magic. Far better than the hot springs at Tiberias; that's a dodgy cure for sure. There have definitely been some changed lives around here – people seeing for the first time, the lame now out working in the fields, earning a fair wage; not hanging round the gates begging. I guess he's made Capernaum a better place. Our village too. And he is a nice fellow. Always smiling, always with time for people. But today he's got all heavy on us and I don't like it. He's never asked anything of us before. He's known his place. There was a feel-good element to his message, assurance that God loves us, that kind of thing. Only there had to be a catch and finally he's come out with it. He won't be drawing the crowds from here, that's for sure.

In fact, people have started to leave already and he's still talking. I nudge you again and finally you get to your feet next to me. You raise your hands in an apologetic shrug at Jesus and cast a longing glance at him over your

---

[20] Ellicott's *Commentary for English Readers*, Warren's *Recovery of Jerusalem* and Thomson's *Land and Book, Central Palestine and Phoenicia* are among many commentaries that tell of this discovery at Tel Hum, thought to be a credible site for Capernaum.

shoulder as I lead you out into the white sunshine. We blink as our eyes adjust. 'Ah, that's better, I couldn't wait to get out of there.'

'That *was* a bit rude,' you say to me.

'I don't like how you talk down to me when Jesus is around. I am still your father, always will be.'

'Couldn't we have let him finish?' you say.

'Why exactly?' I pull off my prayer shawl that covered my head and brush damp hair from my face. 'I always knew he wanted something from us, that there had to be a catch. Let's go and find ourselves a boat to take us home.'

You are silent for a while as we walk in the crowd. I hate it when you are like this – brooding over something, preparing a speech more often than not. Always a little too clever for my liking – I'd see you as a threat if I didn't love you so much. You never stood up to me like this before this Jesus came and that unsettles me. 'I like him,' you say, finally. 'There's something about him.'

'He wants more than a following,' I remind you. 'He wants us to become his flesh, his blood. He said he wants us to "remain in" him. A complete loss of identity, that's what I call it.'

'Hardly,' you say.

Oh, aren't we knowledgeable now?

'If it's as he says it is, that he's been sent from God himself, I think we'll become more fully ourselves, we'll bloom into the people he intended us to be.'

I am struggling to keep up with you, you are walking so fast, and I'm starting to feel short-winded. I can't answer you back but I will, when I can sit down again.

'And if I become like him, I really wouldn't mind,' you continue. 'In fact, I'd be honoured. Look at all those people who have allowed him to touch their lives – they are simply better versions of who they were already. It's like they've been released, not restrained.'

Now I shrug my shoulders. You have a point when you look at it this way, but I don't want to concede that easily. You go on. 'What have you got to lose, really? Let's be honest, Abba, you have twenty years left on earth, at best. My new sandals will probably last longer than you.'

'Well thanks.'

'I'm only kidding. But you know what I mean. So if he's got it all wrong and we die into oblivion, we won't know anyway and we won't have lost anything. But if he's right… Just think! He says we'll live *forever*.'

'You always were gullible.'

You say nothing and I enjoy the opportunity to catch both my thoughts and my breath. 'I blame your age,' I go on. 'How can you be expected to reason like me at your age?'

'But his ability is coming from somewhere, and there's nothing evil about him – not a trace of self-centredness, no cravings for power, no quest for possessions. I think he'd give away his last meal, go hungry so we wouldn't.'

'He'd just make himself some more. Conjure it up out of nowhere.'

You look exasperated by me and sigh. 'Don't dismiss him yet, that's all I'll say. We owe it to ourselves to really find out if what he says is true. What we'd be throwing away – well, it's just not worth it.'

I stop walking so that I can perch on a low wall and you jump onto it in one swift move, still with more energy than you know what to do with.

'He's upsetting the old order,' I tell you. 'The Pharisees don't like him.'

'Good. They're a pompous lot, most of them. I'd rather listen to Jesus any day. At least he's real. He's not bound up in laws and observances – he's all about living. It's certainly been fun, being on his trail.'

'Yes, well, I only came to keep an eye on things really. Just as well I did.'

You roll your eyes at me. 'You can't make every decision for me, Abba, not at my age… And especially not this one. You're needing to make your own mind up too, and not in a dismissive way.'

'I'll sleep on it. You can't rush these things, for sure. I need time to work things out.'

'Or time to wriggle out of them? Don't miss out, Abba.'

You spot a wandering street vendor selling bread from a basket and I put a coin in your hand and send you across the road.

I watch as you make your way to him, that swagger of youth in your walk, that confident assumption you carry with you that you can manage life, that it will never beat you. If only you could see with the wisdom of years, feel a few disappointments. Then we'd see what confidence you'd place in this Jesus.

You return and place a flat cake of bread in my hand and I nod my gratitude. 'So you seem pretty sold-out on following him still,' I say, tearing off a piece of bread and placing it in my mouth.

'I am. More so by the day.'

'I'm interested –' I say, stroking my greying beard. Your face brightens with the old childish exuberance, but your smile drops as I go on. 'Only tell me about this one. All through your childhood you had your own plans. That fascination of yours with the ancient trade route and how you might exploit it... What happens to all that now? Where's your meaning gone? *Your* meaning, not Jesus's – yours.'

'I'm not really bothered any more, and it was only a pipe dream. I want God in my life and everything else can fit in around him. I know he's calling me. I think he's calling you too.'

I laugh at you but I fear it sounds insincere.

'You know it, deep down.'

I choose to let that comment go.

'I can't forget his words: "No one can come to me unless the Father who sent me draws them to me," that's what he said. You can't get any more meaningful than that.'

You look at the bread in your hand for a time before you start to eat and I know what's running through your mind. I turn from you and eat mine quickly. 'Time to make our way home, lad,' I say to you.

'You head on if you like. I might just stay here for a few hours. I'll be back before nightfall.'

'Make sure you are. And leave that Jesus well alone.'

'I can't promise that, Abba. You know I can't.'

For the biblical account of this story see John chapter 6, verses 22–59.

That's what you are

'Come and lie with me. No one will ever know.' I'm startled and think there must be some mistake. I look at his face to see if this is some cruel joke, if he's drunk or his mind warped, but he stares back at me, defiant.

'No!' I say, with more strength than I knew I had, my curls shaking as I leap back from him, falling over my eyes and catching in my mouth. I lift a hand to push my hair out of the way, but he intercepts and now my hand is in his. I pull and turn to go but he grips my hand tightly, then takes my wrist with force, holding my arm above my head so that I cannot escape.

'No!' I say. 'Let me go! I will scream, I will –'

'And who will believe you over me? I've seen your glances, your flirtatious ways – you know you want me.'

His greying beard is repulsive and scratches me as he forces his face into my chest. The small leather case that's strapped to his arm is digging into my back, causing me to wince.

'I am betrothed!' I tell him.

'To my brother. Family property, and while he's away *I* am looking after *you*.'

'Looking after? That's a joke. And you, a Pharisee!'

'Shut up and obey me. If you make a scene, I will pronounce your flirtation to all of Jerusalem.'

With that he pulls me to the floor and tugs my tunic up to my waist. 'I'm a virgin,' I tell him. 'You'll hurt me. And my husband will know, he'll be able to tell –'

'Your husband? There will *be* no husband unless you do as I tell you. Now embrace me, caress me *here*,' he says, moving my hand onto that which I would not touch. I can feel him responding, though there is no life or intent coming from me.

'Behave as I tell you,' he says with a threat in his voice. 'I can hurt you, or this can be pleasurable. This is your choice.'

And so I act the part, writhing and responding to his touch, though inwardly I am shuddering. The sooner I can make him reach his moment, the sooner he will be off me and gone. I can feel the long fringe on his tunic brushing against my legs as he moves on me and I shut my eyes tight.

'There…can…be more…of this,' he says, with hot breaths in my ear, 'Once…you are…wed. Mendel's work will take him away often, and this… suits…me,' he says, with a final thrust.

Just then there is a commotion and I hear someone pull back the shutter over my head.

'They are here,' says the voice, 'and I can see all the detail we need. Look, she's enticed him and they are entangled!'

There are other mocking voices and he removes himself from me, pulls down his tunic and stands up. I reach for the blanket and cover my dignity, what's left of it. But there is more – for he's grabbed me by the wrist again and is pulling me towards the door. 'An adulteress, that's what you are,' he says, still out of breath, his face wet from the exertion.

I cannot believe it.

'He forced me!' I scream. 'I am but a girl, I know nothing of the ways of men!'

'She knows nothing of the ways of men!' he mimics. He looks at me now. 'Mendel says how intelligent you are, how he discusses much with you. He dared call you his equal! Perhaps this will teach you to stay out of men's affairs. He says you are flirtatious too, he has told me! Cunning, not intelligent.'

But I'm not… am I? Or is it true? I can feel blood winding its way down my leg, evidence, if they needed it, of what has taken place. I fear it already shows on the back of my pale tunic. Perhaps I've wet myself. Perhaps this is all my imagination turned wild, my fears of my brother-in-law at last admitted to myself. But no.

He pauses for a moment and I wonder if he is regretting his actions, but it's only to straighten his shawl and cast an eye over his gown.

Now he is dragging me out into the market square and people are staring at us. He has a fist of my hair, his fingers caught up in it as he yanks me in different directions, and another Pharisee is tugging me by the arm. 'He's preaching in the temple,' says a voice from behind us. 'Take her there, then see what he has to say. He'll be caught out, whichever way he chooses.'

There is laughter, proper laughter from the gut, and I am appalled.

I have been set up it seems, caught in another of their petty battles, except this time my life is at stake. Betrothed girls can be stoned and they see no value in me; no worth at all. Old men and women have stopped what they are doing to stare at me. I know most of these people – there is our talkative, knowledgeable neighbour, and here a group of girls that I have grown up with: Elizabeth, Yael and Rivkah; I look away, though this hurts my scalp all the more. A young man I don't know spits into my face as soon as I turn my head. Do they think I'm someone else? Do I look like some prostitute they know? Perhaps they've all mistaken me. They will realize soon, won't they?

They drag me into the temple to where the man called Jesus is sitting with a crowd around him. Some get to their feet and make a way so that I can be deposited in front of him. Jesus stands up, too. My head hurts but I try to blank it out, for there is worse to come. Where are they going to stone me? Right here? Will they let me speak? What do I say? I was on my own, sewing, when – no, I had been asleep. Was I on the bed already? Was that it?

'Teacher,' they say, several of them speaking at once, the sarcasm rich in their voices, 'this woman was caught in the act of adultery. The law of Moses says to stone her.' I hear *his* voice amongst them and cannot believe his audacity. My head is given a final yank as this would be brother-in-law lets go, then pushes me forwards with both hands so that I stumble.

'What do you say?' they ask Jesus.

I fix my gaze on his feet, and to my surprise this Jesus stoops down and crouches in front of me. It's as if he's shielding me, putting himself between me and the mob deliberately. The look he shoots me is reassuring – full of pity and kindness, though I dare not hope to get out of this. Yet I feel safe and time slows, almost to a stop. He starts to write in the dust and I shut my eyes, absorbing this quiet moment and the sense of his warmth that I have, for I know it's all about to start over again. I open my eyes and he is still writing. My tears land in the dust but his words remain, channelling them like little rivulets. I feel calmer than is logical and begin to read his words: I think they are from Jeremiah but I cannot be sure. Somehow he's deflecting the attention away from me and onto them, for I hear a nervous clearing of throats and shuffling of feet.

Jesus rises now. It is intriguing, for the fidgeting stops and all is quiet. At last he speaks: 'All right, but let the one who has never sinned throw the first stone!'

There is a purity about Jesus that makes me feel conscious of my own failings, as a dove before a lime-washed wall shows it to be grey. He knows I'm not responsible for *this*, but I'm far from blameless. I don't want him to examine me too closely – for if he knows this about them what does he know about me? I get the feeling he'd have been just as compassionate if I had been complicit – it's about the heart, about turning from our errors and towards God. Yet I know that I've been an angry person – my younger siblings taunt me just to get a rise, as if my outbursts are amusing. I think too that God has been an irrelevance to me before now. Oh, I should stop this – he's dealing with their sin at this moment, not mine. But I should make my peace with God, for someone may yet stone me...

He is down at my level again and writing more words, which again I find reassuring. I put my arms over my head and crouch down even lower so that my chest rests on my legs and I am an impenetrable ball. I listen to my breathing; it is slow and steady and I feel amazed by my courage. I think Jesus has something to do with it, and I am starting to believe what many of the good people say about him; I have heard that he is the Messiah. I think they are probably right, for I feel protected and covered as I rest here, as if he is somehow watching over me and defending me from harm. Will I hear my own breathing for much longer? Where are the stones, or do they intend to drag me again, away from him and his kindness?

The silence continues until I hear footsteps, but they are moving away from me, not towards. The passing of feet continues and now I wonder if they have all gone. I open one eye first and lift my head – then the other and steady myself with my hands on the floor to look all about me. It's true – they have left us!

Jesus is still crouching on the ground and I wonder if he is praying; he is certainly concentrating on something very hard. I stand and stretch, turn about in a circle with my arms open wide in a freedom I could not have anticipated.

Now Jesus gets to his feet and I feel his good will once more. He looks into my eyes with audacity, his very kindness penetrating through to my soul. I can see that he knows me, that he doesn't believe me a harlot or a disgrace.

'Where are your accusers?' he says. 'Didn't even one of them condemn you?' He is smiling broadly and gestures at the empty space around us.

'No, Lord,' I say, for he is that to me now. I know that he is the Messiah and I am overwhelmed.

'Neither do I,' he says as the tears roll down my cheeks and drop into the dust once more. 'Go and sin no more.'

I smile at him and wonder if he can feel my gratitude. I suddenly feel very hot, and grab my hair with one hand that I lift off the back of my neck. I look down at my tunic – it is torn at the shoulder and there is a footprint just above the hem. If I wash and sew it will it show?

I want to know how this changes things with my betrothal. I will tell my husband about him, and tell him that I am nervous of my brother-in-law, though I cannot explain to him why. Will the locals gossip anyway? Could there be *any* hope for me?

And yet there is always hope from here, for there is Jesus, and if all else fails I will follow him. I know there are women who do this, travelling from place to place, sharing his stories and helping those in the crowd who want to talk with someone, but aren't quite brave enough to speak to him. I may only be fifteen but I know my mind well enough.

I will follow him even if my life continues here, in this place. I might not see him again, but I can follow him here, in my heart. *Pardoned, that's what you are,* I tell myself. *That's what you are.*

See John's Gospel, chapter 8, verses 1–11 for this story.

Bible scholars all agree that this situation was orchestrated to trap Jesus. As a Jew, Jesus would not have had the right to pronounce the death-penalty on anyone; if he had succumbed it's thought he would have been reported to the Roman officials.

Why do I portray a teenage girl in this story, when we may have assumed she was a 'woman-of-the-world'? In Deuteronomy 22:22–4 we learn that stoning is specified when a 'young woman, a virgin who is engaged to be married' is involved.

It is highly plausible that the woman in this story was framed for the Pharisees' own purposes. David Guzik suggests there were 'pre-arranged spies sent to witness this affair', and points to the fact the man should have been brought along, too.[21] *(See again Deuteronomy 22:22–24.) He quotes Boice's opinion that "Under these conditions the obtaining of evidence in adultery would be almost impossible were the situation not a setup." He also refers us to Barclay, who states, "They were not looking on this woman as a person at all; they were looking on her only as a thing, an instrument whereby they could formulate a charge against Jesus."*

Yet despite their deplorable actions, that no doubt had drastic consequences for the woman, she gains something precious: an understanding of who Jesus is. She refers to him as Kurios, ("Lord"), sometimes used by the Old Testament prophets in relation to the Messiah. I like to

---

[21] David Guzik, *Study Guide for John 8*, Blue Letter Bible. Online resource.

think that somehow her life was changed for the better, though living with the stigma it produced cannot be underestimated.

The blind man

I have never understood why people talk about me as if I'm not here. I mean, just because I can't see them, they do owe me the courtesy of including me in the conversation. 'Rabbi, why was this man born blind? Was it because of his own sins or his parents' sins?'

Well excuse me, I *am* sitting in front of you!

I feel a heavy hand on my shoulder and sense the person they've asked is crouching down next to me, not about to talk over my head. 'It was not because of his sins or his parents' sins,' the man answers.

Now that is refreshing to hear.

His is not a voice I'm familiar with so he won't know my name. His consideration so far means I'll excuse him for not addressing this to me. 'This happened so the power of God could be seen in him,' he goes on. The power of God? In me? Now this is something new. Perhaps people will show me favour – even just a little would be nice. To think, I might not be neglected. He's talking again, this time about a sense of urgency that's needed in doing God's work, and about how he is 'the light of the world.'

The light of the world.

Light.

Bright white light that I see flicker through my eyelids that he touches. It feels cold and he's spreading something on them; I've heard before that spittle has restorative qualities, especially when the person is important, or heard of God. This feels heavy and cold on my eyelids though, like he's added something to it.

I am not used even to seeing light. People have asked me before if I see light or shapes or anything at all. I'd answer them, 'Does your big toe see anything?'

'No,' they'd say.

'Well that's how it is for me. I don't see. That means I don't see *anything*,' I'd explain. My eyes have no function; or at least they *didn't*, for now I at least know what light means. What white means too – the absence of all ill, the colour of purity, of a cooing dove, as my mother told me when I was small. How strange this is. Something is happening and all my senses are on high alert as I wait for him to speak again.

'Go wash yourself in the pool of Siloam,' he says.

Slowly I get to my knees and I feel this fellow standing next to me and taking a hand, then placing an arm around my back to steady me. I wouldn't do this for anyone but the man has a kindness about him and I feel sure that he has helped me already. 'Jesus' they are calling him. This makes sense, for I have heard talk of him, though I've never been able to get to where he's speaking. Now the crowd are gossiping – 'Aaron's got mud on his eyes, he thinks washing it off will see him cured!'

'Look at him go! The old blind beggar is hoping he'll see.'

'He's not that old, he just looks it. Withered like an unwanted fig.' There is laughter.

'Thorny, that's what he is. He's so prickly he's got thorns. Thinks he has the right to be exasperated by what we say!'

Oh, I can hear them. Yet for once I'm not angry – I don't even care.

'Are you coming? I've got to see this!'

Some voices are shushing them but I can cope. If only they knew what I have to put up with; we blind folk are supposed to be respected, but most people can't get beyond the stigma, think it is self-inflicted. I don't care. Jesus has done something for me, and it's not finished yet. I feel like Naaman the Syrian, sent off to wash seven times by Elisha,[22] but I think just once is all I need.

I steady myself with a hand on the dry stone wall, reaching out ahead and then taking a tentative step, then another and another, until soon I hear the noise of splashing water and laughter. Yet in a moment there is complete silence. It is an intense, ringing silence, as if the people here are watching me, as they must have when Jesus spoke. I suspect some have followed me here. I sit down on a wet slab and ease myself in, feet first, and the coldness laps at my ankles. Now it reaches up my legs as far as my knees. I slide myself forwards to where it is deeper, then scoop up water in my hands and splash it over my face until it drips from my beard and down the length of my back.

And, oh! These must be colours! Colour everywhere that sings, shouts – above me, all around me. The tang of wine, the sweetness of grapes, the chill of a deep cave. I see figures moving about, sound coming from their mouths, what must be arms moving. I rub the moisture from my eyes and blink, and

---

[22] 2 Kings 5:1–19.

now everything is clearer still. I hold out my hand at arm's length – my dirt-filled nails gleam in the sun and I rub my thumb along their sharp edges; I flex my dry wrinkled knuckles and watch them bend as I fold my fingers into my palm. I am healed! Then I shout it, 'Oh, I am healed! I can see!'

The sky is vast, a brilliant domed ceiling that stretches above me and reflects in the pool of water. Even the temple cannot be as beautiful. What colour is that? How do you describe it? It's like the scent of muscari flowers that my sister would hold in front of my nose, or the sound of a ram's horn blown from the temple, long and clear; it is, simply, perfection.

Now faces are crowding in too close and I turn and make my way to the edge of the pool. I want to find Jesus – I want to thank him. I have so much to ask him, so much to tell him. But no sooner am I out and dripping onto the floor than the people are gathering around me again.

'Aaron, can you see this?' says one, holding something long and thin in front of my face. 'What is it?'

'I don't know. It looks like it may have come from a tree over there.'

They laugh.

I take it and grasp it in my hands. 'It's what they call… a stick,' I say, finally and with confidence.

The laughter is even louder now.

'How do you even know what a tree is?'

'I have touched them, I have felt them. Just because I was blind, I wasn't without experience, you know.'

'Was blind. He *is* blind.'

They are talking about me again, as if I'm not relevant. Now even more faces have gathered around me.

'Isn't this the man who used to sit and beg?' they say.

'No, he just looks like him!'

'It *is* me,' I say. 'I am the one. Yes, I am the same one!'

'It's the Sabbath,' says an old voice that I recognize. It is a neighbour of mine; I hear him outside long after nightfall, sharing gossip with his wife and children. Doesn't he care that I've been made well?

'Who healed you? What happened?'

I explain my story and to my surprise the crowd seem agitated – do they not see the good in what he's done?

'Where is he now?' they all seem to ask at once.

'I don't know,' I tell them, and before I've even had time to dry off in the sun there's a strong man on each side of me. 'You must tell the Pharisees about this,' they say. 'That Jesus is a wanted man.'

***

We are in the temple now; well at least this is progress. So many steps and they wouldn't let me take them on my own. Yet they must believe me for I've never been allowed in here before, such is the prejudice towards a blind man. I'm sure God never intended that we be barred, and I'm no different on the inside to how I was yesterday; yet I am and will continue to be seen as inferior. Did my poor eyes make me unclean? Still, my faith is as strong as theirs; perhaps stronger, for I believe in Jesus and know that he's life giving… I believe that he's from God himself. This lot are bent on rules and not relationship with God, as far as I can make out. We have walked past the sellers in the court of the gentiles and through what they're calling the Beautiful Gate, beyond which no blind man has ever gone. Oh, what a happy day this is! Old Gad, a friend of mine, has been in the gentiles' area, but none of us could walk further. They would say our presence defiles, as if our blindness condemns us…. Oh, but Jesus! All this is because of him. I fear he is God's glory, transforming this place and its people. He has changed me; he has healed –

I have been brought before them now: the Pharisees, the so-called pure, separated ones. My story is being told by my neighbours – it's their version of things, and still I am not asked to speak, as if my inferiority has been appointed for life. They look stern and their garb sets them apart – much of it's what I know to be black and they appear unapproachable.

Oh, now they ask me. So I explain Jesus's actions, which should be enough.

'This man Jesus is not from God,' says one, 'for he is working on the Sabbath.'

Debate springs up among them, and finally they return to me: 'What is your opinion about this man who healed you?'

'I think he must be a prophet,' I say. A *prophet*? Who am I kidding? Why didn't I have the courage to come right out with it? Yet even this riles them and so now they are sending for my parents.

My parents. Will I recognize them? I would rather have had this reunion outside of the temple, in our own home. Granted, it's still me, but I feel like a new person, and I want to acquaint myself with their features in private. This should be a tender moment, not a time of challenge and rebuke.

It's of no matter, for the locals are leading me out now, after a nod was given in their direction. I make my own way down the steps, for I think they're sure at last that my eyes work as well as theirs. I suspect they want to disown me and dare not be seen showing me kindness. I wonder where I should go, what I should do. I'd like to find Jesus and talk to him. I'm feeling more like one of his and less like I belong here. I have never felt less welcome; anyone would think I'd committed a crime; that Jesus had. It's been a day of revelation indeed.

The locals stop me at the base of the steps and draw me to one side. 'You are not to see your parents when they arrive,' says a voice, familiar from insults. 'You might confer. You are to wait here with us – it was the Pharisees' order.' They crowd around me and block my view. I feel like one of those birds they keep in there, ready for slaughter; there's such scope in me now to fly, yet I'm restricted by their fear, here only for their purposes.

Their group seems to grow as we wait outside and they point at me and heckle. I am used to their antagonism though, and choose not to get drawn in. Oh, I can see! Nothing can break me now! They surround me on all sides, but they can't stop me looking up at the sky – it goes on and on, and my eyes are drinking it in; the years of thirst won't be quenched for a while. Nothing matches it – how vast is our God who made it! Now a flock of birds soars and my eyes follow their path, over the temple and beyond. What speed – and their wings carry them up and on! I watch as they disappear into the distance, then I study what must be clouds building directly overhead – I want to touch them, to trace their outline with my finger. How must they feel? I've always needed to feel everything to understand. And this healing – I've felt Jesus's kindness, felt love. I'd have felt it even if I still couldn't see, but *I can*! No one can take that from me.

I am alone in my thoughts for a while; there is just so much to process. There is a shuffling of feet as the crowd start to bore of watching me. One or two wander off. I think I have lost my novelty. I expect the Pharisees are giving my parents the interrogation they intended. I hope they are gentle with my mother. The shock of today may just be too much for her.

Soon I catch sight of an elderly couple making their way down the steps. A young Pharisee leaves their side to come over to us. 'Take him in again,' he says. The crowd around me parts, and my eyes follow the twosome, now that the view is clear. They seem intimidated and are walking quickly, heads down, as if in a hurry to get away. They must have seen the crowd around me, suspected it was me over here, but they were not brave enough to look. I watch as they make their way down the hill, their steps quick and purposeful. What was said to them? What outrage did they pronounce?

I watch as a man about my age takes my left arm, then a youth holds my right, and I am led back up the steps and into the temple again. They don't need to hold me so tightly – I'm not about to run away! Is it a sin to be healed? To be whole? I worry I am a scapegoat[23] for Jesus… What will they do to *him* if they do this to *me*? We retrace out steps too quickly, for I want to take in the beauty of this place, if I may. Will I have to disguise myself to return and enjoy it?

And so I am before the Pharisees again. I could hear them arguing before we even turned the corner to face them for a second time. I've lost all patience with these elitist men and determine to answer them tersely and honestly now.

'God should get the glory for this, because we know this man Jesus is a sinner,' they say.

This *man* Jesus. How threatened they feel by him. And by me.

'I don't know whether he is a sinner,' I tell them. 'But I know this: I was blind, and now I can see!' I pull at my tunic that is still wet and feeling tight around my neck.

'But what did he do?' says one. 'How did he heal you?' asks another.

'Look! I told you once.' They don't frighten me and politeness is getting me nowhere. 'Didn't you listen? Why do you want to hear it again? Do you want to become his disciples, too?'

Did I just say that! Now they are uttering expletives and cursing me, declaring that *I* am one of his followers, not they. I would like to thank them for the compliment but I must be careful not to take this too far. Yet I find myself saying more than I ever meant to, and my closing words stop me short: 'If this man were not from God, he couldn't have done it.'

---

[23] See Leviticus 16:8–10 for the original scapegoat reference.

If this man were not from God. Were not from God. I think I have made my mind up. I think I had even before he'd healed me. In fact, I've never been more sure about anything.

Now they physically march me out of the temple and the locals are gathering around me again. It is an even bigger crowd than before. 'And don't come back!' I am told.

Like I would want to.

'You'll be hearing from us,' says another. He pushes me from behind and I have that familiar feeling of reaching out to steady myself; an unknown arm pushes my hand away. 'There will be rules for you, conditions. You will be discussed.'

'Don't expect to get away with this,' comes a voice after me.

I will not turn to look at him. Now I'm glad that my tunic is wet for it's cooling me down. I can feel the heat in my cheeks and I begin to run. Running through the temple… what an outrage! My legs must be showing, but that's the least of my humiliation, or so I'm told. I have no dignity… there's nothing to lose. Appearances! And all for what? The only important person to treat me with dignity is Jesus, anyway. It's what he thinks… that matters. This isn't something I've been able to do before; a blind man doesn't run. He is frightened of falling. I cannot fall physically, and spiritually there's no height for me to drop from now… Not that there ever was. I've always been told mature men don't run… shouldn't run. Yet I have years to catch up on…years! A childhood when I sat like an old man. A depressed adulthood. Where am I even running to? Should I go home? Oh, but I'm not ready. I shall run to my old begging spot; catch up with my friends and tell them about what's just happened. I fear they will be even less welcome at the temple now, but we mustn't be bound by fear.

***

'How does it feel?' old Gad asks me. 'What's it like to see?'

'It's…amazing,' I tell him, catching my breath. 'I'm going to ask Jesus if he'll consider healing you, too.'

'What does he look like?'

'I don't know, he'd healed me and I never got the chance to thank him – they'd marched me off to give my account to the Pharisees. Nothing out of the ordinary, is what they say. But I suspect you can see his kindness in his face.

In fact, it's coming at you before you even meet. There's a presence about him, a warmth, I've never know-'

'I think he might be coming,' says Gad. 'I can feel it.'

'How astonishing,' I say. 'It looks like he's come to find *me*.'

This is surely Jesus. There's such a knowing expression on his face, like he's meeting an old friend and has heard of all that's passed.

'I was hoping I'd see you again,' I say. 'I mean, *see* you for the first time.'

'Do you believe in the Son of Man?' he asks me.

'Who is he, sir? I want to believe in him.' Of course I know; I just want to hear it from him, get some clarification. Especially if I'm to follow him, as I want to.

'You have seen him,' Jesus says to me, 'and he is speaking to you!'

'Yes, Lord, I believe!' I tell him. 'Oh, I am so grateful to you! That you would do this for me! Thank you, Jesus, for who you are, for what you've done. For coming to me. How incredible, that you sought me out a second time. I want to follow you, Lord...'

He tells me of how he came 'to give sight to the blind and to show those who think they see that they are blind.' I understand what he's saying, and right on cue some Pharisees step out and challenge him.

'Are *you saying* we're blind?' says the first in a confrontational tone. Then others amongst them ask the same.

If the cap fits.

The biblical account of this can be found in John's Gospel, chapter 9:1–41. The close geographic proximity between the temple and the pool leads me to wonder if the once-blind man would have been taken straight inside to meet with the Pharisees. Being 'cast out of the synagogue' or 'unsynagogued' was a general term suggesting excommunication; there is debate about how much of an outcast the man became and for how long. We don't know for sure where his interrogation by the Pharisees took place, whether in the temple or a synagogue; it could even have been outside, but I choose to use the temple setting for it would have been rich in symbolism for him.

Martha's tale

You can't stay cross with Jesus for long. Most often, you realize that *you* are the one who should adjust, rather than he. But this time I'm not so sure. I mean, how could this possibly be planned? Yes, I think this is one occasion he's got it wrong, and the consequences for us are catastrophic. I fear my own commitment to Jesus will fail now. I fear things will never be the same. I've told him he should have got here sooner, then none of this would have happened. I really thought he would have turned up in time – I fully expected it of him, going by his past appearances. *Look* at him, though. Just look. I have never seen Jesus cry before – I mean, I have heard that he does, especially when he stands over the city to pray. I would go with them if I could, though I do walk in the olive garden, just to feel close to him. But look at him now: those sobs are reverberating through him, causing him to shake, and my own loyalty to him is stirred. He looks caught out, as if this grief has taken him by surprise.

I have sometimes wanted Jesus to know pain. To really feel it. Yes, that sounds harsh, I know. It's just that I'd thought it was different for him; easier somehow. It's strange but now I feel more confidence in his capabilities, not less.

It makes me less alone inside.

I think Mary triggered it. Was it the sight of her so upset? She said exactly the same thing to him that I had: 'Lord, if only you had been here, my brother would not have died.' We'd said it amongst ourselves, but coming from *her* – well, it was shocking. Even so, her words weren't accusatory but innocent; inevitable, almost, as if they had to be said. She picked up one of her long crazy curls and twiddled it distractedly between her finger and thumb, as she does, her face up close to Jesus's in her usual way.

'Where have you put him?'

Those were his words.

So now we find ourselves walking towards the tomb, and people are coming out of their houses and off their roof tops to watch the spectacle. I fear they are not going to leave us alone.

Jesus doesn't seem to notice and he looks as preoccupied as the rest of us. Yes – there is anguish in his face; genuine pain. I notice it is lined and he looks older – can ageing happen this quickly? Perhaps it's my imagination. One thing is for sure: no one can say now that life is easy for him, that he doesn't know what it is to feel loss. And he doesn't even have to be here with us – we've called him 'Lord' for months, for we know who he really is, where he is from.

I drop back and put a hand upon Mary's forearm to hold her back, too. I don't need to explain. He's so disturbed by this, yet I think he's crying about something more. His groans contain anger, like there's a swelling of emotion in him, and I just want to hide. It's too powerful, too upsetting.

Now I think I don't like seeing Jesus like this. He's provoked and I worry about what he'll do. Will he roll back the stone and storm inside? Weep over the dead body? His passions are always way beyond our own and his unpredictability frightens me. I do so fear he is upsetting Mary, too. I think he's frustrated that life is as it is – or rather that death is. That it comes to us all and robs us, separates us from those we love, puts that giant chasm between us. Looking at him, it's as if something significant has finally dawned on him, a profound realization has got to him. Even now I'm still not completely sure what it is.

***

The crowd are muttering disparaging things and I hope he cannot hear them. If only they knew how much he's surrendered for us, how he's sharing our humanity on every level; God's own son, the King of Heaven treading our dusty paths, feeling our wretched pain. 'This man healed a blind man. Couldn't he have kept Lazarus from dying?'

Oh, shut up, all of you. I mean, just shut up and learn from him.

Jesus walks right up to the tomb itself and places a hand on the stone. The crowd keep a safe distance now, drawn yet revulsed by him. We move forwards and stay by his side, though. 'Roll the stone aside,' he says.

People are staring at us – I can feel it, though I am looking Jesus hard in the face, willing him to engage with me.

'Lord, he has been dead for four days,' I say. My voice is wobbling. I'm touched that he cares this much, but he's not thinking straight. 'The smell will be terrible.' I fear he's not even listening.

'Didn't I tell you that you would see God's glory if you believe?' he replies.

It's clear he's serious, and when he's intent on something there's no point fighting. So they roll the stone away.

'Father, thank you for hearing me. You always hear me, but I said it out loud for the sake of all these people standing here, so that they will believe you sent me.'

His tears are forgotten now and a calmness has come over him as he engages with his Father. It's as if the rest of us really aren't here. Then his voice booms forth, 'Lazarus, come out!'

I hold Mary's hand and she buries her head into my chest. I look for the both of us, my arms wrapped around her.

It is very quiet here now. No one says a word, and even the birds have stopped singing, as if waiting with us to see what will happen next.

I see his shadow first. A very long shadow that emerges from the tomb before he does, while a light shines from the depth of the tomb. We hear the scuffing of stones beneath his feet. And then he appears – my brother appears!

'Unwrap him and let him go!' says Jesus.

Mary and I set to work. I take the cloth from his eyes, keen just to touch him, to feel him again. Yes, I know it is him under all this; my brother's familiar sturdy frame is unmistakable. His curly hair is damp to the touch, slick with the ointment we used. I can feel his cheeks are cold from the chilly tomb, my fingers pulling away involuntarily as I work, though in my heart I don't want to let him go. Not now. Not ever.

He sees me once the bandage is off and his dimple is back beside his eyes. The old life and vibrancy, that kind warmth of my brother, is seen in his gaze.

Mary has released his arms and he places them around both of us. Customs be damned.

The biblical account of this can be found in John's Gospel, chapter 11:1–44.

Dead man walking

Bethany used to be such a quiet place. Pshaw! Oh, what an outrage we now face! Here, on this mountainous slope, we'd felt cut off from Jerusalem, though it's only an hour's walk away; this wood-fringed ravine tucks us away from the rest of the world most excellently. Or it did. A desirable village location, part of the area known as the Garden of Olives – that's how we like to think of our place of residence. Who would not want to live here? Seclusion can be wonderful, but it has its drawbacks. I step away from the crowd and watch Martha and Mary as they link arms with each other and walk home. They are talking excitedly and throwing their heads back in laughter. Lazarus still has a crowd around him and he is turning to them one at a time, answering with as few words as possible. He never was one to say much. Now he extends his arms and rotates them to show they are in fact real. His smell reassures us that he is real enough.

Those fanatical sisters of his will be impossible now that *he* has been here again to perform his trickery. It *is* outrageous! May I go as far as to say they will make our village quite unpleasant. Blasted do-gooders. Lazarus was dead and buried four days ago. You couldn't have mistaken the wailing, and, I have to admit, four days without food and water would ensure he was dead, even if he wasn't to start with.

They could have managed without him – they are wealthy enough, living in that spacious house that could accommodate all the village residents. But no, they had to go and pester that Jesus and bring him back to the village again. Pshaw! There's nothing quiet about the man. Nothing discreet. There's the façade of it for sure, the *appearance* of a good man, but the reality must be something else. It's his presence that I find so distasteful – there is a calm authority about him, like no one can challenge him. Blasted fellow. And he seems to see right into you – I will not meet his gaze, for he is one to speak his mind. Still, I'll do my best to make sure he won't be back – we can protect ourselves, we are not subject to the whims of others.

With a show of anger he shook as he commanded this dead man to come out of his grave. And the stench! I feel sure he had begun to putrefy, for it doesn't take long. What an outrage – opening up a tomb like that! Jesus's friends are leading him away, probably so he can go and have a good wash. I'm following from a safe distance. I wonder if he'll ever get rid of that smell or if it will always linger around him. Lazarus, the dead man walking. No doubt the children will have some fun with that.

My gullible neighbours are tattling like womenfolk and some have braved the tomb entrance to peer inside. 'You coming, Malin?' they call to me. 'Not I!' I reply. How ridiculous – I would never join them in their carry on! Still, no matter. Defiled they might be, but we must get to the bottom of these hoaxes. Alas, I feel that ultimately it is my responsibility, for I'm the only one of any standing around here. Who would take most of them seriously in Jerusalem? Yes, unless I do something we'll never hear the end of it. Surely this Jesus fellow needs to be stopped. Blasted lunatic! The villagers will thank me in time, once things have returned to normal. There are, of course, those who are taken in by him, who think him marvellous. It is my job to protect these simple folk. I'm going to slip away to Jerusalem shortly, once I've been home and got myself ready. Let's see what can be done about him. With swift action on my part I don't think we'll be suffering his presence around here again.

Someone is coming along the path – I turn my back to look at how far I've come, fixing my eyes on the trees beyond the cemetery until I hear his footsteps beyond.

It was another Galilean – his family weren't here a year ago. Pshaw! There are too many Galileans settling in Bethany for my liking – it must be why that Jesus fellow feels so at home. That, and the free board and lodging. Does he even have a home?

I worry about Lazarus's ongoing influence too. I stop to inspect a loose rock in the dry-stone wall before moving on. How will we silence that outrageous family? If we were rid of him, the sisters would be flattened, and of course Jesus couldn't come back, with no man in the house to visit. Gone would be their hype, their zealotry, surely. It's hell to be around – the earnest Martha, always out doing good, the emotional Mary, both always affecting the character of this place. It's partly down to them why there are so many sick roaming around these parts, knocking on their doors, begging for refuge. Pshaw! 'You want the large white house at the end of the road,' we tell them. 'You can't miss it,' but invariably they do. It would be a cleaner, healthier place with their influence gone. If this gossip is allowed to continue, just imagine what could happen here! People endorse those women at their peril. We'll have a poorhouse before we know it, or a lepers' colony.

Of course, it doesn't help that our distance from that most holy city meets with the criteria set out in the temple scroll. We, too, would quite like a radius within which no unclean persons may pass, but that is perhaps the biggest drawback in living away from bustle.

Ah, nearly home. Now, I must just go in and smarten up – change into my best tunic, oil my beard, find my polished staff. Prepare myself for the long walk. As Bethany's most notable representative I must appear the part.

***

Where is that pompous old fool going? I mean, Malin is quite ridiculous and I fear what he is up to. Yes, he's really not to be trusted... Can I stop him? But how? And what would I say? Oh, I do so fear for Jesus now. I mean, we needed Lazarus back, but what has this done for Jesus's safety, his future?

I step to one side of the window, just in case he glances over his shoulder to catch me. He looks set for a journey, his distinctive saffron-coloured tunic tucked into his belt, his staff in hand. No one else has a tunic quite like that, and you never see him with that stick unless he's off to Jerusalem.

Oh, but he mustn't!

But he probably would.

He's just the sort of person to hate Jesus – he's always looked down on us, objected to our acts of mercy, our hospitality for all. Where will it end? And the brisk strides he's taking, dust flying up with his foot fall and every strike of that staff as it hits the ground. He has such a purpose about him! I should tell Mary – I do *so fear* this won't end well.

Jesus and the others are out in the central courtyard. Earlier I'd caught them talking in hushed tones about getting away. 'Where are you going to?' I asked Cephas then. I placed a large pitcher of cold water on the tiled floor, and a bowl of the sweetest black grapes on the low table, but I could see they were not interested in refreshment.

'We can't tell even you,' said Cephas. There was an apology in the shrug of his shoulders and the heavy sigh, as he put his hand slowly across his cheek, then over his beard in thought. He nodded in the direction of Jesus for explanation, and immediately I understood. 'He wouldn't have you put under any pressure, or be at risk of interrogation,' he went on. 'You will say with a clear conscience, "I know not where they are." For few can be trusted in Bethany now. We're leaving when it's dark and no one is to follow.'

So I turned and left them to their discussions. Yet that picture of them in my courtyard will stay with me – I fear they are in great danger now. I mean, the greatest danger possible. Jesus was animated, pacing the room, talking with expressive hands and sending them serious and impassioned glances. He would look at them each in turn, a certain sadness in his eyes, like a father who is sending his sons to war. His gaze would stay on his subject as he turned and started walking, then he'd fix his sight on another. I don't believe Jesus feels nervous, but there is an energy about him today that even he seems unable to deal with. I feel sure they are to be entering a difficult phase. I hope this isn't all because of me. *I* was the one who ran out and fetched him; who told him he had to come, not thinking of the risk it would be to all of them. I hope he can forgive me.

Lazarus has shut himself away – Martha, I need some space, he told me – and Jesus had suggested he get some rest. Not that he looks tired; I've not seen him looking this well in years. He emerged from those wrappings with the glow and plumpness of an only child. I mean, you wouldn't think he had lost so much weight, or that his skin had been taut and fragile, like a butterfly's wing. His grey pallor and staggering walk made him look like a dead man even before it happened, *but now* – I'm reminded of Lazarus aged twelve, with the same joy and exuberance he had before Imma and Abba passed away.

Where is Mary? What *am* I to do about about Malin? Perhaps Jesus and the disciples should get away before nightfall – this just feels so risky. I don't think they're always that organized, or able to look ahead, see what's coming. I know I often think of things that never occur to other people. But when I tell them I'm told that I'm fretting – it's just that my mind doesn't stop. And so now, what should I do, what should I say? I really don't feel good about this one. I fear there's no way I can tell them now. I mean, they sent me out as my nervous presence is a distraction, yet I know they need me.

Oh, I must stop worrying, I know I must. Chains of anxiety link one scene of my life to the next, and Jesus says I gain nothing by it. I know he's right. He smiles at me with unending patience and tells me to let go. He knows more than is humanly possible – how could I forget this? For sometimes I do find marks where I have dug my nails into my palms, and I don't even realize I'm doing it. And what can Malin do anyway? We have *Jesus*. He's victim to no one – not even Malin and his schemes for a better Bethany. What possibly could motivate the man? I mean, what does he think he will gain?

***

Bethany, several weeks later

'Martha, leave that. I'll sort it out later.'

'If you could just tidy up a little, Lazarus. He'll be here soon, along with the rest of them. I have so much to do – loo-'

'Of all households on earth, we're most blessed,' I tell her. 'What joy is ours!' I shut my eyes and take a deep breath. It's a habit I've developed since my return from the dead. It's what I remember doing when I came round – taking the air into my lungs and feeling in awe. I like to recapture that moment – *his* moment. The joy it brings me often makes me laugh – I just can't stop myself. I open my eyes now so that I can look at her – she has her back to me as she stoops to straighten the large rush mat in the middle of the floor. 'That he chose us as his friends, Mart, is one thing. But that he demonstrated his power over death – it is extraordinary.' I cast my gaze over the veranda and in the direction we'll see him return, that dusty track out of Bethany that we've all trod so many times.

'I know, but Lazarus, please could you just sit over there? I want to sweep underneath that settle. I fear the house looks a terrible mess.'

I lift my feet for her and smile.

'It's the same old you, but you do sound older now that you're back with us. That, and a little daft.'

'Really? I hadn't noticed.'

'Why are you laughing so much these days? You're worse than before. I mean, these are dangerous times.'

'Oh, they always were. Anyway, why are they coming back so soon?'

'It'll be Passover that's drawing him. Has he not thought? Of course, they'll be looking for him, and now more than ever.'

'You need to trust him more, Martha.' I shut my eyes to breathe deeply again and amazing peace overcomes me. What joy it is to know him! I start to laugh, but as I look at her, I can see she's not impressed.

'I do trust him, more than anyone,' she protests. 'But I worry about him, Lazarus. Surely you do too?'

She's gone again, into the courtyard to sweep, though she's done it already this morning. Her rhythmical strokes invade my thoughts; living with two women has its challenges. I've never needed a wife. They are devoted and wonderful, and the depth of their love has touched me. They manage perfectly well without me, yet apparently I am needed to make their lives feel complete. What a blessing they are! They have always been competent, running the home when Imma and Abba died in such quick succession. I'm ashamed to say that I cannot remember our mother's face, though everyone says Martha is just like her – tall, willowy, with long strides that the rest of us struggle to keep up with. What reassurance that resemblance brings me! She has a nervous energy that means there's not an ounce of flesh on her. Oh Martha, I want to say, if you could just relax. Her dark eyebrows almost meet in the middle, that heavy brow adding to her seriousness when she asks yet another of her troubled questions.

She always was persuasive; I rarely argue with her – never through choice and only through necessity, when she is worrying herself into a hole. Neither did our parents, so Mary tells me. Martha doesn't realize how beautiful she is, and has no time for her appearance; always the uptight one, she has to express her love through her deeds for others – it's so natural to her. What a contrast there is between my sisters! Only a couple of months ago – but how long was I gone? Only recently, anyway, I witnessed a scene that said it all…

'Mary, I fear it's another suitor. I mean it's the really keen one,' Martha told her. Her eyesight is sharp and she misses nothing. We were all on the roof, enjoying a game together. Mary scattered the shell counters across the floor as the three of us rushed down the stairs, Mary instructing us as we went: 'I'm not home – you understand? Tell him *no*, I don't want *anyone*!'

'What a nonsense!' I said. 'He's handsome and he's besotted –'

'Our parents aren't here,' she said, looking for somewhere to hide. 'No grandchildren needed. *You* are the only family I need.'

We watched as she concealed herself in the tall wicker basket, pulling the lid over herself as he rapped on the inner door.

'What a kind offer!' I said to him. 'I will be sure to pass on the message!' I heard her squeak in protest from inside the basket and it wobbled slightly. 'Oh, excuse me,' said Martha. 'I fear I have hiccups!'

He didn't look convinced as I opened the door for him and sent him on his way.

I don't think Martha has had one suitor. What a strange situation, anyway, with no father to ask. Are they intimidated by her brilliance? I would never risk disrupting any advances made in her direction. I have always felt myself to be more like Mary – something of a risktaker, a little carefree. Mary is always understood, and can demonstrate her loyalty with such affection. Poor Martha. Still, nothing would ever get done around here without her.

I listen to her sweeping now that still continues. She does make me feel a bit guilty with her constant bustle. What a problem she is! I always think of her with that bandage around her wrist, that she uses to tie back her hair – it may become the fashion one day. So might the smell of healing salve that follows her around, that she's always applying to other people: cinnamon, cloves or spearmint, and never sweet-smelling flowers. Sometimes she gets me to sniff her wrist because of a new one she has invented – 'This one is really good – you should try it,' she says. They all smell the same, I tell her. 'Oh, but the healing properties are better in this one – you'll see.'

She loves Jesus so wholeheartedly, as he epitomizes everything she's ever stood for. Except his version is backed with power and not worry. If he hadn't brought me back it would have been hard for my sisters to see him. There is already gossip; there has been for a while. They love him, but not like *that*. It's ironic really, for nothing could be further from their minds, but I've heard what people say – that he and Martha would be a good match, but that he prefers Mary. What a joke! They are wrong on both counts. My sisters love him with a purity and his intentions towards them both have always been honorable. I think they will never marry anyone, but of course the neighbours like nothing more than to speculate.

I don't want to marry either – I'm really sure of that now. Time is short, life is urgent; I even wonder how long I've got. I've heard the whispers about me, too, and seen the fingers pointing me out to a rather official looking visitor to Bethany. My existence is rather awkward for those who would have Jesus discredited. I don't mind at all; I cannot wait to put this world behind me, and to be where Jesus is heading. What joy will be mine – even greater than this! I shut my eyes and think of how I will transition into God's wonderful presence. I would rather not leave my sisters behind, though. I wonder why they chose to involve him. Was their grief really unbearable? They must have known they were putting him at risk, but then perhaps all of this was inevitable.

Oh, to be in eternity! What a day that will be, when we arrive there. I've been asked what I saw when I left my body. I cannot say. I *will* not say. The significant thing is this: he brought me back. That he is able to do such a thing! It confirms what I always knew about him in my spirit, what I always believed. If anyone fears death, they should look to him. Why did he call me home? Out of kindness to my grieving sisters? Out of pity for me? I think it's more than that. He wanted to demonstrate his power over death, his Lordship. It's not because I'm anything special; perhaps he chose me because I *am* so ordinary. I like to think I'm trustworthy too; no one has ever had any reason to doubt my testimony before now. And for sure, they couldn't doubt this as there were so many witnesses. What a case this is! I am a problem, indeed.

See John chapter 11 for the biblical account.

Martha, Mary and Lazarus's ministry: I like to speculate on the hospitality of Martha, Mary and Lazarus and have left the subject open-ended in the text quite deliberately. I suspect they were naturally generous and socially outward-looking, and their ministry may have been formalized as time went on; these are, however, simply my own thoughts on the matter. Nonetheless, there is good reason for all the surmising. As Bethany sits at a low level, a few miles out of Jerusalem and unseen from the temple, it is considered a likely location as a centre for the sick. Pilgrims would have stopped there, on route to the capital, weary and no doubt foot-sore, too. Further speculation surrounds whether the siblings were of the Essene tradition, and running a place of refuge for the sick, the homeless and the traveller.[24]

It has been moving for me to think of the regrouping of Jesus and the disciples after the raising of Lazarus, and the implications of this for their visibility. The Bible talks about how they got away to Ephraim, an obscure location thirteen miles north-east of Jerusalem itself. I suspect they travelled to it at night, away from suspicious eyes. From this wild spot the disciples would have been able to see anyone coming; it provided a panoramic view, sitting as it did, high up on a hill. I like to think of Jesus praying from there, looking out onto the plains of Jericho and beyond. It would have been a quiet place for consolidating knowledge and preparing for what was to come. Time alone with his Father, and time to get himself and the disciples ready. A time in the wilderness at the close of his public ministry, which no doubt reminded him of his forty-day seclusion before things began just a few years before.

There is a myth that is perpetuated concerning Lazarus – that he was a changed character after being brought back from the dead: miserable, in fact. Theory has it that he didn't smile after his resurrection, as he was so deeply affected by what he saw during that time. It is said that he smiled only once, when he witnessed someone stealing a clay pot. He is said to have remarked, 'the clay steals the clay.' I struggle with all this. Firstly, Jesus knew what he was doing in bringing him back. Secondly, he was brought back by Jesus, so he would have been whole, not damaged. Jesus's healing is always complete.

---

[24] For more information on this see Brian J. Capper, "The Church as the New Covenant of Effective Economics", *International Journal for the Study of the Christian Church* 2, 1 (January 2002), 83–102.

The Lord needs it

I'm not sure how Jesus's friends got to hear about me though, to be fair, I am known around these parts as a wealthy man. I inspect my new tunic for creases as I walk – I think it hangs beautifully. I'm considered something of a leader, too. My opinion is often sought on local matters and always given. Everyone must know that architectural design has advanced in Jerusalem because of me, and, indeed, Bethpage itself is much smarter because of my advice and investment. Perhaps the fact they've chosen to use my donkey means they've singled me out. To be fair, it is a perfectly reasonable assumption. 'The Lord needs it,' was all the explanation I was given. I had to inform my wife who was out visiting a friend; she loves that donkey and if it were gone without explanation she would have been sure to panic.

I'm catching them up now; not that I need the donkey back, for I trust Jesus completely. The day he swindles someone or thieves is a day that's not worth living. Still, I wish Jesus was more dynamic. To look at the man you wouldn't guess his celebrity status or know he intends to lead anything. If today is going to be *the* day he could have tidied himself up a bit, but he never was image conscious. A bit of personal care never goes amiss. That aside, he can certainly deliver, draw a crowd. I can hear them shouting from here: 'Hosanna!' They are waving palm branches over their heads and the children are skipping and dancing. If he didn't *intend* to claim power today he surely must have agreed to in his spirit by now. He wouldn't want to disappoint a crowd this size and I think they've made the decision for him.

Yet I'm worried about the logistics of this: how can one man with a few enthusiastic followers overthrow anything? The Romans have held our people oppressed for so long, and I wonder exactly what he intends to do. To be fair, he could really do with me as one of his disciples, I feel. But now his following's so big I'm not sure how easy it would be to have him take me on. I'd be more a personal advisor, a campaign manager; perhaps I could share the role, once he's got to know me, of course. With his power and my management skills we'd be phenomenal. Still, it looks like he's going for it now. I think the best thing for me to do is to follow along and oversee things. Who knows, perhaps I'll find a way in. All I really want is to help Jesus to be the best he can be. Just a small measure of arrogance goes a long way, and I do think he's lacking in worldly leadership skills. Yes, the Lord needs it. After all, what leader have we ever known with such a humble disposition?

***

'Come on, Breina. Let's get you home. They seem to have abandoned you, and their claims to instate Jesus as king. What was that all about? He's returning already and he hasn't done anything!'

My donkey seems to understand as she nuzzles into me, but then she looks away in the direction of Jesus. 'I wouldn't bother with him,' I tell her. 'So "your king is coming to you. He is righteous and victorious, yet he is humble, riding on a donkey – riding on a donkey's colt."[25] Well, it wasn't *him*. What a letdown. Still, you may do it yet.'

She brays some sort of understanding and we turn for home. I was right all along; he isn't kingly material. A king should be commanding and with a strong presence about him, a prideful look that shows who he really is. I think we were mistaken. Not that I was taken in by it all; not really.

We make our way through disgruntled looking crowds – I pass a woman consoling her son, and an old man commanding a small child to find his tunic on the way back home. There seems to be quite a crowd of us returning and the disappointment hangs thick in the air, like the smoke that will waft over from the temple in just a few days' time. I will gladly give an elderly person a ride back on Breina if I need to; there might as well be at least some point to this journey, after all.

'That's the donkey he rode on,' say the people as we pass on by. It's as if we are tinged with shame. 'Poor donkey,' says one little girl. 'He wasn't to know,' says her father after me, not expecting me to hear.

My attention is caught by a small family group who seem to be walking at the same pace as me. Before long I am up behind them. 'He did nothing!' moans the young man to his wife. 'I was ready to follow him! I really thought he was different.'

'Right up to the Golden Gate – then nothing,' she replies, pulling her shawl further over her head to protect her eyes from the bright sun.

'He was always talking in riddles. Never could understand him.'

'What of all those healings?' asks their lad, who is almost a young man himself. He turns round in front of them, his arms outstretched and a stick in one hand, which he waves at them.

'What of them?' says his father, adjusting the baby on his back.

---

[25] Zechariah 9:9.

'And Lazarus?' the lad continues.

'Yes, Lazarus. He does pose something of a problem.' The man lifts a pondering hand to his beard while supporting the young child with the other.

'I think there's something we're not getting. You saw the way Jesus cried when we looked down over Jerusalem. Heard his words about "the way to peace". We can't abandon him now,' the lad goes on.

'He's messed with your head, my boy,' says the father. 'It's time things got back to normal around here. It was a provocative act but he didn't follow through. He doesn't know what he's about himself, I'll be bound. Stay away from here on,' he finishes.

The lad has lost his energetic manner now and drags his stick behind him so that it draws a line in the dust.

'We should have reported him instead,' the father continues, but the son isn't engaging with him. 'The Pharisees want to arrest him – there was probably a reward in it.'

There is a long pause and the wife and son seem caught up in their own thoughts. But then, 'some of them were in the crowd,' the boy tells them. 'They'd accepted him, it's all getting better, just you wait and see.'

'It's so quiet on this road now,' says his wife. 'I preferred it with all that singing.'

'False optimism,' says the man.

'Well, I did kind of like him.'

He shoots her a stern glance but she either doesn't see or chooses to ignore it. 'He made it a better place, or makes it. I expect he'll be back with Lazarus and his sisters by nightfall.'

'Like I said, stay away.'

Their conversation saddens me and I allow some distance now to form between us. Dare I say it, I think their son is right in his belief in Jesus, though wrong in imagining the authorities will warm to him. Walking behind them has forced me to really weigh this up. The palm branches are turning limp and some have already shrivelled after just a few short hours. I still can't shake the image of Jesus from my head, the triumphant king, the one we have all been waiting for. He hasn't acted as we'd anticipated, but I don't think his story is over yet. Perhaps I should have left Breina in Jerusalem; then they would have had to return her to me. I'll find another reason to talk to them, though. Perhaps a campaign manager isn't what Jesus needs anyway. It's followers to grasp what he's about and trust his leadership. *The Lord needs it.* To be fair, I don't really have anything better to offer, and I think I might give it a try. If they haven't arrested him already, that is.

The biblical accounts of the triumphal entry are found in Matthew 21:1–11; Mark 11:1–10; Luke 19:28–44 and John 12:12–19.

In this narrative the Jews were expecting Jesus to lead them out of Roman oppression. They failed to grasp what Jesus's Messianic mission was about, and anticipated revolution rather than peace.

We must be wary of asking Jesus to live up to our expectations. Who is leading: him or us? His purposes aren't always obvious, so we must be careful not to be like the 'hosanna' chanters in this story, who proclaimed Christ as king, but only while he matched their perception of what a king should be.

Bad for business

'Just who does he think he is? God or something? Who is *he* to say we can't use the temple like this?' The boy watched as his father struggled to guide their one ox down the steps while he spoke, pushing it across with his shoulder so that it didn't step on his feet. A much younger boy, meanwhile, darted in and around the little group, as if energized by the encounter.

The father stopped and waited for all eyes to be on him for dramatic effect – '"Get these things out of here. Stop turning my Father's house into a marketplace!"'[26] His mock-Galilean accent and exaggerated arm movements made the boys want to run for the hills, but he didn't notice. Rather he looked into the faces of all the gathered men. 'How exactly is our economy supposed to run without business in there? The man is crazy and he needs to be stopped. He wants us to abide by his rules, his ideals – well I'm sorry, but I don't see him putting bread in my children's mouths.'

The older lad looked away, trying not to let his father catch his eye – they never were hungry, though he often wished his family did business out in the open, where he could kick a ball around with his friends. He had to stop him going on – his father was downright embarrassing; several of his front teeth were missing and the dissimilarity between him and Jesus couldn't have been more striking. There was something wonderful about Jesus, something commanding – now he really did hold your attention for all the right reasons, as you wondered what he'd come out with next, what he'd *do*. He rubbed a hand over his face and thought he could smell the faint lingering aroma of the palm frond he'd been holding the day before. 'I'd heard rumours...' he heard himself say, but then he thought better of it.

'What was that?'

'Oh, nothing. Just something someone once said about a miracle of his. It's really nothing.'

'They say he has *magical powers*,' added his little brother, his eyes wide with wonder that he could hold a crowd as well as his father. The older boy knew he'd be in trouble, and, as always, now the brat had started he couldn't stop. 'Give him your packed lunch and he can –'

---

[26] John 2:16. There is debate over whether Jesus cleared the temple twice; I have included words from what some think was the first incident, but the pronouncement was authentically his, regardless of the conclusion you draw.

'Doh! Oh, Ben, take the beast down to the next platform,' said the father to his responsible son. 'Oh, dear. Let's all move down a few steps. I'll clear that up later when all of this has died down.'

'Never was the best surface for steps – gleaming white marble. How can anyone expect to keep that clean?' said the man who'd been selling oil inside the temple.

'I've always felt the exterior too dazzling. Particularly with the sun bearing down in all its splendour,' contributed one of the money-sellers, overtaking them.

'There will be a whole lot more cack to clear up inside too – what with all those frightened animals. He hadn't thought of that, had he?' said the boys' father to his friends again.

'You do have to watch where you tread around here, but it's a small price to pay,' said the oil-seller, wiping his moist forehead in the sun. 'We're a thriving community, a thriving temple. He should be pleased. How long we going to stay out here in all this heat? We going to go back in? It's not like us to be pushed around.'

'Not until I see him come out,' said the father again. 'I'd quite like to swing for him, but not in there. It'll keep.' He stopped at the bottom of the long staircase and gestured towards the Mount of Olives – 'I remember a time when we would sell right over there, at the far side of the valley. The animals used to enjoy sheltering under the shade of the trees.'[27] The ox followed his arm and gazed off into the distance, as if included in the conversation. 'Over time we got a little bolder, a little closer, until it was recognized by all that it was just easier to sell inside the temple itself. It's meant we can charge a better price too, as far as we're concerned – you know, for the convenience. I don't know what his problem is.'

'It *is* supposed to be the Court of the Gentiles,' said the lad. 'I guess it's not easy for them to find a quiet space to pray here – I mean, it's half market, half...'

'You've got a right one there, Levi.'

'Whose side are you on?'

'Yours of course – I'm only saying. It just can't be a house of prayer for all nations right now.'

---

[27] Carson, D.A., *The Gospel According to John.* (1990). Pillar NT Commentary, 178.

'Jesus is being pedantic. Why's he so bothered about them anyway? He's just making an issue out of nothing. He's a bloody trouble-maker and he should go back to Galilee where he belongs. You got that, son?'

The noise of bleating made them all turn their heads to see a sheep tumbling down the steps. It righted itself and was soon followed by a tall, thin man bearing a large lamb under each arm.

'Hello Eli, has he thrown you out too?'

'I was only passing through with this lot. We all do it...'[28]

'Is it safe to go back inside yet?'

'I wouldn't. Give it an hour or two. I'm going back the long way round. What a nuisance – jumped up foreigners, who needs them?'

'You got through this time, though.'

'I was running, believe me!'

'It's bad for business. Very bad,' said the father, shaking his head slowly, with exaggeration.

'I promised that I'd deliver these sheep personally – nothing but the best service for old Yosef.'

'You going his way again?'

'Of course, it's all part of the deal around here; the temple does alright out of us, anyway, and we get something in return. Tis a pity that old Bethlehem still keeps providing the temple with the sacrificial lambs – now that would be good business for us. We don't work on that scale, anyway.'[29]

Shared grumblings were uttered before the man went on – 'But I wonder, what person has grown up around here thinking this is solely a place of worship? Plenty of employment goes on here besides the priesthood. Everyone knows the temple is famed for its outward beauty, but what goes on inside...Well, ...'

---

[28] Pulpit Commentary on Mark 11:16: 'the shortest cut was through this court and by Solomon's Porch. The distance would be greatly increased if they went round it. So the priests permitted servants and laborers, laden with anything, to take this shorter way through the great court of the temple.'

[29] See notes at the end of this tale for information on Bethlehem's sacrificial lambs.

'What if God's like that – like him? They say that's what he's claiming. I mean, we heard him ourselves – "my Father's house",' added the boys' father.

'I'm a godly man – I think we all are. We make our sacrifices, obey the law as much as our neighbours,' said one old seller.

'They said he was going to come in yesterday, that he'd arrived all king-like with everyone bowing down in front of him. I'd thought he'd been in to recruit more followers but that never happened,' joined another.

'Oh, he looked in alright. I'd heard that. Some say he was choosing his moment.'

The older lad didn't know where to look, what to distract himself with. 'I've heard him speak,' he said. His father shot him an accusing look and he knew the interrogation would come when they were home.

'Go on. What do you say in his defence?' said an old and well-respected seller of incense who had been quiet until now. They said they always smelt him before they could see him, but the accolade could have been worse. 'We mean you no harm,' he told the boy, the reassurance evident in his kind eyes and leathery, well-worn smile lines as he spoke. 'We just want to understand what motivates the fellow. It's baffling, wouldn't you say?'

'I think he really wants people to know God – to understand his love, to get right with him. You know, if this is God's *dwelling place* it can't be that nice for him, can it?'

'We're only at the outer edge. That's not where he dwells,' said one or two.

'It's symbolic,' said the lad, confident in his delivery now. 'He wants clear access to himself. This is meant to be a place of blessing and yet inside it feels like we charge for drawing close to him. There seems to be a cost attached to everything.'

For once his father was lost for words, but his younger brother did look impressed, and he came to sit beside him on the step, shuffling in so that their bodies touched, as if the association might rub off on him, the connection with this Jesus might be his, too. Yet now the lad had found his courage and it didn't matter to him what anyone thought. If he didn't explain this to them, who would? 'We hear that he is a jealous God. I think Jesus is wanting to make it clear that this is to be a holy place – not full of dung and dodgy deals,' – his younger brother sniggered – 'of exploitation and buying privilege. That's all.'

'That's *all*?' said several together.

'Perhaps in another era, but not here, not now. Not in my back yard,' added the oil seller.

'Well until Jesus provides me with another livelihood, I'll be in there,' concluded the boys' father, his leadership evident in that he was the only one still standing, and it was a convincing performance. '*I* have more right to be here than him – *I* was brought up here, learnt to read here.' The others nodded their respect at him, for his companions could not read themselves. 'To me, it's the place of God's provision. Dirty and smelly it may be, but it's the only temple I've ever known. I don't intend to move on any time soon.'

The lad stood up to take the ox for his father. It might help his cause if he could show himself to be helpful, a little bit more responsible. *Hosanna to the Son of David!* Could he ever risk adding his voice to that again?[30] Perhaps he would persuade his family – he was a match for his father in speechmaking, he'd decided, anyway. Perhaps it would all get better from here. Perhaps it might.

See Mark 11:15–19 (I follow this account and have Jesus simply look into the temple on the day of the Triumphal Entry, returning, presumably the next day, to deal with the exploitation there). See also Matthew 21:12–17, Luke 19:45–48 and John 2:13–22.

Much can be found in commentaries about the role of Bethlehem in providing the lambs for the temple. (See 'Welcome, Little King' story.) Ellicott, writing about Luke 2:8, says 'The statement in the Mishna that the sheep intended for sacrifice in the temple were pastured in the fields of Bethlehem, gives a special interest to the fact thus narrated, and may, perhaps, in part, explain the faith and devotion of the shepherds...'

See also the blog by Howard Hewitt. It is interesting to consider the parallels with Jesus's own life; the sheep, born in Bethlehem, would be brought to Jerusalem on foot on a Friday, ready for slaughter: 14 March, 2014 Story of Bethlehem Sheep More Than Legend. https://blog.wabash.edu/immersionlearning201314/2014/03/14/story-of-bethlehem-sheep-more-than-legend/

---

[30] In Matthew 21:15 we read of children in the temple, exclaiming, "Hosanna to the Son of David!" I suspect many of them were accepting of Jesus, even when their parents weren't.

Malchus's tale

I should be used to crowds by now – I've dealt with enough of them. Yet I feel very uneasy in this one. The reason? This Judas is a problem for me. I mean, what a vile man, what despicable conduct. He's waiting with me and he's looking shifty, like his eyes can't settle on anything. He intimidates *me*, but how? I don't like his height – I have to glance up at him, and his gangly legs mean he could outrun me. The man keeps clearing his throat, like he wants to make a speech. Yet why? He is amongst his foes – you can't change sides that easily – and he doesn't fit in anywhere. I won't engage with him, for sure; that he is selling out like this proves to me he wasn't worthy to be among them anyway.

My strong dislike of him is making me question what we are doing more than anything could. Dare I admit it? I've always struggled to see Jesus as dangerous; that's a thought I could never own up to. Yes, there was that provocative moment when he arrived on a donkey, but he went home that day having achieved nothing. That said, he returned to cause havoc here in the temple, but even then there was an overriding sense of goodness that I got from him. No, I cannot see him as an *evil* overthrower. But he's a *risk*; of course he is. Our task would be easier to take if we could set out to find him unaccompanied, at least for me. Pilgrims are lodging everywhere, though, setting up camps across the landscape like flies on a wound. There are estimates that Jerusalem's population has swollen to 100,000 this week; we must surprise his followers by night or many would come to his aid.

I can see the tension in Judas as he waits beside me; there is a vein bulging in his temple and sweat causes a sheen that glows on his forehead. He's even holding his own club, which I can only assume he intends to use on his group, and I can see how tight his grasp is. No, he is not one of them and I suspect he never was.

The noise is increasing as the temple guard assemble around us. And the smell. Has nobody washed? Yet there is fear in the ranks as we all know how popular Jesus is about these parts. A full moon hangs heavy in the sky already, burdened like a woman with child as it is at every Passover. It will certainly make finding Jesus easier.

A gong is sounded and all falls quiet. Final instructions are given about no one returning until Jesus is found, and to expect resistance, even trickery; we all know the stories about him, which is why such an army of men has been called upon. It does look quite outlandish, for sure, and we are not the full force yet. My master gestures for Judas to step forward and he clears his throat again, then wipes his brow, his nerves showing now that his moment has finally arrived. 'You will know which one to arrest when I greet him with a kiss,' he says. 'Then you can take him away under guard.' His arm shakes as he receives a pouch of coins and he will not look at anyone.[31]

The command is given and the row of guards at the front of the courtyard start to move. They lead on to the neighbouring garrison that belongs to the Roman guard. It is unusual for us to operate with them in such a way, and it increases the gravitas of the occasion. We are waved in and a group of well-armed, very tall Roman soldiers step in front of our group, marching in unison to an exit that will take us from the fort and across the Kidron Valley. I have of course seen this bridge of the Red Heifer before, a raised walkway to the Mount of Olives, but I've never walked on it until now. The effect? It makes me feel very important, for sure. It has been agreed by our leaders that Jesus *must* be captured tonight, or we do not go home to our beds. We are doing the right thing, I think to myself, as my stride falls in with Judas' and the soldiers' that march either side of us. They are setting a fast pace that isn't natural for me. As we set out down the slope I get a sense of the scale of this operation. I mean, there are now seven rows of soldiers before us and the flaming torches and lanterns light the way like the brightest stars, though darkness hasn't completely fallen. I think it shows we are not to be meddled with, but small flickering lights usually speak to me of peace. There won't be much peace this night, for sure.

My master had said 'It's better that one man should die for the people'[32] and of course he is right. I'm sure that he is. I mean, that fellow came in from Bethany to tell us he'd seen Jesus raise a man from the dead. I remember it well – this local was a respected figure certainly, with an impressive staff and distinctive golden tunic. Others from Bethany followed, all concerned about the effect Jesus was having on their quiet neighbourhood. But the religious community here saw more than that; without Jesus's death there could be revolution, it was said, and they stayed up well into the night for days, discussing how to bring Jesus to justice, devising this plot and that. And my

---

[31] In Mark and Luke's Gospels Judas is promised money before the event, whereas in Matthew's Gospel he is given the money when the arrangement is made. Mark 14:10–11; Luke 22:3–6 and Matthew 26:14–16.

[32] John 11:45–52 and John 18:14.

part? I simply observe on these occasions, and try to anticipate where their decisions will take me. Their conclusion is the only logical one – of course it is.

My friends think me very brave. But I only say and do what my master commands, and he is uncompromising in his expectations; some say he is reckless, but you can't hold onto power unless you have an attitude of ruthlessness. It's never been done before. Well, not in my lifetime. Caiaphas is the brains behind my actions, but it's meant I've seen a lot of Jesus and his disciples over the last few months. I don't think his followers like me very much, but I am only the messenger. They would be surprised if they knew that I'm interested in what they have to say; my job prevents me from asking what I'd like to. Oh, I have to admit, I am confused, for sure. Trying to kid myself just isn't working. And why? I've been taught since childhood that there *is* no supernatural; that signs and wonders are never what they appear, but Jesus's life has been full of them, and I cannot dispute how people's circumstances have been irreversibly changed. That's of little consequence, for it all ends here, tonight, with his arrest.

How must I behave? I must show no mercy. Now is not the time for my sympathies to find expression; I must suppress these thoughts and concentrate on the job in hand.

With the fast pace that the soldiers have set we cross the valley in a very short time and Gethsemane is no longer a green backdrop but an amalgam of gnarled olive trees and dust paths leading into darkness. Can we do this? Was nightfall really a good idea? But as I look behind me, I can see we'll have the mountainside covered – there must be hundreds of our men out tonight. Judas steps forward now and leads the way as the ranks of soldiers stop to let us through. He knows these tracks well and takes us into the depth of the wood. I think I see people lurking at the edges, but as torches are placed near the trees it is clear they are only the contorted branches that have flexed and grown like limbs, with the same thickness and natural sway.

Darkness seems to have fallen very quickly and there is an eerie quiet, despite our number. There seems to be an absence of birdsong, too. This is not the place of beauty I anticipate, for I've been here before and often think of it, when the demands of my job encroach on me. Soon Judas strides ahead and this time we find the shadows closing us in are not branches but people, and sleepy ones at that. These are the branches of a still summer's day. We had expected more resistance; they may as well have woken from a dream!

Judas walks straight up to the man standing in the centre and kisses him on the cheek. 'Rabbi!' he says. It's unfolding like a very bad dream, though I know I *should* feel pleased. I mean, its mission accomplished and this great army was unnecessary, for sure.

'My friend, go ahead and do what you have come for,' Jesus replies. And his manner? He doesn't look offended and there is an air of inevitability about him, like he blames no one. I actually feel very sorry for him and can't help feeling he deserves better.

Jesus's followers stumble to their feet and soldiers move in and grab him. Yet Jesus steps towards them and they stop. 'Who are you looking for?' he says.

'Jesus the Nazarene,' they answer.

'I AM he,' Jesus says, and it's as if something explosive is released into the atmosphere, for we all fall backwards, physically stung by his words. Is this happening? But it is, I feel sure. His declaration is not lost on me, and none of us can stand on our feet. I feel disorientated; drunk, and try to steady my vision by grasping with my hands, but there is nothing to hold onto. *I AM he.* I'm reminded that this is why such a group has been sent to arrest him, for it was likely he'd demonstrate his legendary power; yet I'm feeling even more uneasy now, conscious of a pervading sense of this man's goodness. Could it really be that he *is* who he claims to be? Jesus could run away at this moment, but he waits for us with such calmness.

I don't want this to go any further. I mean, I want it to stop.

'Who are you looking for?' he asks a second time.

'Jesus the Nazarene,' we reply.

'I told you that I AM he,' he says. 'And since I am the one you want, let these others go.'

Slowly we struggle to our feet and now the guards are looking both defensive and afraid. What do we do? There are more soldiers acting than we need, all keen to claim the glory that *they* were the ones to arrest him, and his followers are getting agitated. 'Lord, should we fight? We brought the swords!' they say, with the enthusiasm and ill-preparedness of young boys. Cephas has recognized me, and as if laying all the blame for this at my feet, lashes out with his sword, as if to kill me!

Has he? Is this some fatal wound? The pain is excruciating and I lightly touch my neck, then the side of my face to feel what he's done. I think my ear is missing!

'Aagh,' I shout and stumble again to the floor, my head in agony, my left hand searching the ground in amongst the new-fallen olive blossom and the dried rubbery fruit from last year, my right clutching at my head. I shut my eyes and scream before trying to explain, but find I have lost the ability to speak. Not a sound comes out of my mouth. Can they not wait just a moment? Let me find my ear at least? Though I'm not sure what good it will do.

I stop and look at my hands in the torchlight. My right hand's covered in blood and I return it to my head, feeling bone beneath my palm before it's wet again to the touch. I catch sight of my brother who must have come with us, his face lit up by a lantern that he holds from a long pole. He knows it's me, and the horror on his face confirms for me what has just happened.

'Put your sword back into its sheath,' Jesus says. My hearing is muffled but my good ear still works. 'Shall I not drink from the cup of suffering the Father has given me?' he finishes.

I don't know what I am doing and find myself standing in the way of the guards, in front of Jesus. It seems I am crying, though my sobs are silent and lost on everyone else, who seem more concerned with getting Jesus tied up and ready to go. Jesus turns to the crowd now and rebukes them, but strangely there is kindness in his words even now. Still he doesn't seem to blame us, though he tells us we've had plenty of opportunities before now to arrest him. He says it's been preordained, which makes me feel somewhat better, though my wound is still killing me.

To my surprise he now turns the attention to me. 'No more of this,' he says, to his disciples I think, as he is resigned to the fact he's being arrested. Then he steps closer to me and touches the side of my face, where my ear belongs. At once it feels better – there is an energy surging through it and it is warm. Most of all, it is no longer painful. Slowly, nervously, I touch it, and it feels as it always did! I felt sure it fell to the ground, and the blood still stains my hand and tunic. I will return tomorrow as soon as it's light, before I'm needed, and hunt for it. It is the most bizarre of things. How many saw what happened? Cephas surely knows what he did and he is still sat on his haunches, his hands over his face. He could've gone to prison for that, or have been sentenced to death. For my part, I want to let this go, and there is now no evidence to prove what he had done. He is a lucky man. I suspect Jesus did this for him as much as for me. They say he had plans for them all, though I wonder how effective they will be without Jesus as their leader.

My master will not entertain talk of this, for sure. He regularly instructs us all that miracles do not occur; cannot occur. I am walking, hearing proof that he is wrong, which will certainly be a problem for him. It's best that I say nothing at all.

They have tied Jesus's wrists now with rope and his followers seem to have fled. We will see Caiaphas before long. I hear some shouting behind me, and as I look I see a naked man running back to the olive grove, the guard holding his tunic in his hand that he's wriggled out from. 'Leave him,' says another soldier to him. 'They won't be causing us any more problems. It's the last we'll be seeing of them, I'll be bound.'

I can see Cephas lurking behind an ancient tree, and the next time I glance back again I see him following us from a safe distance. Jesus is just level with me now but I dare not look at him. I can see from the corner of my eye that they are treating him roughly; there is no need for that. I really cannot look at him. He's healed my ear and yet I am still a part of the mob returning him and it makes me feel so bad. Does he understand that I have no choice? I believe that he is who he said he was, for sure, but I am still Caiaphas's property, and he is not known for his mercy.

Oh, what do you do when you know your master is wrong on something? When he's chosen his battle with the king of heaven? I could explain. I owe it to Jesus. Yet the others will deny it happened and make out it was all in my imagination; there's no scope for admitting Jesus did this, and it wouldn't change anything, except my lifespan.

He can save himself, for sure. Of course he can. He's already demonstrated his power, so I just need to hang back and wait for him to act. He'll come through, and when he does, I hope he'll take me with him. Does he know I am on his side now or will I have to speak out? I wonder if my voice has returned. Even my name mocks me; 'my king', I hear, whenever I am called. I have found the true king yet I am unable to follow him. Still, no one will know what goes on in my heart.

See all four gospels for this story: Matthew 26:47–56; Mark 14:43–49; Luke 22:47–53 and John 18:1–11.

On Judas, the traitor

It's not always easy being the young one.[33] Most people assume you don't have their level of wisdom; they don't even bother to consult you on the important stuff. But I know that, in my case, something significant could have been averted, if only they'd listened to me. I shouldn't keep on like this, I know. The fact is, I really can't fault Jesus – he's been the only one to recognize any strength of character in me. He's told me things he wouldn't tell the others and I just love that. Yet he seemed to think his choice of disciples was spot on and not to be questioned. He surely can't think that now.

So most of us are together again… All except for Cephas, who's been gone all night, Judas – the traitor – and, of course, Jesus. I hope we get Jesus back easily enough – there was no point to his arrest, he hasn't done anything wrong. They have nothing to hold him on, but the events of last night felt monumental, like they'd have some eternal consequences. And the way Jesus prepared us all, he seemed to think it was the beginning of the end for him.

I haven't slept properly all night. I should have stayed with Jesus but it all got too much for me so I just came away. I really don't know what for, but I'm here now and the questioning probably ended hours ago. James has been snoring in the corner and Didy keeps calling out random words in his sleep. I wish he'd stop. Truth is, I think he still feels frightened. I think we all do. The only decent sleep I had was in the garden when Jesus had instructed us to stay awake. I felt drugged, or as if I'd drunk too much wine, but of a very potent variety. There was a strange, heavy atmosphere, the sort you feel before a massive storm, only this was one hundred times bigger, more intense. Like walking around inside a colossal headache that's on the outside of you – if ever a place can feel pain, contain emotion, that garden did last night. That was even before the crowd arrived with flaming torches and lanterns, with *weapons*. And then he kissed him. 'Rabbi!' he said. Of all the insults, of all the shameful ways of man. Cephas was wild with anger and brought his fishing knife down on the high priest's slave. I keep reliving that bit in my mind. He'd sliced off his ear, but even then, Jesus was thinking of others and bothered to heal the guy. I can't wait to talk to Cephas about it. Now he is a true disciple.

I wonder how Judas is feeling right now. He's lost his chance with Jesus, and so many would have loved to have been in his position. We trusted him – perhaps not as much as Jesus did, but we trusted him all the same. Last night

---

[33] See note at the end of the story if you want to know who this disciple is.

I thought he was leaving our supper to run an errand, but I see it all now. *He* was the one who sat next to Jesus last night and dipped his bread in the same bowl. I hadn't realized then. Jesus does speak in riddles; we're often not quite getting what he says. Truth is, it's a bit embarrassing really. There are only so many times in a day you want to ask for clarification as you start to feel a bit stupid. Especially when you are the youngest.

I hate Judas right now, really hate him. I don't think Jesus would mind, not in this instance. We'd tried to think of him as a brother. So at times it was clear his faith wasn't as strong as ours, but we made allowances for him there. He objected when Mary washed Jesus's feet with nard – as she poured that amber liquid over his feet, he looked disgusted, and his words told us exactly what he thought; not that we were in any doubt. I didn't like the smell much either but it was more than that. He wasn't worried about the supposed waste of money – he just couldn't handle such devotion; it made him squirm inside. Looking back, he never had the same level of tolerance with the crowds, but Jesus didn't give up on him, so we took that as a sign he was trustworthy. He even put him in charge of our finances, which settled any doubts we'd given way to. But this! Outright betrayal of our Lord, and all for what? The rumour is it was over thirty pieces of silver – some meaningless metal with no eternal significance. Did he even know what he was doing? Had he always been evil or was this one moment in time that has defined him forever?

To have been around Jesus as he has, to have seen the miracles – the water into wine, the healings, the miraculous meals for thousands – was his spirit not even slightly stirred? He's had Jesus explain *everything* to us, but he thought his life was more important. Just how do we begin to understand this? I need to go back right to the start, look for clues, see if I can make any sense of it. I think now that Judas tried to make himself seem more godly than the rest of us. Made out that he could see what we couldn't, like he was spiritually more aware – now I know it was all a sham. He was always so gushing, so full of compliments, and such a charmer. He must have been incredibly skilled at faking emotion. It must have been tiring too, always pretending to be someone he was not. He had always been quick to take offence – it was like stepping around broken pottery on the floor, always saying to him, 'No, that's not what I meant, Judas wait, Judas, look....' He was often seeking attention, saying and doing things to get a reaction, I believe now. You'd think that would wear off in the presence of Jesus. Why did he even call him? Was there ever a point to all this? Will we ever know?

And then there was his 'sense of humour', his jokes, often a little risqué. Suggestions of a couple's intimacy, comments verging on crude. That kind of banter wasn't uncommon before Jesus – but we'd all moved on. The things Jesus talks of absorb us completely and leave us with no time or emotional space for impressing the world. Judas was interested in the ladies too; he'd always linger with an attractive woman who wanted Jesus's attention, ask her more questions than were really necessary. 'I haven't seen you around here before,' he'd say. 'I've come to see Jesus,' she'd reply. 'I can help you get closer to him, wait with me a while' – these were the comments he'd come out with. But Jesus trusted him, so we let things go. I'm convinced now we should have warned him.

How can anyone make sense of what Jesus has been doing unless he is the Son of God, as he told us? No one else has that power and authority. With Jesus it's never to receive praise, he's always pointing to God the Father. One look from him, from his eyes that seem to blaze, they're so alive, and you know he's read you – he holds your gaze and looks deep inside you. He must have known what Judas was up to, what he was really about. Yet there is love in them too, so much love. Perhaps that's what he couldn't cope with. But if I was Judas I would have walked away from the group if I couldn't handle it. I mean, imagine listening to all Jesus said and realizing, 'I'm one of those sinners,', 'I'm that thorny ground he's speaking of', 'I'm a goat, not a sheep, I don't like it when he calls my name' – Jesus tells these stories so that we realize, that we see our fallenness, our need and want to belong to him, so that we want to receive his help. He could've talked to Jesus about his struggles, owned up and at least got some conversation going. Said, 'Jesus, can you help me find a way out of this?', 'Jesus, I haven't been able to trust you with this yet, it's silly really. It's because I'm worried about such and such. What do you recommend? What should I do?'

But he didn't want to.

Truth is, for Judas I think it was all validation of who he was, and that he was fine with. Perhaps he got a kick from being on the inside and seeing us weep with Jesus, hearing us intercede – but didn't he pray? It certainly sounded convincing. Oh, I really don't know any more. He'd fast with us, he said all the right things (mostly), but he's sold out and now they have taken our Lord away. I really do hate him. I wish we'd never seen him, associated with him, that his name and ours had never been said in the same sentence. We've wasted so much time listening to him, trying to counsel him and confiding in him our secrets and longings. What an evil, evil man.

I can't wait any longer for the others to wake up; we need a plan, to decide on what we must do from here. Is there anyone we can go to, any way of speeding up Jesus's release? The cockerel is crowing, people will be up and about. I think I'll go and join Cephas again now.

See Matthew 26:47–56; Mark 14:43–50; Luke 22:1–6; Luke 22:47–54 and John 18:1–13.

This story is from the perspective of John, one of the two sons of Zebedee, and a very close friend of Jesus.

The temple priest

'Don't get too attached,' I told the children. 'You'll be eating him for supper!'

There is laughter that for a time competes with the bleating.

'My daughter wanted to hold ours. "This one's not for knowing," I said to her. It's been hard on her – we arrived in Jerusalem days ago!'

Laughter again, and this is just from those at the front of the crowd. Aren't they even remotely disturbed by this uncommon darkness? I fear from where it came, and why.

All these sacrifices! If it were not bad enough that we must sacrifice for our own people, we have to ensure a daily sacrifice for Caesar. It's relentless. Yet this time of year is the worst of all. Every Jew within reach of Jerusalem needs to know a sacrifice has been made on their behalf. Still, we keep those shepherds of Bethlehem in business.

More and more men press in until there's barely any standing room left. I'm relieved when the doors close them in – the sooner we start the sooner it's over, and it's never a job I enjoy. There is quiet from the men now and the bleating seems to get louder, the pitch higher, with a pleading quality. I do think they sense what's coming; I've served at enough of these sacrifices to have a fair idea.

Three blasts from the silver trumpets, like a final judgement: I fear they condemn us all. Their gleam reminds me of those thirty silver coins and I can still hear their chinking sound from within the bag, passed to me last night. I was asked to count its contents and I remember its weight in my hand. It all happened so quickly and now it cannot be undone. We priests have sentenced a man to death and he's out there now, dying. What did we expect? Yet I feel sure he was innocent, and no amount of sacrifice will ever make up for our deed. There was in us all that need to impress – how ludicrous. That mock trial, the humiliation we put the man through; all so needless, so cruel.

Lamps are lit behind us so we can see what we are doing. Not that we want to. Well, I don't. There's no accounting for the others.

The first man steps up with his lamb and I put the cold blade to its throat while he holds it close to his chest. I press a bowl against its white fleece to collect the blood. It spurts and I am glad my tunic is red today, for no amount of scrubbing would conceal the stain. My fingers are wet with blood and it drips onto the floor. Soon I am ready to pass the bowl along the line and the next victim is handed to me. I seek His forgiveness as I do this, for the irony is not lost on me; a sinner used in such a ceremony. Such blood on my hands. Such blood. May He be merciful.

I hear a loud groan from further inside the building – it's more a shout of lament. This is a dark day indeed. I pause with the knife poised until the cry ceases. Now the very ground feels unsteady and I widen my stance before resuming. I am tired but is there more to this? The men are packed in here so tightly that it's hard to tell. We began this slaughter yesterday and I barely slept last night – it always weighs heavy on my spirit. The smell still lingered when we got up this morning – the smell of the burned innards and skins; I wish they would take them away whole and deal with them in their homes.

I press the knife firmly into the neck of this new lamb. He surrenders without a fight and I feel the life leave him in my hand. The creature is still. But that Jesus was causing havoc; perhaps this place will settle down again. They say he wanted to become King, which we couldn't allow.

The dead lamb is taken from me and then the next man hands me his. This one struggles and I tuck its legs under my arm as I wield the blade. It really won't keep still and I pause to think. I don't believe it was in Jesus's nature to have us killed, though that was the justification I kept hearing. My greater fear was of the chief priest; if I hadn't complied I would have been demoted. I could have lost my job if I'd resisted the general will amongst us. Demoted from what though, I now wonder. How could I have stood up for him? What difference would it have made? There was such overwhelming hatred of him, such resentment, that my small voice would have made no difference.

The lamb that I am holding bleats extra loud in my ear.

For specific details concerning the earthquake and tearing of the temple curtain, read Matthew 27:45–53 (darkness, earthquake and curtain); Mark 15:33–9 (darkness and curtain); Luke 23:44–6 (darkness and curtain).

There is forgiveness for everyone who asks, even those who feel theirs is the worst deed ever. I believe there are many who fit into this category, who assume the sin that holds them is beyond God's mercy. The cross states clearly that it is not.

In Acts 6:7 we read 'So God's message continued to spread. The number of believers greatly increased in Jerusalem, and many of the Jewish priests were converted, too.' Surely some of these priests would have been among those who mocked Jesus and condemned him to death. My character is one of those who would have found salvation, in time. I think we can all relate to his feeling of powerlessness, and can probably remember a time when we haven't spoken out on Jesus's behalf. I hope his story is an encouragement to you.

At the cross

'Mary, we should go,' you say to me, and you tug urgently on my sleeve.

'But I have to be here for him,' I tell you. 'We can't leave him alone, I can't _'

'It's not going to help you,' you say. 'There are others here for him, witnesses who're not quite so involved with him as you. No mother should witness the death of their son; let alone in such a gruesome way. And it's getting so dark, Mary.'

'Oh, it is, too. I really hadn't noticed.'

'Well I had,' you say, and you go on talking, but I fail to register your words. 'Nature…confused,' that's all I hear. 'Have you seen it?' you ask.

'What? What was that?'

'While you've been watching Jesus, I've been studying that spider in the tree beside us. It's been taking down its web.'

You are throwing your arms about like it's really important, like it means something. I think you are simply too afraid to look at the cross.

'Oh, that's unusual,' I say.

I don't know why you have the urge to talk, but still you carry on. 'Like I said, all of nature is confused – the birds have stopped singing now that the light has faded. Listen – not a tweet to be heard, not a squawk. I even saw some small bird fall to the ground while you were distracted – it fell to the earth like a stone tossed down into a dry well.'

'Mmn.'

'This day can't possibly get any worse, so won't you come away with me?'

'Oh, of course. He said "And a sword will pierce your very soul," too.[34] I'd forgotten.'

'What?'

'In the temple, when Jesus was in my arms.'

---

[34] Luke 2:35.

I try to make out his infant features in the maimed figure on the cross. He is too far away and now, I am losing him for good. If we could –

'Mary, you're tired and upset,' you say, interrupting my thoughts. 'This has been the most traumatic day, why won't you come?'

'An old prophet said that to me long ago,' I tell you. 'I pressed those words down and tried to ignore them and it worked for a while, but now I understand.' My thoughts take me back, and it's an easier place to linger. There we had stood, and it had felt like such a happy day. Joseph had taken our baby and put him in the old man's arms, and I'd felt such pride, for to have been chosen felt the most awe-inspiring thing.

Looking back now, I realize it was the most terrible destiny, for both me and my boy. Dear Joseph hadn't lived long enough to see it. But why has God allowed all this? How could he possibly plan such horrors for his children? It *is* hard to make out even his form now through the tears; it's like looking through a waterfall, knowing people are standing on the other side but being unable to see them. Perhaps it's just as well.

'Mary, it's turned so cold,' you say to me. 'A change came in the air with the darkness. Come on, we really should go,' and you link your arm through mine.

'Just a little longer, I can't leave him.'

And so we stay and you stop talking for a while. But then, 'Mary, you are too quiet and this day too sinister,' you say at last. 'We really must go now. Look at you, you're trembling – I simply can't let you stay and watch any longer.'

I widen my stance to stop myself from swaying. 'You go,' I tell you. 'I'll be fine. I'll come and find you when it's all over.'

'I'm not leaving you,' you say, and I'm aware of you still beside me as I stand. My gaze is back on my son and I can see more clearly now as my crying has lessened. You seem to have finally given up your quest to move me on, which is just as well.

So could this be what God had singled me out for? Was I specifically chosen to suffer? If only mothers could decide the future for their children – make them all safe and secure, tuck them up in heaven's mercy as we at first truss them in swaddling bands. Wrap them in, wrap the world out so that it cannot touch them – not now, not ever.

Those kind hands of his had never hurt anyone. How they once fitted inside my own; it was always something I'd cherished, how neatly his little hand fitted in mine, with my thumb just long enough to reach around the outside of his. Since then they've healed so many people, and have been lifted to heaven in prayer and in blessing every day. His energy in serving others seemed endless then – he never turned people away, even when he was tired or hungry or just feeling run-down. It could be the small hours and he'd come to the door to see who it was and how he could help. Those feet had walked miles to seek people out and bring heaven's anointing. Now look at them; nail-driven and hidden under a flow of blood; every last drop of his kindness bled out of him and onto the ground below. I can see that from here. Oh, it's all so wrong and no one understands.

'I must go to him,' I mutter in explanation, grabbing my tunic in one hand and running as fast as I can before you put out a hand to stop me. What has my whole life been about if not to care for him, to be there for him?

I run as close to the cross as I can but a guard steps forward and positions himself between us, to prevent me from getting too near. What is it to him? He will never know what it is to be a mother – he'll never feel that fierce love burning inside, a dangerous love that will do foolish things for its offspring. My own children have never really understood it. Not even Jesus. I doubt whether God does – why would he put me through this, otherwise?

There is a friend on either side of me, and I can feel the presence of someone behind, too.

And then a voice. 'Dear woman,' it says, and I look around me at my closed-mouthed friends, before looking up and realizing it is *him*. My boy is talking to me, even now, at his most desperate hour. And 'here is your son,' he goes on, and as I turn round properly I see it is John who had walked up behind me and stopped. He looks almost as upset as I feel and is barely able to stand, as if a violent pain grips his abdomen, though on those words his back straightens and his face appears to shine as he looks from Jesus to me.

If that's not enough, he continues to speak to us, every word laboured, jagged and torn with pain. But there is no doubt in what he's saying, and the way he looks on us, his meaning is abundantly clear. 'Here is your mother,' he says to John, who is crying again now. There is an echo in his voice, and the strength it takes him suggests to me this is his last effort for the world. Most people would be up there feeling bitterness and resentment to the very end, but not him.

Did he just nod at us? It wasn't certain, but his intentions are unmistakable, and now I feel a hand on my shoulder. Dear John. Dear Jesus – always thinking of everyone else, even at this most awful moment.

I feel all disorientated as I realize it's still *him* up there, that he hasn't changed, that his love is still going on, relentless, as ever. But there is something more – I can't balance and neither can anyone else, for I look at John who has stumbled to the floor, and the guard has jabbed his spear into the ground and is hanging onto it, fear written into his face. Then I realize you are still with us, too.

'What was that?' I say.

'Hold onto me,' you reply. You pull me down to the ground and we crouch, trying to steady ourselves with our hands pressed firmly on the floor in front of us, for it is surely shaking, and even opening up in places. The very earth feels terror today. I may at times have been accused of possessing an overactive imagination, but I've been proven right so far. It began with the pregnancy which was all God's doing. Ever since there have been those who are quick to point the finger, even suggesting I'm nervy and highly strung, but it's always God working out his way in my life. Sometimes I feel a helpless bystander, as I do here. Oh, couldn't there have been a better way? Why did it have to come to this?

The sheep on the distant surrounding hills have started to bleat in unison and I can hear a child crying. I don't want to look at my son now, but something forces me to, and as I glance up I can see from his face that he is gone. The day is still dark but that look of surrender is unmistakable.

At once I turn away.

The ground beneath my fingertips begins to quieten and I look at you and John. There is an understanding between us as we get to our feet. We find ourselves walking back now, stepping over the cracked ground, jumping over the chasms that have appeared, though I don't remember setting off. The streets are deserted; I think most people ran for their homes as soon as darkness fell, but at last I don't feel afraid. I keep thinking of how he looked up there and it won't leave me alone. Now I think of it, it seemed as if he was accomplishing something. I have seen a friend in childbirth and held her hand, and the expressions weren't so different. It was as if he were birthing something too, bringing something to pass. Ridding the world of something very evil and transforming it. I have to think on this and remember who he was... Who he is. For this isn't the end for him, I feel sure of that. Faith is surging again, though I cannot account for it. My boy came for a purpose and I really don't think he missed it. My God isn't a God of failure or of missed moments; he's a God of triumph, and what he sets out to do, he accomplishes every time. The tears are coming, uncontrollably, though I feel sure they shouldn't. John understands, though he says nothing. I think you do, too.

See John 19:25–27 for the moment when Jesus provides emotional care for his mother and John in the form of each other. The 'you' in this story is imagined and is my way of giving you the reader a way into the scene as you wait with Mary and support her.

Joseph of Arimathea

'Eliezer, I fear I have been the most distracted host. This will not have been the Passover you were expecting, but I hope you've found the accommodation comfortable. I'm something of a troubled man. Do you have time for a chat before your family leaves? Share some bread and olives with me, overlooking the valley.'

You recline on the settle but I am too distracted to relax myself, though glad I've found a listening ear. 'I have always been slow to come forward in life,' I tell you, 'and, if I'm honest with you, have learnt to live with many regrets. Perhaps I'm no different from anyone else in this, you included. But there comes a point when you think, I don't care about my so-called reputation any more, I don't even care what happens to me; some things are too important to leave floundering. I only wish I had adopted this boldness earlier in life, but here we are, and perhaps talking to you will help me decide what to do now.'

'That's a big responsibility,' you say. 'I'm not sure I can advise you, for we don't know each other well.'

'Well, if you could just sit and listen,' I reply. 'I ask nothing more of you. I have so much to tell you that I'm wondering where to begin. I think I need you to understand where I'm coming from, to find a point of connection with me, so let me ask you a question. Have you ever joined an organization, or taken on a responsibility, then wondered about the wisdom of your decision? Have you thought you might be able to maintain your scruples – that you'd make something work, even against all sound advice, with the voices you trust encouraging you not to go there?'

You nod.

'So that was me. I have always loved Scripture and tried my best to live an honourable life. The Lord became my passion many years ago, and so it became natural for me to want to devote my life to this. I became a member of the Sanhedrin, which, of course, meant I could vote on all the important decisions. It wasn't without warning from my friends. "You'll have to compromise," I was told. "They're not all godly men like you, many are in it for themselves." My closest friend even told me, "You'll become all self-important, just like the rest of them. We might as well say goodbye now." I was determined to be different, though once I was on the inside, I could see it would be impossible to maintain my standards – if I was to stay in post I'd have to ignore many things. I was even told to dumb down my passion. I was informed that part of our reason for being was to maintain the status quo, that I should enjoy my position of privilege and see it as God-given, recognizing the poor were as such due to their own fault and divine judgement. "Harden your heart," I was told. "Don't bother us with more tales of pathetic woe," and "Make a name for yourself. You want your community to respect you. They don't. You're soft, a walk-over."'

'Well, it has been hard to balance this with my personal faith. On occasions my private devotional time would slip. I told myself I was doing an important job, that God needed me in this post, and so I remained. But then *he* came along and my inner life was in turmoil.'

You look confused but I cannot stop my flow of words.

'It was as if he'd moved into my head and rearranged all the furniture,' I say, 'so that I no longer had anywhere to place my usual thoughts; my level surfaces were turned upside down, my inner scrolls written over with new words and commands. I am talking about Jesus.'

Now I can see you understand.

'Of course, I had known him almost from his birth and took a special interest in him, especially after his father died and there was no man of the house. I had heard all the stories about him from when he was small – the angels at his birthplace, the visitors from the East bearing gifts for a king – what I knew of the young Jesus was his profound, deep knowledge of God and his caring nature. He always was a remarkably good child, exceptional in fact. But a change came over him a few years ago. No one saw him for several weeks, and once he was back he was speaking about God wherever he went, challenging people, healing them, even bringing deliverance, or so I was told. I didn't know what to think and it troubled me. For a while I kept my distance. Of course, there were mutterings amongst my ranks, and they got worse and worse as the months went by. I was forced to ask myself if all I'd heard about him was actually true.

'It was my friend Nicodemus that swung it for me. He too was drawn to Jesus, but he did something about it very early on. One dark starless night, when he felt sure no one would notice his absence, he took himself off to find Jesus and ask him some very frank questions. Jesus got going with what was on Nic's heart before he'd got beyond the pleasantries, talking about how to enter the Kingdom of God and how to have a meaningful spiritual life. He told him about being born again, by the Spirit of God. Then there was more. He talked about how God sent his own son, not to bring judgement but salvation, for those who believe in him. That gave us much to think on. I've always respected Nic and we had many a long conversation together after that…God's son…did he mean, could he be…?

'I felt an inner conviction that Jesus was speaking God's truth, and I started mingling in the large crowds that gathered around him. I tried to look official, as if I was monitoring what was going on, but secretly, in my heart, I was yearning for this kingdom life he was talking about. I would turn up at the gatherings I heard whispers of, the ones that I knew weren't so public and my Sanhedrin colleagues would know nothing about, but still this wasn't enough. One day I went up to Jesus when he was on his own, trying to get some personal space I suppose, but he welcomed me with an outstretched arm as if he were expecting me. Looking back now, I am pretty sure he was. One of the amazing things about Jesus was he always had time for people. His disciples were very protective of him and thought many of the people he helped were timewasters, but he had that knack of knowing exactly who needed him, and by that I mean *really* needed him. He could see beyond appearance and manner and to their deepest need.

'Well, we talked long into the night, watching as the sun set over the city and lights flickered from the distant windows. He told me how he often went up there to pray – it's called the Mount of Olives, and it was one of his favourite places. It's strange to think how I found him that day; it was as if my feet knew where to go and led me out of the city and up, my mind completely disengaged. It was so good to catch him on his own, to know that he still had time for me, as he did before he became so popular.

'Even after that special day I was always on the fringes of his group and could never identify myself as one of them publicly. Slowly his disciples realized I was not there out of ill motives. I felt they had it so easy, for they were at the centre of things and had him around all the time. What a privileged position to be in. Of course, I would have exchanged all my lot for theirs – my wealth, position, power – but it wasn't to be.

'To my shame, I followed Jesus secretly for a very long time. Looking back, I know I could have done things differently, but I got there eventually. I have struggled with how I failed him, but now I realize I couldn't have changed anything, for somehow it was all part of his divine plan. That makes it much easier to live with. Of course, I still feel a failure though. I did grow bolder once I knew what they had planned for him. I stood against their schemes and told them I could not endorse the crucifixion. For once I raised my voice, even shouted at them, no longer the walk-over they had me down as, but it did no good.

'I cannot tell you how ill I felt on Friday – the most awful Friday I have ever known. I had so expected his kingdom to come on earth that I really hadn't foreseen that most terrible of days. I shut myself away when I woke and wept, praying for it all to stop. My forehead dripped sweat as I wrestled and implored, and when finally I stood, I felt faint as pain expanded in my skull. It was pain that was too big for its confined space, like a tree that erupts through a stone floor, pushing its way up through crevices between the rocks. I had to lie down but I couldn't settle. All I could think of was that if I'd spoken out in favour of him, perhaps I could have stopped it going so far, but I was an outright coward. I had tried to stop them, yes, but I hadn't put myself on the line; I hadn't explained I was one of them or put up any real resistance at all.

'At that point I'd really had enough of myself. What use was I to the world, I thought. I was a disgrace, and I decided that my life didn't matter any more. To have followed him secretly was worse than not following him at all. I wanted to do away with myself, but that would gain the world nothing. I could, I decided, give him a decent burial at the very least and speak of him as I should. I would identify myself as one of his own. I even began to wonder if I might try to reform our flawed legal system. But then the awful realities of all this began to reach me. So here was my quandary: my fellow members of the Sanhedrin had pronounced him a criminal, and unless I told them of my familial links he would be assigned to a pit with all other law breakers, and no record of him would remain. This was just too much. I knew I had to explain myself to Pilate, and I hoped it would be enough. My extremist Sanhedrin peers would stop at nothing, so I had to reveal everything, and it actually pleased me to think of how I might be ostracized once they knew.

'I set out at once, and was relieved to find Nicodemus waiting outside my house. He must have known how I would react, for the love of God was burning inside him ever brighter too. I took myself to the market to buy a length of the best linen cloth. The seller opened her mouth to speak, probably to ask what the cloth was for, and to tell me she had a cheaper variety that would be just as thick if it were burial. But then she stopped herself, knowing I was too full of grief to even care. I could feel the woman's sympathy then and I couldn't look at her, so I carried out the transaction with downcast eyes. Nicodemus had told me that he wanted to buy what was needed to anoint the body. He'd mentioned myrrh and aloes. I said to him to have it all delivered to the cave and we agreed a time; there's no way he'd be able to carry it all on his own. I even doubted there would be so much available at such short notice: seventy-five pounds worth. He said it was to be a royal burial and I wasn't going to argue. I had already decided that we would use my tomb, the one I'd set aside for myself in some grandiose, self-important moment.

'I made for home with the cloth tucked under my arm, and what happened next was both strange and terrifying. The sky began to darken, slowly at first and then all at once, so that I struggled to see my hand in front of my face. I crouched on the ground and began to pray, and after a few minutes my eyes adjusted to the light. Of course, it felt like a heavenly condemnation, a rebuke for all mankind, and I was undone. The darkness stayed around for hours, and quite honestly it suited my mood anyway. Only when I felt sure he had to be dead did I set out to find Pilate and ask him for the body. It was mid-afternoon and the sky had started to brighten at last. I know I was seriously sleep-deprived, but I'm sure that as I started towards Nic's house the ground shook...in fact, I wondered if I'd felt a tremor minutes earlier. Now several rocks fell from a wall at the end of the path and birds flew up into the air and began to screech. It was a day of much madness, of terrifying happenings, and it helped to have a purpose at last, to be doing something useful.

'We visited Jesus en route, just to be absolutely certain. It was not a sight I was prepared for – I mean, how could you be? Every last trace of life had left him, every vestige of dignity and respect had been ripped from his body in a day of utter torture and violence. They had not been content simply to nail him to the cross. On his head they had rammed a crown made of the sharpest thorns and blood had trickled down, over his face and down his neck. He must have tasted the blood in his mouth as it reached his lips. There were a few yellow flowers on this crown, and the thorns were of the longest and sharpest kind imaginable. His body had been slashed in several places and he looked disfigured, almost beyond recognition. But we knew it was him – beneath the swelling and the bruises was that same honest face, that same look of patience that seemed to say he could take whatever was thrown at him – in life, in death. There was still no hatred to be seen in him – would he really have been that passive? I doubt he even cried out but just took it. What we saw was beyond contempt. The most perfect, godly man I've ever known, degraded in this, the most horrific of ways. He had never lifted his hand in violence towards another, had only ever used his hands to heal and they did *this* to him. Some of the women were watching from afar and I wondered if they had seen it all. I wondered how they would ever recover.

'Pilate didn't seem surprised to see me and granted the body without argument. He did send for the centurion for verification that Jesus was dead, but this seemed only a formality and I paced the courtyard, counting my steps in each direction until he returned. When I was given the nod I retraced my route and found Nic waiting for me at the side of the road. We walked on in silence together. I find it hard to recollect how we managed to lower the cross to the ground, and how we found the strength to remove those nails from his body, but somehow we did. I recall tossing the crown away in anger and watching it fall into a shrub, from the likes of which it probably came. Before we knew it, we had wrapped him up and were carrying him to the tomb. We let the women follow on behind us, for they needed to be sure where they must come to, to grieve and pay their respects.

'I have supposedly polluted myself, but that hardly matters. It's only an outward expression of my inner state, and besides, it wasn't contact with him that was polluting – quite the opposite. He was pure and holy; nothing corrupt could cling to him and certainly couldn't be transmitted by him. Well, even to think of it is a complete nonsense. So I am 'defiled' for seven days and have to stay out of the way this Passover week, but that's no bad thing. There's no way I could attend anything anyway. But here's the most amazing thing, why this whole muddle is not all that it appears... What I have to tell you is this: there is a rumour going round now that he's done it. I mean, really done it. That he's *risen* from *the dead*. Of course, I have been to check on the tomb and it is indeed empty, the soiled linen headcloth now neatly folded up, as you might courteously leave your sheets for your host after a night or two's stay at their house.'[35] You smile at this. 'Imagine his satisfaction as he tidied up and prepared to leave that awful tomb, for him a mere stopping place. Though I think the excitement was too much for him, as the cloths that wrapped his body had been tossed aside. The stone itself would not have been easy to remove and there were guards standing by all through the day and night. There is a new atmosphere in there this Sunday morning, and it seems as if the birds are singing more loudly today, that the sun is shining brighter. On one level the possibility is completely incomprehensible but on another this is logical and right. Of course, it does make sense of all that he used to say.'

'That is an incredible story,' you say. 'It explains much, too. The sky turning black, the earthquake, the sombre mood of nature herself.'

'So what does life hold for me now? I can honestly tell you I don't know what I am going to do. I think I am probably a wanted man. I could keep

---

[35] John 20:7.

company with the disciples, but I think they've locked themselves away somewhere, and besides, I would only sully their reputation even more. I might get away from here, at least until the rage dies down. I'm pretty sure they won't want me in leadership any more, but no matter. Unless they can acknowledge Christ as Lord, I want no part in their official religion. Of course, I am going to pray about where I should be, what I should do. I think I'm going to take myself up to his special place on the Mount of Olives and just wait for his guidance. I think he has a way of leading us when we seek after his will with our whole heart. For once I feel almost proud of myself – or at least as if I've contributed something meaningful to his story.'

'I feel sure you have,' you say.

'Well, the strange thing is that when I pray to the Father now, I know that he hears too. I know that Jesus was God all along. That's a comforting thought.'

See Matthew 27:57; Mark 15:43; Luke 23:50–56 and John 19:38.

Talking nonsense

'Open up! Quick, you *must* come!'

The door in the gate has slammed and you are banging on the inner door with your fists, now slapping it with the palms of your hands.

I unlock and usher you in, running back to pull the gate and glance down the road. 'Mary Magdalene! Do you want them to know where we are?' I tell you, as you wait for me in the courtyard. 'Get inside, *now*!'

The others are standing clear of the doorway and leaning against the walls until I have locked the door behind you.

'Nate!' says Thaddaeus.

'What?'

'Go easy on her. Calm it.'

Now we see you're hysterical and we wonder at your sanity. It's been said you are histrionic, which is perhaps a little unkind. I think they were just jealous of the depth of your friendship with Jesus, so it's no wonder you're struggling today. I know Judas was one who grumbled about you but look what we know about him now; he never could handle devotion.

I pull open a shutter to let in some light, but just a fraction, and you have our full attention.

'You must listen, all of you,' you say, in between your euphoric tears. I had hoped you'd hold it together better than this. You'll find this situation has upset us all – some of our group are weeping and you are not exactly helping matters.

Now you claim to have seen Jesus. Cephas pushes past me and runs out of the door – the fool. He hasn't been in his right mind since the events of Friday. He can look after himself and we have to leave him to it.

'Calm down,' we tell you. 'You haven't slept – neither have we.'

'I *have* seen Jesus,' you say again. It's not only your voice that's trembling – it's all of you.

'You're talking nonsense!' I reply, and my hand lingers on my black beard. Others agree, but not all are quite so cynical as me – 'How can you be so sure?'

comes Didy's voice from a dark corner. 'Was it his shape in a crowd of people? But then is it crowded outside already? It's still early.'

'I've met with him,' you say, cutting through our confusion. You are not wild now but calm and you seem exasperated with us.

We exchange glances around the room, looking each other in the face, but not you.

'Met with Jesus? That's wishful thinking,' we tell you.

Now you resume your mad woman's tears, demand that we find him, invite him in. Welcome him home.

'That's all over. We can't know him now, sister,' says Andrew, a kind consolation in his voice as he speaks to you in quiet, measured words.

'But you *can*. We can. It's what he died for. Don't you see? Come with me,' you say. 'We'll find him together.'

'It's too risky. We could get caught,' says James.

'You're asking too much,' says Philip, shaking his head at you.

'This is crazy but I need some fresh air,' says Didy. 'I'm going for a walk, if only to prove you wrong. There's nothing I hate more than false hope. Don't be surprised if I'm gone all day, lads. I can't handle the tension in here.'

'Walk her home, Didymus, will you?'

'Have you heard any of this?' you say. 'He's alive. It's not over – it's only just beginning! I'm not going anywhere until you listen to me. Don't stop believing. You must have faith, ...'

'You need someone looking after you, and you can't stay here,' says Matthew, gesturing for Didymus to turn and show some compassion.

'Go and get some sleep, Mary,' I tell you. 'Sometimes you can want something so much that you convince yourself it's happened. It's called delusion and it's not helping you.'

See John 20:1–18; Luke 24:1–12; Matthew 28:1–10 and Mark 16:1–11. The accounts vary on whether it was just Mary Magdalene or a group of women who told the disciples and some commentators splice the accounts together, working out a chronological sequence of events, with the empty tomb causing Mary Magdalene to run off and find Peter and John, first encountering Jesus on her own. While it is hard for us now to be certain, the gospels all are very clear on this: Jesus had risen from the dead and made many appearances to his followers. The apparent lack of collaboration between the gospel writers strengthens the Bible's authenticity, to my mind. [36]

***

'You're talking nonsense!', 'How can you be so sure?', 'That's wishful thinking'. These are all things people say to Christians now. We, like Mary, try to explain our personal encounters with him. She states, 'I have seen the Lord', which is what we Christians say, in a way – that he's met with us, is knowable. I wanted the reader to identify with Mary, and to be both comforted and challenged by what she says, and our need to do the same. (See 1 Peter 3:15).

---

[36] See 'Answers in Depth', *The Sequence of Christ's Post-Resurrection Appearances, Where Exactly Did Jesus Appear, and to Whom?* by Dr. Elizabeth Mitchell on March 21, 2012.

Just girl talk

Jesus understood. At least *he* valued her, gave her and the other women a role to play. They never felt like they were on the fringe of things with him. It was quite something that he had appeared to her and her friends first. Yet it carried with it a sense of responsibility – he'd entrusted her with the message that he was alive, and she couldn't let go of that. Ah – here was a thought! She would be known for *this*. Before it was 'the Mary from Magdala – the one who was demonically oppressed.' Never mind that *he* had delivered her. Jesus never judged her harshly, even before he'd freed her. She'd left her home town to follow him; to support him, yet still her old reputation followed her around. A past life that she was defined by. But now –

'They wouldn't even have survived without us,' one of the company announced, breaking into her thoughts. This was Joanna, and she was used to more appreciation than this.

'Well, that's hardly true,' Magdalene answered. 'Jesus can make a meal out of nothing, and it's been a privilege being able to provide for them. He didn't need us, not really. But now he does.'

'What's so different?' Joanna replied, taking a handful of the overripe, large green grapes from the bowl. They had forgotten to eat over the last few days, and now their appetites were returning.

'Well, if the men aren't going to spread the news about what's happened, we must,' Magdalene told her.

'They'll come round, anyway. But I had thought they'd trust our account…' said Mary, the wife of Cleopas. She sighed and began plaiting her hair in a distracted fashion, looking way off into the distance through the open door. It was as if she expected Jesus to walk through it any minute. Perhaps he would.

Salome knelt beside her and took over, beginning the plait again for her. 'Here, let me. You're tired,' she said.

'It's nothing personal on their part, Mary,' said Magdalene, fingering her shell pendant distractedly, her one link from home. 'They need to hear from him themselves. Too much hangs on it for them to rely on someone else's account.'

'Jesus wanted us to tell them,' said Salome. 'Dear Jesus.' No one said anything for a minute – it was just the sound of hair swishing through nimble fingers. 'There, your hair looks amazing,' and she handed her the end of her plait to appreciate.

'Well, we've prepared the way at least. We need to leave the rest to him,' said Magdalene. Ah, was she really able to convince them of this? They carried more than enough worry around with them and it never was *his* will.

'So what exactly happens now? I mean, where do we start, what do we do?' asked Joanna. 'I'm not looking forward to going home. I'll be in trouble for coming, for passing on what I knew about the trial and torture. Word will have got round that I'd gone to follow him.'

'You'll just have to update them all. That will really give them something to talk about!'

'Yes, well. We'll see. I mean, it won't be easy. Chuza worries about his job.' She smoothed her tunic and there was just the slightest suggestion of a growing bump. 'What else do we have to eat? I really am so hungry.'

'We have some dried fish and some raisins, we should save them for the journey. Perhaps we'll find something to buy on route too.'

'I said to my husband yesterday that we'd walk back to Emmaus together, just the two of us,' said Mary, wife of Cleopas. 'With some time away from the others I might be able to convince him. Besides, I've missed him.'

'But that was yesterday. Everything's changed. Just think on it. I imagine you'll be walking in silence most of the way if he's rejected our message.'

'We'll be home by nightfall. I think he plans to get away early so...' – her voice trailed off into nothing again as her thoughts took over. 'No, I'm sure we'll be witnessing together before too long. I know he'll come round. What about the rest of you?'

'Getting back to Galilee is no easy feat. Should we travel back with the men?' asked Salome.

'What, really?' replied Joanna.

Where was their confidence in God's protection?

'What makes you think we'll be safer with them?' Joanna continued. 'They are wanted men, surely. I don't think we're safe until Jerusalem is way behind us.'

'But you might see Jesus again. He wants them to leave for Galilee – the angel said Jesus is going ahead of them to Galilee, that they'd see him there.[37] I think you should stay close to them, even if they do find us irritating at the moment. Stick together as a group – the prospect of seeing Jesus again should be enough to keep you going. We don't have that to look forward to in Emmaus,' said Mary.

'Where is Jesus's mother?' asked Joanna.

'I think John and Peter are looking after her,' Magdalene told them.

'I don't know why her own sons don't take care of her,' said Joanna, smoothing her tunic again.

'Rumour has it they're not yet believers – not all of them, anyway. They will be. Give it time. I mean, how could you not be?' Magdalene replied.

'I can't wait for her to see him,' said Salome. 'I've got to be there when it happens. Can you imagine? I remember when she was first pregnant with Jesus – the trouble she found herself in, having to explain that. Oh, the strife! She thought Joseph had left her...'

'I keep trying to relive what happened today. I can't believe I didn't recognize him at first... I thought he was the gardener!' said Magdalene. 'How embarrassing is that?'

'Well he does look different. Not any less himself though,' said Mary.

'We were so upset too. I think my vision was blurred because of my tears. It was only when he spoke that I realized. He used to tell that story, "my sheep hear my voice and they know my name." His voice is unmistakable – it always will be. If ever a voice could carry kindness and authority, his can. There's such tenderness in it, you just have to stop what you are doing, are thinking, and listen. I love his voice. I can't wait to hear it again.'

'We won't forever though, will we?' said Salome. 'Isn't he meant to be joining his Father? I mean, it's mission accomplished, isn't it?'

'Well, he's made a way for us to be there, too,' Magdalene told her.

'But what happens in between?' said Mary. 'The rest of our lives without him. Can you imagine that?'

---

[37] Matthew 28:1–10.

'Everything has changed though, hasn't it?' said Joanna. 'I mean, the angels, the empty tomb. He's changed history, and well, the place just *feels* different. I can't help thinking there's more to come.'

'What more could we hope for?' joined Salome. 'We should just be glad that we've known him. That we've been privileged to be a part of his story. People are going to be talking about us, wondering what it must have been like for years to come.'

'We're in the end times now, surely, anyway,' Magdalene said. 'Ah, even when he does go back to heaven, it won't be for long. He knows how weak we are, how we need him. He'll find a solution to our missing him like he does everything else. And think on what he's accomplished for all mankind. It's a small price to pay. We'll look back on it all from heaven one day, but until then, we've got a message to share. *His* message.'

'Well, I hope it goes down better than it did with his disciples,' said Mary. 'I'm no great speaker at the best of times. He can use me, but I don't think I'll be much good at it.'

'I'm pretty useless myself,' added Joanna.

'If we get to see him again we'll tell him, explain how we're willing but feel so helplessly ill-equipped,' said Salome. 'He might have some tips for us. Something. It was so easy to talk about him when he was right here, among us. All we had to do was point, say to people, "Come with us, we'll introduce you." What happens if no one believes us? What happens if it all fizzles out, like a damp fire?'

'Do you think he went through all that for it just to 'fizzle out'? We can't let that happen. I won't. Ah,' she said with a smile, 'we've just got to imagine that he's still with us, even when he does go back home. Think of him watching on, cheering us on and encouraging us. It's all we can do.'

'You're right Magdalene,' said Joanna. 'Do our best and see what happens. Carry on with what we were doing, whatever the cost. At least now we can tell the end of the story, and it's a good one after all. He's *alive!*'

The cast of women

In the gospels we are told of a group of women who witnessed the crucifixion, the empty tomb and the risen Jesus. (In some accounts we are given names, but often terms such as 'many', or 'among whom' are used.)

Joanna was at least present at the empty tomb. In Luke 8:3 we learn that she was wife of Chuza, who was steward to Herod Antipas. I suspect she was among the 'many women' at the cross.

Also at the cross was Mary, the wife of Clopas. I like the idea that it was she who was with Clopas (thought to be Cleopas) on the Emmaus road. Salome (who some think was Mary's sister, and so Jesus's aunt) was at the cross and went to the tomb. Mary Magdalene is key in all the accounts. She is the woman who is repeatedly mentioned before the others and is thought to have been the leader among them. Jesus's mother was of course at the cross.

Thinking time

'Thaddaeus, stop humming!' whispers James in my ear. I start to drum my fingers on my knee but from his sigh get that this is irritating him, too. Ha, I wonder what Jesus would think of us if he could see us now, this subdued group of men who are barely talking. There is at least *plenty* of time for thinking, and I shut my eyes as I lean back on the cold stone wall – I can feel the ridges in the supposedly smooth plaster, and shift my back into a comfortable position. We're doing *everything* in this room: cooking, eating, sleeping, hardly venturing outside for anything as it's just too risky. With my eyes closed I'm realizing how revolting it's starting to smell... I don't think we've washed in days, not since before it all happened, and the stress has made us sweat more than ever. I try not to breathe too deeply as I rest in my thoughts.

We felt pretty sure it was him last Sunday night – I mean, if I'd been alone I may have convinced myself I'd seen a ghost, but we were all here – well, except for Didymus.[38] I start tapping my foot now and my sandal is creaking. We keep them on at all times in here, such is the sense of danger, the possibility of having to run for our lives. What I would do for some air! The courtyard is easily overlooked, and the gate doesn't shut properly. So here we are.

We'd doubted the women's version of events, and were in part relieved that we hadn't seen him; it's always awkward when you meet someone again after having let them down. But he wasn't accusing; 'Shalom,' he said, showing the deep-raw wounds in his hands and side.

Yet here we are eight days later, the door still locked[39] and barricaded, as if nothing has happened. Nate glares at me now – I stop the tapping and stretch out my legs, crossing my feet at the ankles. We're no longer singing hymns, shaking the building with our praises, as we did after he appeared. The fear of arrest quickly got the better of us, and it only takes one person to be jumpy, quick with the 'shushes'. I uncross my legs and let out a long sigh. *Lying low* is what they call it, though we do walk around in here. I really am struggling. I want to talk at least and I must have bruises from being elbowed in the ribs so often. I have a lump on the inside of my lip from biting it so many times. I find that I'm chewing on it now.

It is rather dark in here, day or night – we keep the shutters drawn at all times. When beams of light do pass through the cracks I can see my friends

---

[38] The origin of the story of doubting Thomas (or Didymus), found in John 20:24–29.
[39] John 20:26.

look tired. I think we've all aged these last few weeks, and I wonder how we move on from here.

Cephas is sleeping fitfully and moans every now and then; he's not sleeping well at night but is up and roaming, tripping over us as he goes. 'I'm coming, Lord,' he says then, 'so wait right there. Keep the boat steady lads.' There's always a pause as he plays it out in his mind and we dare not interrupt him. Right now, Andrew is sharpening a stick with a knife, for no apparent purpose. Nobody seems to mind *his* expression of anxiety. Yet the rhythmical splicing is soothing and my own breathing slows and deepens, the smell of the room less intrusive now. And there is silence.

'Peace be with you,' comes a voice, and my heart starts to beat very fast. I keep my eyes closed for a moment longer to absorb the sound of his voice that's so dear to me. Yet I'm aware that suddenly it's very bright in here, and I have to open them to see him! He hasn't thrown back the shutters but is just radiant with heaven's glory.

We always were slow to grasp things, but I'm pleased to see he hasn't given up on us. We all stumble to our feet and stand around the room now, motionless and moved to tears. All restlessness has completely fallen away.

He gestures to Didymus to come and stand beside him. 'Put your finger here, and look at my hands,' he tells him. 'Put your hand into the wound in my side. Don't be faithless any longer. Believe!'

Well, that told him. Ha, Didy had been going on for days about how he didn't believe us, and it did wear us down. I think that's why we were rarely talking in the end. No one had any valid suggestions as to what we should do from here either. Yet for Jesus to instruct him so means he's heard *all* of our recent conversations. I can't help but feel somewhat ashamed.

Didymus sniffs hard and wipes his eyes and his nose with his sleeve, then stretches out his arm, extending it slowly until his fingers have no choice but to touch his wound. I wait for Jesus to wince as Didy now prods with two fingers, but he doesn't, though he appears to brace himself. I think this is nothing, after all that he's been through. Didy now sinks his fingers into the gaping hole. I look away for a moment – it's just too gruesome.

'My Lord and my God!' he declares to Jesus, stepping back now and letting out a quiet sob. Jesus puts a hand on his shoulder. 'You believe because you have seen me. Blessed are those who believe without seeing me.'

Didymus looks at his feet, his tangle of curls hiding his emotion but we all know exactly how he's feeling. I'm so glad now that he didn't pretend to believe us. We're all such cynics when it comes to anything new and, astonishingly, we still needed more reassurance ourselves, if the truth be told. Ha, Didy always was one to speak his mind. We never do ourselves any favours by keeping our questions to ourselves; one thing I've always known about Jesus is that he wants us to be frank with him, share what's troubling us. It's only then that we can begin to deal with it and move on. Otherwise the question just stays at the forefront of our minds and we can't get beyond it.

Jesus leaves in the same manner that he arrived – that is, avoiding the locked door altogether. I wish I knew how he did it.

'Well, how *did* he do that?' says Didymus, as if reading my thoughts again.

'Not more doubts, please,' says Nate.

'I'm done with that, friends,' he says, shrugging his shoulders up to his ears, and rumpling his brow in embarrassment. 'That was the real Jesus and I touched his actual flesh, put my fingers in his side. So how does he –'

'No more questions,' we tell him.

'I guess we should unlock this door,' he now says, removing the planks of wood that we'd wedged it with.

'Shouldn't we keep the door locked, just for tonight?' I ask him.

'For what reason?' says Didymus. 'I feel sure he's protecting us.'

Our silence is well and truly broken and the chatter continues into the night. Soon I get my head down and just listen in – finally I'm tired, now that my anxieties have passed. Tomorrow we'll be bolder; less frightened, and maybe we'll get out of here – ha, at last! I have much to think on. Didy's getting something of a teasing from the others, but it's good natured. And he's a better disciple than me. I think we all benefit from his directness, for he often says what the rest of us are thinking. I wish I could be more like him. He's always included in discussions; the others ask him if *he* considers something a good idea. As for me – ha, I rarely get a mention! I'm completely overlooked. Of course, it's a privilege to be among Jesus's close friends, but I get the feeling no one's *ever* heard of me when we've been out among his wider group of followers. There's a reason for that – I'm unexceptional. I haven't been known for putting myself on the line, or for saying what others are thinking. I didn't even get to keep my original name in this group – not because of my own fame, not because Jesus thought me worthy of a better one, but because Jude is too close to Judas, and well, *everyone* knows about him. If I was exceptional it would've been alright, people would have been able to tell us and our names apart. Instead I'm just Thaddaeus[40] by default...my name should mean 'praise' but no one notices what I say, to God or to anyone else. Unless they find me irritating, of course!

When we couldn't understand Jesus, Didy was right there with our thoughts. During that last supper before he died, Jesus said he was going to prepare a room for us, explaining 'And you know the way to where I am going.' Didy said to him, 'No we don't know, Lord,' and I felt so relieved. He told him plainly, 'We have no idea where you are going, so how can we know the way?'

Then Jesus came out with one of his most memorable sayings ever: 'I am the way, the truth and the life. No one can come to the Father except through me.'[41] This prompted the rest of us to ask a couple of our questions, but we wouldn't have interrupted him if Didy hadn't done it first. I think the end result is that Didy's bolder than the rest of us, and his devotion to Jesus is unmatched, just so long as he's sure about things.

Some say he's a bit clueless, a bit of a nutter, but I don't think so. I remember that time when Jesus wanted to go to Judea to see Lazarus. We thought our friend was just ill but Jesus told us in no uncertain terms that he was *dead* and he was going to bring him back. We told him that the Jews had just attempted to stone him there. But Didy replied 'Let's go, too – and die with Jesus.'[42]

I *wish* I could be more like Didymus. I just know that of myself I'm so inadequate, nowhere near as good as the rest. On that first visit Jesus *did* say he's sending 'power from heaven'[43] to help us. Now that I do need. Perhaps, in my weakness, he'll fill me more than most.

For the biblical account visit John's Gospel, chapter 20:24–29.

---

[40] The names Thaddaeus and Jude never appear in the same book, supporting the widely held view that they are the same person. Thaddaeus is listed in Matthew 10:3 and Mark 3:18. In Luke 6:16 and Acts 11:13 Judas (not Iscariot) is found.

[41] John 14:6.

[42] John 11:16.

[43] Luke 24:49.

What were the disciples' movements after the resurrection?

My own personal interpretation is that they stayed in Jerusalem for a time – Mary runs to the disciples on the Sunday morning, having been to the empty tomb. That same day (John 20:19) the men were locked behind a door when Jesus appeared to them (they would not have made it back to Galilee in a day). Eight days later they were still behind a locked door – I expect this is the same door.

We know that Jesus had instructed them to go to Galilee (Matt. 26:32; Matt. 28:7 and 10). It is my belief that this was what he'd originally wanted for them, but they dithered behind the locked door and didn't have the confidence to set out. As a result, he met them in Jerusalem the first time and told them to wait for the Holy Spirit there (Luke 24:49). Had the disciples received the Holy Spirit to some degree before Pentecost, when Jesus had returned to heaven? I think it's possible, and we at least know he had breathed on them at this point in the gospel accounts (John 20:22–23).

Do you love me?

'Do you love me, Cephas?' She brought her face up close to mine so that our noses almost touched, and looked deep into my eyes, as if to find the answer there. For it seemed she doubted me, too. But didn't she trust me? As I pulled back, I could see the question written into her raised brows, and the frown lines that were unfamiliar to me. Where was the smile that I so love?

'How can you even ask that?' I replied, and I took her hands into mine and rubbed reassurance into them. 'Of course I do – you know I do.'

'Only I wondered if you were coming home, you'd been gone so long.'

I wondered how she could be so selfish? For I doubt she really feared for my safety. It was just an excuse to vent her frustration, yet I love her so. 'You *knew* what was happening, I had explained everything,' I said, pulling her into an embrace. 'You could have come with us.'

'I was looking after Imma. You know I can't leave her.'

'Ahem,' came a voice. We never do hear her coming. 'I'm fine, I think you'll find – have been ever since Jesus visited me that day. You don't need to keep fretting over me like I'm some small child. The fevers are a thing of the past. You should go with Cephas sometimes – he needs you more than I do.'[44]

***

Do you love me. Can she really doubt it? She appeared to be cross with me, offended, and so I found my way onto the beach for a while; some of the others have had the same idea. And so, I wonder how warm their own homecoming was. If only she knew what I'm going through.

After the usual greetings we sit in our companionable silence, each alone in his own thoughts. There are things I still need to work through. I still can't get over that he even appeared to me, before the others saw him. For I was astonished to see him and so relieved. So he really has conquered death, and when he said he doesn't condemn me I could see that he meant it. But what shame on my part! And with a towering failure like mine, perhaps he felt he *had* to see me. Surely I'm the biggest failure to have ever encountered him. He'd wasted his time with me. The reality is this: I'm no longer good enough to do his work.

---

[44] See 1 Corinthians 9:5.

Oh well, life goes on. It's back to all I ever knew. 'I'm going fishing,' I tell the others, picking up the large net I've been repairing for the last few days; for once a fisherman, always a fisherman. My good wife saw me leave the house with it, so she won't expect me home till the morning. Perhaps another night without me will do her good – for it will give her time to think on what I said.

To my surprise, the six who are with me say they'll come too...I can't forget how Jesus told us we'd each go to our own way but this lot seem slow to catch on. I felt he meant forever, not just on that most dire of nights. It's over, finished. I let him down in the most monumental way and that life with him has gone. For what's the point even trying to share about him now? Everyone knows my story, this lot included, but old habits die hard, and they still see something of the leader in me.

As the water laps at my ankles I start to relax. There's nothing like a strong breeze and a good catch to buck up one's spirits. I can do this, at least, I tell myself. Yet the night passes slowly, with not even a single fish obliging us for our trouble. It seems that now I fail even at this! I fear God himself is against me, and I wouldn't blame him. There's only so much failure he can take from any of us, and I suspect he's given up on me. How can I really hope for anything more?

Soon a ruddy sunrise breaks on the horizon and starts to spread its warmth across the sky in colours of promise that my spirit cannot match. There is the smell of a charcoal fire in the air, but perhaps I'm just hungry. Today I can't even feed my family; I think of them back at the house and I know I should join them. We felt that our homes would be the first place they'd look for us, so we had to keep some distance between us. The smell is unmistakable though... That servant girl rattled me that night for sure. Which of those men was she trying to impress? I shouldn't have stood so close to the fire if I didn't want to be identified, and I shouldn't have opened my mouth; not if I couldn't speak up for him. My stupid accent gave me away anyway – who was I trying to kid?

Not only had I utterly failed at his arrest but I continued in my error, repeating that terrible denial, until his eyes fell on me.[45] That sealed it. Of course God doesn't want to know me, and I can only expect greater troubles in life from here. Oh, God, have mercy.

---

[45] Luke 22:61.

189

A voice from the shore interrupts my ponderings, and it is much needed. 'Fellows, have you caught any fish?'

'No,' we reply. We can't see the man and this does feel quite ridiculous, conducting a conversation at a distance of more than a hundred yards.

'Throw out your net on the right-hand side of the boat,' the voice returns, 'and you'll get some!'

So we do, and the boat starts to topple with the sheer weight of the catch. I've been here before...but I need to let these thoughts go, for my memories of our times with him now haunt me. Just then John says in my ear, 'It's the Lord!'

But of course! For why else would this happen, for what other purpose? I pull on my tunic and throw myself into the water, swimming as fast as I can, then staggering onto the beach. If I can just... get to... shore quickly enough... he might stay. Catching my breath is hard, but I want the chance to talk to him on his own, for him to know just how sorry I am. I have had time to formulate my thoughts now; that first appearance of his was such a shock to me that I questioned if it were even happening.

He's done this for them, of course he has, not me – for my actions were underscored by my three denials and he heard them all. Yes, the courtyard was full of those who'd arrested him, still there with their clubs. But wasn't it all the more important that I stood up for him? What would it have mattered if they had done away with me there and then? For that is what I feared. My tears gave me away and yet no one arrested me. By then I didn't care. My life could not have been any worse since then, my shame any deeper.

The giant catch, though, it's like being called a second time.[46] But he wouldn't, would he?

As I approach the shore I can see the charcoal fire and Jesus is standing beside it, welcoming me. He knows it all; he witnessed that scene, and now he's extending his arms to me and bids me come. I just don't get it. How this fire reminds me that he saw it all, that he knows everything.

I can't look at him and fall to my knees in front of him, covering my face with my hands.

---

[46] Luke 5:1–11.

The boat has landed for I can hear the others, their laughter and shouts fill the air like they did in the early days, after the wedding feast, the first haul, the first healings that we saw. I know I'm not good enough for all that now.

'Bring some of the fish you've just caught,' Jesus calls to them and, still without looking into his face, I turn, glad of a part to play. The others leave me to it, keen to receive Jesus's greeting, and I drag the net off the boat myself. It is as laden as it could be, yet it doesn't tear.

I can see them all together as I make my way up the beach. They haven't bothered to look back at me and they look just fine without me. I sidestep a rock amid the sand and drag the net carefully so as not to catch it.

I hand Jesus a fish and he puts it on the fire for me, then gestures for us to sit and eat what he's already cooked. He makes a space for me to sit down next to him and I eat some fish in silence, still unable to meet his gaze. I never thought I'd eat with him again, but he's torn off some bread and hands it to me. My own hand trembles as I take it from him. I eat the entire meal without speaking. I am dropping morsels of fish, and finding it hard to swallow what does make its way into my mouth.

The meal over, Jesus waves the others off to count the fish and turns to me. 'Simon, son of John,' he says, 'do you love me more than these?' Not *Cephas* then. What was I expecting?

'Yes, Lord,' I say, 'you know I love you.'

I stare at his bare feet, the wounds still visible and terrible, the scabs still fresh and new, though darkening now at the edges, crusting up as they tighten on his skin. I look up and out to sea for what seems a very long time.

'Then feed my lambs,' he replies.

I think that means I have permission to serve him still, that I've not been cast off forever.

But he asks me again, 'Simon, son of John, do you love me?'

He is taking some convincing, but why am I surprised? 'Yes, Lord,' I tell him, 'you know I love you.'

'Then take care of my sheep,' he says.

I think he's accepted my answer at last and there is an easy silence.

But then, in the lull of conversation, he asks again, as if he really doesn't trust me: 'Simon, son of John, do you love me?'

'Lord, you know everything,' I say. 'You know that I love you.' I steal a glance at him; his face is still swollen from its hours of torture, still recovering.

I stare into the charcoal fire and a feeling of peace floods me as I remember those three awful fireside utterances of before. He's allowed me to proclaim my love for him over each one of them, and he has spoken out my commission. I may never be worthy but I *am* called.

I look at him properly now and I can see the trust in his own eyes, that are also full of tears. It's not that he doubted me, I think at last – it's just that he needed me to speak out my own resolve.

Now he goes on to explain my future to me, that sounds as if it will be challenging. As I study his bruised and scabbing face I really don't mind. Perhaps it will give me another opportunity to declare with my life what it is I really think of him. And as if to affirm the resolve in my heart, he says to me again, 'Follow me.' The same call, the same location and a second chance.

Of one thing I am sure: I will not be the same from here. And so, let this be a life laid down, lived as he intends.

For the biblical account visit John's Gospel, chapter 21, verse 1–end.

Peter's encounters with Jesus

I believe that Peter had already encountered Jesus personally after the resurrection and it had just been the two of them. (See Luke 24:34 and I Corinthians 15:5). Jesus would have known how broken Peter was and how sorry, and it is just like him to seek out the downtrodden. We know from elsewhere in Scripture that if we take one step towards God, he comes running towards us, and Peter's renewed commitment has already been seen in his running towards the empty tomb. Jesus has appeared to the disciples as a group too, on a couple of occasions, but I think Peter still would have felt down on himself and unworthy of any leadership responsibility. He really needed this time with Jesus on the beach for him to grasp what Jesus wanted from him, and to understand he still had a purpose. This feeling could hit any one of us, though we may feel our commitment is unshakable.

Know that Jesus comes running towards you and has not given up on you. No perceived failure on your part is insurmountable on his, so long as you genuinely want to belong to him.

Coming home

'He's coming home, *he's coming home!*' The phrase rolled in over the hills and plains, swept over the roof tops of the eternal city and into the very corridors of God's holy dwelling, towards the inner courts where he had indeed made his home. Who started it, no one could be sure, but its echo carried with it a certainty that was not for disputing. Meanwhile, the first to declare his return were still on earth, but good news always travels fast.

'He's done it!' said an angel who'd longed for this day for over thirty years, his wings hanging limp since he first learnt of Christ's intended departure. It had been their default position anyway; he'd still worship with all of his might, but his inclination was to rely on his own interpretation of events, which limited what God could do through him. Being in the loving Father's presence brought him joy, yes, but he'd felt things just hadn't been the same. This angel now parted his lips, and out came the pain and longing of thirty long years in a torrent of worship, where he declared the Son's worthiness and profoundest of wisdom. He wept over his Lord's compassion and his own past folly, deciding then he would become the best servant; not that he wanted anyone to notice. The honour it was to serve him, and he was coming home!

'How do we get this place ready?' said an angel who loved to dwell on the deep love of the Lord. 'What a homecoming he deserves! Nothing will be good enough for him, no tribute worthy for him now – not that it ever was, I mean, what could –'

The archangel cleared his throat rather loudly. 'Indeed,' he said, but even he felt his knees start to buckle and he flexed his wings to steady himself, holding them rigid until he could contain the emotion. 'What a change this has brought.' They had never seen him like this, so visibly choked, and watched as he shook his head in wonder and breathed deeply, his eyes closed. The rest of the angels had to look away then, and bowed their heads. 'There are not words...', continued the archangel, but his speech trailed off into nothing.

A long silence ensued, until one of the wisest and most considered angels hummed her intention to speak. 'Imagine the reunion between Father and Son,' she said. 'Oh, it is too much,' and a shiver began at the tip of her wings and rippled through her until her feet left the floor and she found herself up on the ceiling. 'Oh, this always happens if I dwell on him for too long.'

'Too long? What is too long?' came a voice from below her, and soon the companion worshipped with her from the highest vaulted ceiling, followed by others, all caught up in the Spirit and basking in God's goodness. The angel who had carried a sadness for thirty years now soared into the air, weaving between them and pushing his wings to their limit as if they were new, the mercy of God propelling him in a way he didn't believe possible. He would be trusting every word his Lord said from then on.

And so the streets were brushed, the walls and gates polished, but it was irrelevant really. *He* was coming home. What more did they need? What more could they ask for? It was what they'd longed for, but there was no time to get ready! They would never be ready. How he had proven himself – not that he needed to. There could be no one more worthy.

'What's he doing now? Why isn't he back?' called an impatient angel who always surprised with his maverick comments. Though his words were acceptable, one or two of the throng often raised a questioning eyebrow when he spoke. He never held back and felt entitled to ask what was on his mind, usually being the first of the throng to speak out. Now he dropped down to the floor after a quick inspection for cobwebs on the highest golden arches, landing with a thud; he only knew two speeds – fast and take-off.

'He's putting in a few appearances,' said the second-in-command, his eyes on the boldest angel who was now scrambling to his feet. 'Reassuring his followers, giving them some instructions, that kind of thing, but he won't be long...'

The community of angels gulped hard, felt a hardness in their throats, and many began to cry.

'He's coming home,' said a slow angel who always brought up the rear.

'We *know*,' replied several angels at once.

'No, I mean, *he's on his way*. I heard it outside from the pair who told the disciples not to stare up into the clouds. They raced ahead of him to bring in the news, just so there could be no mistake. It's our turn, you know. He's coming *right now* –'

They grasped each other's hands and squeezed their eyes so they were tightly closed, some beginning to lift into the air until they were all adrift from each other.

'Oh, it's too much,' said one.

'What should we do, what can we say?' said another who remained on the ground. 'Oh, how do we respond? He's the King of Kings, Lord of Lords, he's –'

'Just be yourselves,' said the archangel who stood beside him. 'I must warn you though, he may look somewhat different.'

'How?' said the outspoken angel, and they all gathered round now to listen to the archangel's reply.

'You see, he's fully God and fully man now. He so loves them that he's not going to let that part of his identity go.' The archangel paused for a moment and blinked hard to regain his composure. 'He has holes… in his hands and feet, where the nails were driven through.'

'He could heal that, no problem,' said a faith-filled angel.

'Oh, they will probably heal over a bit in time, but it's as if he doesn't want them to, and he certainly won't speed it along. Perhaps he'll keep them forever. You see, they are important to him – symbols of his love for them, of who he is, what he stands for… What he's done. Every time they look at him they'll be reminded that they are forgiven, complete. His brokenness for their wholeness. It all makes perfect sense, when you think about it. But you must be careful not to stare.'

Not all the angels heard the entire speech, for some had fainted and fallen back on their wings, to be lifted into the air while their hearts caught up with their minds. His overwhelming brilliance was going to be too much for them, and he would awaken them slowly, as the news began to settle inside them. Two or three of them would open an eye as his radiance fell on them, then shut it tight before they felt his hand on them and knew they had to go on. '*It's you, it's really you,*' they would say. The reunion was going to be immense.

The stronger ones among them began to line his entry route, but still many were overpowered by the extent of his love when the time came. They roused themselves, shook out their feathers and raised hands in worship, only to realize he had passed them already, catching just a glimpse of his glory as he made his way home to the Father. Others fell onto the ground or knelt, closing their eyes in fear and reverence. He would catch up with them all, in time.

It was fitting that the Father would be the first to properly greet him, though. No one was worthy to witness that moment, and none would be able to stand. The fullness of God's love, the wonder of this completed task, had shaken heaven and earth, and acknowledgement must come, first in the throne room, then in every heart of man. Eternity was changed, forever changed, and it would take an eternity for his created beings to even begin to understand.

Inspiration

Simeon and Jesus portrait, Andrey Shishkin

The Three Marys, Henry Ossawa Tanner

The Disciples Peter and John Running to the Sepulchre on the Morning of the Resurrection, Eugène Burnand

Still Doubting, John Granville Gregory, ca. 1990 and The Incredulity of Saint Thomas, Caravaggio.

Printed by Printforce, United Kingdom